Love
is What
You
Bake
of it

Book One in The *Meraki* Series

Effie Kammenou

This book is a work of fiction. Names, characters, businesses, organizations, places, events, and incidents are either the product of the author's imagination or are used fictitiously. Any resemblance to actual persons, living or dead, is entirely coincidental.

Printed in the United States of America

First Edition:

10 9 8 7 6 5 4 3 2 1

ISBN 13: 978-0-578-60978-2

Library of Congress Cataloging-in-Publication Data TXu 2-172-450

Kammenou, Effie. Love is What You Bake of it

Cover Design by Deborah Bradseth - www.tugboatdesign.net

Author photo by Daniel Krieger

Meraki

A small Greek word with a complex definition. In essence, it means to put your soul into something—anything done with great passion, absolute devotion, and undivided attention—a labor of love.

In dedication to my husband, Raymond, for your patience, encouragement, support and love.

Acknowledgements

To my husband, Raymond, and my daughters, Eleni and Alexa, for your never-ending support and encouragement.

To my sisters, Kathy and Jeanine, who inspire me with their compassion and kindness.

To Valerie Gildard, my most trusted beta reader—the first set of eyes on my manuscripts. Thank you for your attention to detail.

To Rett Tyler, author and critique partner / beta reader. I value and respect your opinions and suggestions.

To Marisa and Chris Raptis, who brainstormed a subplot in the storyline for this book with me.

To Aphrodite Papandreou, who supplied me with much-needed facts and shared personal accounts of a tumultuous time period in Greece.

To my editor, Katie-bree Reeves of Fair Crack at the Whip Editing, a master at her craft and a pleasure to work with. Thank you for always pushing just that little bit more out of me.

To Deborah Bradseth of Tugboat Design, for this beautiful cover, as well as all my past covers.

To my publicists, Drue Hoffman and Debra Presley of Buoni Amici Press, for your professional management on the publicity for this new release as well as for *The Gift Saga*.

To all my friends, too many to name, who have and continue to support and inspire me—you know who you are. You may have even found traces of yourselves within the pages of my books.

To my parents. To my father, who amazes me every day. I pray I have inherited his longevity and sharpness of mind. And to my mother, no longer with us but never forgotten. If not for her, my first book would have never been written, much less this fourth one.

"Food brings people together on many different levels. It's nourishment of the soul and body; it's truly love." Giada De Laurentiis

Prologue

Kally

July 2011

Gravel crunched under the soles of Kallyope's espadrilles as she stepped from the car. Shielding her eyes with both hands to protect them from the glaring sun, she squinted up at the clear blue sky. Golden rays radiated streams of light in what might be interpreted as joy shining down from the heavens. It was the kind of day Long Islanders dreamed of, as summer weather in the Northeast was often unpredictable.

But today, Kallyope cursed the sun smiling down upon her. Taunting her. Reminding her that everyone but she was brimming with joy as they frolicked at the beach or walked hand in hand by the pier with their special someone. Kally begged for the gloom, some rain perhaps, or even a damn hailstorm. Anything for a drop of sympathy from above.

Even the cemetery didn't hold the air of despondency it should have. The grass was lush and the branches on the magnolia trees hung low, dense with shiny green leaves. Kally made her way down the row of stone markers. Halting before one, she fell to her knees; the moist soil and prickly blades of grass staining her skin. With shaking hands, she ran her fingers along the engraving on the polished granite, the date a blatant reminder that today was only one day after the first-year anniversary of his death. She couldn't bring herself to come here yesterday for fear of who else might have been visiting or at the risk of any questions as to why she, a strange woman, was crying at his gravesite. The evidence before her proved that many had indeed come to grieve him. Fresh flowers covered the grave. Notes, flags and a miniature model motorcycle adorned his final resting place, bringing life and love to the otherwise cold stone.

Collapsing over the lifeless monument, Kally broke down into racking sobs. "Why? Why would you do this to me? How could you leave me with so many unanswered questions?" she wept, her shoulders shaking with the agony of it all.

Hunched over the stone, her mass of long, dark curls draped over her, covering her face as she continued to cry privately. Or so she thought, until a hand rested softly on her shoulder, startling her.

"Are you okay?" a voice from behind asked sympathetically.

Kally turned quickly, relieved it wasn't anyone he had known. Not sure how to answer, she looked up at a set of kind, brown eyes and nodded. Climbing to her feet, she brushed off the blades of grass stuck to her knees and faced the young woman.

"It's a difficult day for me. I guess we all have them," Kally stammered. "Otherwise we wouldn't both be here."

"I've had many days like you're having now." The young woman nodded in understanding as she guided Kally over to a nearby bench. "Do you want to talk about it?"

"Honestly, I wouldn't know where to begin. It's been a year and I've been through more emotions than I can count. Shock, sadness, anger ..." — Kally sighed, averting her eyes from the stranger, — "... regret."

"I know those emotions well. But it gets better. I promise. The ache in your heart will always be there, but it changes into something more manageable." She quietly laughed, self-mockingly, under her breath, shaking her head at her own words. "Here I go acting as though I have all the answers. After all, I've only recently discovered how to allow myself to be happy after loss."

"May I ask who you lost?" Kally asked.

The young woman sighed. "My father died when I was ten, but I'm here to speak to my *yiayiá*. She was who I always went to when I needed to talk or get advice."

Kally looked at her quizzically. "Your *yiayiá*?"

"Oh, I'm sorry, my grandmother."

"I know what a *yiayiá* is. I have one myself," Kally said with a small smile.

"Huh, you're Greek. My *yiayiá* used to say the Greeks have a natural magnetic pull toward each other, and that if we were tiny fish in an ocean of sea life we'd still find our way to each other."

Kally's mouth curved up slightly. "There's a lot of truth in that."

"And speaking of finding people," she said, blowing out a nervous breath, "I'm leaving for Kefalonia tonight to hopefully win back the affection of someone I've been pushing away for years. I just needed a little hug from above before I go. I'm Evvie, by the way."

"Nice to meet you. I'm Kallyope—Kally." She liked this woman. There was a kindness about her and Kally could see her concern was genuine. "Tell me about this man. I could stand to hear something positive at the moment."

Kally listened as Evvie told her briefly of her relationship with Zak, the man she was determined to win back. She had done everything in her power to protect her heart from falling in love so as not to risk losing another person who meant the world to her.

"But then I finally realized that, like the song says, I had learned to live half alive. And I couldn't do it anymore. It's more painful to be without him. So, what was I really protecting myself from? It only took me forever to figure out I was fooling myself into a false sense of security. I just hope it's not too late."

Kally shook her head adamantly. "It's not. If he's anything like you say he is, he'll understand. You have a chance. A good one, too, because he's out there and you can find him. It's not like that for me. Jaxon is dead and I'll never get the answers I need from him."

"I'm so sorry," Evvie said.

"It doesn't matter. We wouldn't have ended up together anyway. That song? It must have been written with him in mind," Kally said bitterly. "Collecting his jar of hearts. I wish I had found out before the accident."

Evvie rested her hand on Kally's shoulder, a look of sympathy reflected in her features. "I think you should put this behind you. It doesn't sound like he was worthy of you. Don't look back and cry over his grave. He doesn't deserve it. You need to move ahead with your life."

"I just wish I had the answers to my questions." Kally sighed. "But you're right, he doesn't deserve my tears." She clasped Evvie's hands in hers. "But you! Go convince that man he can't live without you."

Both women rose to their feet and hugged. "Thank you for taking the time to cheer up a stranger," Kally said with a smile. "I'd love to find out how your story ends. When you get back, you should stop by my dad's restaurant. I help out a few days a week. I'll give you the address."

"We can do better than that. Give me your number and I'll text you."

Kally pulled her phone from the back pocket of her shorts. The girls exchanged numbers, promising to keep in touch. When Evvie walked away, Kally made her way back to Jaxon's grave.

For a moment she stared at the stone, her eyes calm as she considered the past buried there. "I won't be back," she said resolutely. "And I'll never forgive you."

Chapter 1

Kally

September, 2018

The village of Port Jefferson was still bustling with activity two weeks after Labor Day. While most harbor towns and tourist villages on Long Island quieted after the summer ended, this quaint little town never seemed to die down, not even in the dead of winter. A commuter ferry system ran yearlong, crossing the Long Island Sound to reach Connecticut and, in the summer, tourists passed through, many on their way to other destinations.

The main streets were lined with boutiques, novelty shops, restaurants and cafés. There were more ice cream parlors than one could possibly imagine in such a tiny town, the most popular being a small stand at the end of a row of stores in Chandler Square. On any given day or evening, the line would stretch from one end of the strip to the other.

Kally had lived in Port Jefferson her whole life. Unlike her sisters, who had dreams of moving to more exotic places, Kally loved this corner of the world—her corner of the world. In her mind, it had everything she needed—the pier for strolling along and admiring the sunset, a variety of restaurants, Fetch Doggie Boutique to spoil her

Yorkie, Emma, and the Greek Orthodox church she attended as often as she could manage.

Most of all, there was her very own establishment—the one she'd dreamed of opening for years. The Coffee Klatch was a café that promised new experiences while providing a welcoming, friendly atmosphere with its open design, soft pastel colors and floor to ceiling window front. A book nook with cozy couches and armchairs dominated one corner of the space, while tables filled the rest of the area. Glass cases boasted artfully decorated pastries and the countertops held cake-filled glass domes and jars brimming with candy. With several other cafés and tearooms in the area, it had been important for Kally to find a way to distinguish hers from the others. And she accomplished that by offering an international flair. A range of unique caffeine-induced beverages were made available. Greek coffee, *frappé, cappuccino, café-au-lait, café de olla,* and even English high tea were just some of the drinks on offer. And the pastries Kally created to complement each beverage put the icing on the cake, so to speak.

It was Sunday afternoon. Kally had locked the doors to the café at four o'clock and sent the staff home, staying behind to settle the receipts for the day. Satisfied that everything was in order, she gathered her bag and a pile of soiled aprons and headed to the front entrance.

A warm breeze tickled her skin. Closing her eyes, she lifted her face to the sun, smiling at the pleasant afternoon yet regretting that she had no time to enjoy it. Today was her sister, Mia's, name day and Kally was expected for dinner. The Greeks celebrate the feast day of the saint they were named after rather than their birthdays, but here, in the States, they celebrated both. *Double the obligations. Double the family time.* Not that she didn't love her family, but sometimes they could be too much, too intrusive, just too …

Briskly, she crossed the street and walked up the block to the cottage she'd proudly purchased the year before. It was another thing she'd had her eye on for a long time. The fragrant lilacs surrounding the stark white house had always appealed to her. When it fortuitously went up for sale, she snapped it up before the real estate agent had a chance to stake the sign into the ground.

"Emma, I'm home!" she called. "Come on girl, let's go out."

* * *

"It's about time," George said as Kally walked into her parents' home.

"*Kalispera* to you too, *Baba*," she answered in a deadpan tone, one eyebrow raised. "Aren't you in a welcoming mood," she added sardonically.

"My pastry chef quit on me last night. I wouldn't have that problem if you didn't leave me."

Not that again, Kally thought. "I'm sorry." And she truly was, but her father's guilt trip for every decision she made was getting old. "I'm sorry you lost your pastry chef. I'll call my contacts and see what I can do for you." There was no point in defending her decision to branch out on her own. It would just end in another argument.

"Good! You're here," Melina said, glancing out from the kitchen. "The food is on the table. *Elate.*"

"Hi, Mom." Kally kissed her mother on the cheek, handing her a bakery box from The Coffee Klatch.

"Theo, Krystina!" Melina called out. "*Ela.* Come down for dinner."

"Where's Mia?" Kally asked.

"I'm right here," Mia gargled, padding from the kitchen with a half-eaten potato wedge in her hand.

"*Hronia Polla! Na haíresai ti yiortí sou.* Happy Name Day, Mia!" Kally handed her sister a small Kraft paper gift bag tied with a pale blue satin bow.

"Should I open it now?" Mia asked.

"Absolutely!" Kally replied.

A high-pitched, fast-paced, heavily accented voice from the kitchen grew closer. Swinging her trusty *koutali*—wooden spoon—frantically in their direction, she scolded, "*Ela tóra. To fayitó kryónei.*"

"We're coming now, *Yiayiá*. Trust me, the food is still piping hot," Mia said. "I almost burned my mouth on the potato."

Thunderous, uproarious thumps caught everyone's attention as Theo and Krystina stomped down the staircase.

"Did I hear my favorite word? Food?" Theo asked, breezing by without even a greeting and heading for the back porch.

Kally shook her head with a smile. Nothing ever changes, she thought with a sigh.

The temperature had dropped to a pleasant sixty degrees as the sun began to dip lower. Brushstrokes of marigold, rose and lilac peeked through the tall, green foliage that surrounded the Andarakis property, the sky above transforming from sunshine to moonlight without a single cloud to impede the view of its celestial beauty.

Every morsel of food had been consumed—grilled herb lamb chops, Greek sausage called *loukaniko*, grilled branzino with *skorthalia*, lemon potatoes and a *horiatiki* Greek salad.

"So, when are you coming home for good?" George asked Mia suddenly.

"*Yióryios!*" Melina scolded. She only called him by his Greek name when she was mad at him, which was often.

"How many times are you going to ask me that? I like living in the city. I work there," Mia replied.

"The train station is a mile away," he said, pointing his pudgy finger at her. "It's convenient. You can get to work from here."

Mia glared at her father. "It's a two-hour commute for me to get downtown."

"A girl is supposed to live in her home until she gets married!" George slammed his hand down on the teak table so hard that his dish jumped. "That goes for you too." He shifted his focus to Kally.

"And what if I never get married? Do you want to be stuck with me forever?" Kally crossed her arms in challenge. "That old world thinking doesn't apply anymore."

"You should want to get married one day," Melina said. "Find the right man. A good man." She snapped her head around and glared at her husband. "Not a Greek man. They're impossible!"

"*Vre*, Melina," George groaned. "What are you teaching the girls?"

The squeak and clack of the fence gate halted the bickering. "We're here!" a cheerful voice called out. Mia was the first to rise from her seat to greet her godparents at the door. Thalia and Markos were her mother's cousins. Thalia's mother, Rhea, who stood alongside them, gave refuge to Melina and her mother when they left Kalamata. Melina and Thalia had been raised more as sisters than as cousins.

"Efthymia, *hronia polla, vaptistiki mou!*" Thalia said, kissing her goddaughter fondly on one cheek, then the other.

"Thank you, *Noná.*"

Thalia stuffed a twenty-dollar bill in Mia's palm.

Mia laughed. "I'm not a little girl anymore. You don't have to do this."

Thalia winked. "It's tradition."

Melina walked over and took Rhea by the elbow, seating her next to her own mother.

"Krystina, put down that contraption and clear the dishes from the table," George demanded.

Krystina looked up from the screen of her iPhone. "Okay, but only if Theo helps."

"I'm not asking you," he demanded.

"Theo will help your father clean the grill," Melina said, trying to appease her daughter.

Krystina muttered something under her breath and Kally jumped to her feet. "Mia and I will help you, Krys." Kally coaxed her sister to her feet.

Inside the kitchen, Kally was loading the dishwasher as Mia and Krystina carried desserts and dishware back and forth.

"Mom," Kally began when her mother came in carrying a tray of empty glasses. She closed the door to the dishwasher and pressed the start button. "You know you're not doing Theo any favors by letting him get away with doing nothing."

She rinsed out the sink and turned to look at her mother. Melina was placing the cake Kally had brought on a glass pedestal—red velvet with fresh raspberry filling covered with dark chocolate ganache.

"He knows you love him, right? Just as much as the rest of us. So stop compensating or he'll turn out just like Dad."

Melina's face went sour. "By like your father you mean a grumpy, inconsiderate, self-centered pain in the ass?"

Both women burst into laughter.

"Tell me how you really feel, Mom! And you wonder why I have no interest in marriage?"

"Oh, *koukla*, I hope that isn't true. Men today are not like your father. He has old ideas."

"Yeah, well, some of the new ideas aren't so fantastic either."

"It only takes one good man to come along," Melina said. "I was on The Facebook. Did you know that there's a group called Greek Singles? Why don't you give it a try?"

Kally bit her lips together to stifle a smirk. "First of all, it's just Facebook, not The Facebook. Second, no. And third, don't even think about it."

One good man indeed! Kally knew exactly where to find one of those. The only place they existed was in the pages of a good romance novel. And she was heading home to indulge in that fantasy very soon.

"Manifesting is a lot like making a cake. The things needed are supplied by you, the mixing is done by your mind and the baking is done in the oven of the universe." Stephen Richards

Chapter 2

Kally

The Coffee Klatch was an aptly named establishment. It didn't take too long from the day of its grand opening to become a spot where patrons felt at home to linger for extended periods of time, conversing with friends while sharing a decadent pastry or enjoying a leisurely afternoon coffee. The café attracted an eclectic assortment of regular customers and their presence added to the essence and spirit of the café.

Milton and Spyro, a pair of octogenarians she recognized from church, came every day to discuss the state of the world and argue over politics while drinking strong Greek coffee and nibbling on sweet baklava.

Mr. and Mrs. Lawson were once-a-week regulars. They arrived every Saturday morning at nine a.m., seating themselves at a table by the large window. Mr. Lawson was British, his wife, French. A transfer from his company brought him to New York. Kally would have thought they'd prefer to live in the city, but they enjoyed the serenity of the North Shore and its proximity to both the trendy East End of Long Island and the sophistication of Manhattan.

Four different book clubs convened during the course of the

month, as well as a trivia game night, and even a knitting circle. By hosting these evening events, Kally made use of the space wisely, helping to cover her overheads in hopes of breaking even in her first year. But she had surpassed that expectation. Her ingenuity, creativity, and talent creating mouth-watering pastry and warm, comforting beverages, as well as the inviting atmosphere, afforded her a tidy little profit.

Early Tuesday morning, Kally walked the short distance from her home to the café. Today, as she stepped up onto the curb, the toe of her shoe hit a piece of metal debris. Bending down, she noticed a battered license plate littering the sidewalk. Her first thought was to throw it away, but right before she placed it in the trashcan, she thought better of it. *What if it had been stolen? Or what if it accidentally dropped from a passing car?* Pulling a few tissues from her bag, she wrapped up the filthy piece of metal. She'd hold onto it until she had a moment to call the authorities.

Kally preferred to begin each workday in solace. The staff would trickle in slowly, assisting her with the baking and the daily routine of opening. But she relished in that first hour or two when there was no one in her space except the voices coming from her earbuds.

Kally jolted when her best friend, Egypt, snuck up behind her, pulling on one of the earbuds to listen for herself. "What is it today? Show tunes? Mozart? Or one of those audiobooks you get lost in?"

"Don't scare me like that."

"Definitely a romance then. You get so absorbed in them, you don't know what's happening around you," Egypt continued. "What would you like me to work on?" she asked, securing around her waist an apron embellished with the café logo.

Kally wiped her hands on her own signature apron. She had a collection of them. Egypt could usually read Kally's mood from what was written across her chest. Today, she had on an ivory apron with black ruffles. A pink cupcake dripping with frosting hovered above the words, 'Sometimes you just need to eat a cupcake with icing and get over it!'

"Are you trying to tell me something?"

"No." Kally looked at her friend as though she was one card shy a full deck. "What are you talking about?"

"That." Egypt pointed to the writing scrawled on her apron. "Your apparent mood of the day." Pursing her lips, she waited for an answer.

"Oh, that. I had dinner at my parents' home." Kally let out a tiny groan. "Same old same old. My dad telling me I should have never moved out. Dad arguing with Mom. Dad letting Theo get away with murder. Mom wanting to get me on '*The Facebook*' to join a singles page."

"The Facebook?" Egypt giggled.

"Anyway, these are the scones of the day." Kally handed her a large tray. "Dried cherry pistachio. Slip those into the oven for me while I finish the *Tres Leches* Cakes."

Egypt placed three large sheet pans into the commercial oven. Looking for a pair of oven mitts, she noticed the license plate resting on a folding chair in the corner.

"What's this doing here?"

"I found it outside the café door. I called the police station to come and pick it up. I wasn't sure if it was lost or stolen."

Two hours later, The Coffee Klatch was buzzing with activity. Luis, the baking assistant she had pulled from the local community college culinary program, was in the kitchen whisking eggs, two servers were waiting on tables and Kally and Egypt were manning the to-go counter near the front door.

By the time the morning rush had died down, Kally's mop of pinned-up curls had fallen out in random spots, her apron was covered with coffee splatters and her face was dotted with powdered sugar. Before she had a moment to change her apron and freshen up, a police officer walked in, presumably to retrieve the errant license plate.

Egypt came up behind Kally and clamped a hand over her shoulder. "Holy *cappuccino*. That is one hot *macchiato* sent down from heaven by one of your Greek Gods."

Kally looked up to see what Egypt, who was now digging her nails into Kally's skin, was making such a fuss over.

From the corner of her eye, she had seen the blue uniform enter, so had promptly bent down to pull the license plate out from under the counter. But she hadn't bothered to pay attention to which village officer it was that had come by. She knew most of them from the neighborhood and quite a few would stop by for some coffee while on their break.

It wasn't until Egypt's nails had practically drawn blood while she whispered breathy squeals in her ear that she looked up to see an unfamiliar face—a face that looked like it belonged on the pages of a magazine or flashing across a movie screen. He exuded an air of wealth and power and her first impression was that the small-town uniform seemed out of place on such a man. Kally pried Egypt's hand from her shoulder and made her way over to the edge of the counter.

"Hello, officer. I believe you're here for this." Kally handed him the mangled metal. One of his fingers inadvertently grazed hers as he took the license plate. A stab of nerves shot through her as their eyes met and she immediately looked away. Steeling herself, she lifted her eyes back up to him, nodding resolutely. She had done her civic duty and it was best she got back to work. If only her feet didn't feel as though they were cemented to the ground.

Kally wasn't short at five foot-six inches, but the constable towered over her by at least seven more.

"We ran the plate number you read to the dispatcher and the car belonging to this plate was stolen, so thank you for calling it in," the officer said, his voice deep and velvety, despite his professional manner.

"I'm glad I could help." Yes, Kally told herself. He was a good-looking man—thick, dark hair, the kind a woman wants to run her hands through—toned from what she could tell under that uniform—eyes the color of rich chestnuts. He's probably the best she's seen in well, years. But so what? It meant nothing to her. Nothing, she convinced herself as her heart began to thunder in her chest. Looks are superficial. He could be a creep. *Doubt it.* Or an axe murderer. *Ridiculous.* He could have a wife and nine children. *Now that's more like it.*

"Hi, I'm Egypt." Her friend walked right smack into his personal space and offered her hand. "And this is my very best friend and proprietor of this amazing establishment, Kally."

"It's nice to meet you, ladies." He pulled his hand from Egypt's hold, easily looking over her petite frame to address Kally. "Great place you have."

"Are you new around here?" Egypt asked. "I've never seen you before and I know just about everyone."

"I grew up here but I've been gone a long time."

"That's enough interrogation," Kally admonished. "Don't mind her, it's just that we pretty much know all the village police."

He didn't comment further and Kally noticed he hadn't even offered his name when Egypt introduced herself. His conceit and rudeness would make it easy to overlook his outward appearance. She observed him as he assessed the shop. He was either a sun worshipper or one of those naturally tanned humans who had flawless, glowing skin. His hair was as dark as the midnight sky, straight but thick and styled too fashionably for a local government worker.

He eyed the pastries and confections arranged under decorative glass domed cake stands. "I know of one young lady who would love it here."

Egypt's smile faded.

"Be sure to bring her by then," Kally said with a genuine smile. *One point in his favor for complimenting my place.* "Can I offer you a coffee and a scone on your way out?"

"Are you out of cupcakes?"

"No, not at all. Is that what you want?"

"No, but it seems you're pushing them today."

Kally crinkled her forehead. "Am I?"

He pointed to her apron and smirked. "I'll get over it if you will. Whatever that is," he added with a wry smile. "Thanks again," he said, and without another word, he walked out the door.

"Well, isn't he a bit of an ass," Kally grumbled.

"If you mean to say you'd like to bite his ass, I'm with you, girl!"

"Egypt! Seriously. Don't you think it's rude he didn't tell you his name when you introduced yourself?"

"Is that what you're picking on?" Egypt scolded. "You'll find any excuse to shoot down a man. This one is perfect for you. It was like he fell out of the sky as a gift to you!"

"You're insane."

"Me? When was the last time you went on a date?"

Luis, Kally's baking assistant, pushed his way through the kitchen doors. "At least not since I've been here."

"The two of you need to stop ganging up on me. I'm perfectly happy with my life as it is. Besides, you heard him. He has a woman he's going to bring here."

"There is that," Egypt said, sounding deflated.

"If he ever steps foot in here again, that is. What was with you?" Kally asked Egypt. "You're usually Ms. Confident and play it cool around men. I thought those green eyes of yours were going to bug out of your head. You looked like a grade school girl with a crush on her teacher."

"When was the last time someone who looked like that stepped into here?"

"She has a point," Luis agreed.

"Not you too?" Kally groaned.

"I wish!" Luis exclaimed. "I'd hop on that train!"

Egypt greeted a customer at the take-out counter. As she brushed by Kally to make a *cappuccino*, she threw over her shoulder, "By the way, his name is Max."

"How do you know that?"

Egypt rolled her eyes. "It was written on his nametag."

* * *

The next morning, Kally headed to work at the crack of dawn. She'd had a sleepless night and baking always took her mind off whatever was keeping her awake. That Max person had gotten under her skin. There was something about him that kept him in the forefront of her mind. One minute he seemed friendly and the next he got all … professional and formal. When he teased her about the quote on her apron, she wasn't sure how to take him.

Kally didn't know why she should even care. This Max, who never had the courtesy to tell her his name, meant nothing to her. Yet she had tossed and turned all night thinking of the moment when his chestnut-colored eyes met hers.

Kally tied a clean apron around her waist. Today it read, 'Give me coffee and no one gets hurt.' That pretty much said it all. Later, she would change her apron with a saying more appropriate for the romance book club gathering that evening.

* * *

Book club night had turned out to be a great success. Kally started it not only for her love of discussing her favorite novels, but also as another way to gain exposure and much needed revenue for her café. She moderated the romance and classic literature clubs and Egypt took on the other two—mystery/thriller and fantasy/paranormal.

Kally pondered on her relationship with Egypt as she prepared ingredients for a large tray of *baklava*. There wasn't anyone more opposite than she, but they had been friends since the sixth grade when Egypt transferred into her school mid-year. Her parents, both doctors, had worked all over the country before taking permanent positions at Stony Brook University Hospital. Egypt was outspoken and extroverted, whereas Kally was practical and more reserved. Egypt was a free spirit meanwhile Kally felt more comfortable staying in her own lane. Kally envied, in a healthy way, Egypt's exotic beauty—light mocha skin, almond-shaped eyes the color of jade and golden-brown ringlets in a style that only she and Halle Berry could pull off. Kally's own curls were her nemesis. It was her life's struggle to keep them frizz-free in the Long Island climate.

After Kally ran the walnuts through the food processor, she melted large chunks of butter over a low heat while adding cinnamon to the chopped nuts. Finding a rhythm in pace with the soothing, classical music she chose on Spotify, Kally began to assemble the pastry. A wide, natural bristled brush, dripping with butter, coated the first paper thin sheet of phyllo. To Beethoven's 'Moonlight Sonata,' her hands danced repeatedly from the stack of phyllo to the pan and finally to the butter. In time to Chopin's 'Raindrops,' Kally spread the first layer of walnuts over the top of the buttered pastry sheets. And just like that, her mood had shifted from exhausted and irritated to energized and content.

By the time Luis walked in, she had already made a tray of *revani*, four dozen hazelnut macarons and a Cuban *Tres Leches* cake to serve with the book club's monthly selection, *Next Year in Havana*.

"The queen of the Nile is here to grace your presence!" Egypt flung her hands up in the air as she made her grand entrance, all five foot-two inches of her.

"You're in a good mood," Kally laughed.

"And you," Egypt frowned, grabbing hold of Kally's apron bib to read the inscription, "are not."

"I wasn't, but I am now. Baking soothes my soul."

"Honey, it's not your soul that needs soothing," Luis said. "It's your—"

"That's enough!" If Kally let him continue with one of his crude comments, Egypt would've jumped right in. Not that she minded a joke or two but she knew this one would be at her expense and she'd heard enough for one week.

"I'm assuming it's your date that put you in such a good mood today?" Kally asked.

"Do tell!" Luis shimmied over and pulled up a chair, hoping for all the intimate details.

"Na, he was a dud. So boring I could have fallen asleep even after a triple shot of caffeine," Egypt said. "But ... when I got home I had a request on my Etsy account from a woman who bought a pair of earrings from me, asking for five more pieces."

"Fantastic!" Kally exclaimed.

"That's not all. She has a shop in a touristy town in California and she's placing the pieces in her store. If they sell, she's going to commission a whole collection for the holidays."

"This is big!" Kally hugged her friend, careful not to put her sticky hands on Egypt. "You have to tell your parents. They'll be so proud."

"As proud as your father is that you left the family business to run your own?"

"He's just set in his ways, just like your parents had their expectations on what they wanted for you," Kally said. "But once they see you've made a success of your dreams, they'll change their minds."

"Who knows?" Egypt shrugged. "I'll unlock the front door."

George's plans for Kally were purely selfish in her eyes. He should want her to branch out on her own and make her own way, the same as he had when he emigrated to the United States. But his dreams for Kally were small—work in his business until she got married and had children.

Egypt's parents wanted a grander future for their daughter—a college education, medical school and a practice all of her own. But those were never Egypt's desires. Kally remembered how she hated science class and nearly flunked biology. All her electives were in the arts, and forcing her to attend college had been a huge mistake.

Now, at thirty-two, Egypt worked at Kally's café, helping out front but also designing decorative elements to add to cakes and cookies. In her spare time, Egypt created one-of-a-kind jewelry that now sold in several local boutiques.

Kally was stacking books on a shelf for next month's book club selections in a cozy corner of the shop dedicated to selling novelty items when a male voice greeted her.

Turning, she came face to chest with the police officer from the day before. The very one who for some inexplicable reason was the source of her sleepless night.

"Oh, hello," Kally said politely. "Is there something more you needed from me? Um … I mean … regarding the car plate?"

"I thought I'd give you an update," Max answered. His eyebrows lifted in surprise. "Whoa!" He lifted his hands in surrender. "Do you choose those aprons at random or is that a warning?"

"You'll have to wait and see," Kally replied smugly. "The update?"

"Oh, yes." Max brought his attention back to the matter at hand. "We tracked down the car. It was used in a drugstore robbery about twenty miles from here on the South Shore. The car has been recovered and the suspects are in custody."

"Good to know. Thanks." Kally resumed stacking the books.

"So, what do you recommend today?" Max asked ambling over to the glass dessert counter.

"The blueberry scones are good or the individual carrot cakes. Luis, my baking assistant, just finished a fresh batch."

"Who made the scones?" he asked pressing his palms to the glass.

"I did."

"Hmm. I'm not a fan of blueberries. Maybe I'll come back another day. Thanks," he said, pushing away from the display. But as if by afterthought, Max turned back to Kally. "You have a little something right … here," he told her, cleaning a clump of icing from her hair.

And without another word, he left.

As he walked away, Kally stood with her fists planted on her hips, her expression held in a confused scowl.

"What did Officer Hot Buns want?" Egypt asked, bouncing over as soon as Max shut the door behind him. "He was eyeing you with those smoldering eyes." She imitated Max in a goofy exaggerated manner.

"Hardly!" Kally scoffed. "I think he just insulted me. Not a fan of blueberries," she muttered under her breath. "Who doesn't like blueberries?"

* * *

Finally, at six o'clock, Kally closed up for the night. She had barely enough time to go home, shower, walk Emma, scoff down a quick dinner and get back to The Coffee Klatch in time for her book club.

At first, she had begun with only eight members. Now, six months on, the romance book club had seventeen women attending, not counting the three other genre book clubs that met throughout the month.

The corner of the café she had designed for the events was fashioned with a plush couch, a set of mismatched upholstered chairs and a coffee table. It wasn't long before she had been forced to extend the space and add furniture, which turned out to be a blessing as her daytime customers gravitated toward the welcoming spot.

Book club gathered together an eclectic assembly—regular patrons of the café, a few of her mother's friends and acquaintances from her fitness class—women of all ages, the eldest being her own grandmother who, once she heard some of the selections could be on the steamier side, decided she was in.

"I really loved this book," one woman said as she sipped her *café Cubano*. "I learned so much about a country and people I knew very little about."

"Yes, and it certainly makes us realize how lucky we are to have the freedom we do," another woman added.

"I thought it was cruel in a way, never knowing that the one she loved was alive all along," a young woman stated.

"That's reality. The book was based on situations that were common for the time and conditions," Kally said. She looked over to her grandmother, gauging her expression. She had gone through her own troubles when she came to the States as a young mother, hoping her husband would follow soon after. Sadly, that day had never come.

"The book needed more sex," her grandmother blurted out and everyone laughed.

"*Yiayiá!*"

"What? It's true." Her grandmother rose from her seat and shimmied. "I might look old, but inside the fire still burns."

It's a good thing they all knew her and found her amusing, Kally thought. One minute she was lecturing on the reasons to attend liturgy faithfully and the next moment referencing a line from an erotic romance book that should never be repeated out loud, especially by her own grandmother.

"I've chosen a book for next month's discussion that's a true romance rather than a historical fiction with some romantic elements," Kally said, holding up the selection. Some of the women clapped. Others cooed their approval.

"It's a good one! I've already read this one, Kalliope," one of the ladies said, addressing Kally's grandmother of whom she was named after, although her mother played with the spelling when Kally was born. Kally's mother had an unexplainable obsession with names containing the letter Y—Kallyope, Efthymia, Krystina. Melina hadn't named Theo, but if she had, Kally sometimes wondered what she would have come up with.

"I've read it too," Kally said. "And I believe it will satisfy everyone."

"Sat-is-fy," Kalliope dragged out in her heavy accent, her eyes bright with mischief. "I need to get my hands on this book." She began to laugh so hard she threw herself into a coughing fit.

"*Yiayiá*! What I meant was it has romance, mystery, strong female characters and a beautiful location. A little something for everyone," Kally explained. "Behave!" she admonished with a smile.

"She's the best part of the evening," a young girl around nineteen-years-old said. "I wish my grandmother was this much fun."

When the discussion had officially ended, the members began to move about and chat amongst themselves. One of the older women Kally knew from church approached her.

"Kallyope *mou*, you have no boyfriend at the moment, correct?"

"No, Risa," she answered with a hint of impatience. Kally knew what was coming next. Fiddling with the chain of the pendant she wore, she anticipated Risa's next words.

"I didn't think so. I'm sure Melina would have told me if one of her daughters was taken." Risa's smile widened. Cuffing her hands on Kally's shoulders, she continued, "My nephew recently moved back to town—"

A low groan bubbled up from Kally's throat.

Risa twisted her lips in condemnation. "Now hear me out." Affectionately, she took Kally's face in her hands. "Your mother and I have been friends for years. I love all you girls like you were my own."

"I know that. We all love you too," Kally assured her.

"It's time you meet a nice boy and settled down."

"I am settled," Kally defended. "I run a business and have my own home. I have everything I need."

"But do you have everything you desire?" Risa asked. "I don't know anyone who has read more romance books than you. Yet you don't search it out for yourself."

"That's because, for me, romance is nothing but a fantasy. I've accepted that and I'm happy with my life."

"I've never heard anything so silly. There's a lid for every pot."

There's a cliché she'd heard a thousand times. Kally sucked in a deep breath.

"The lids I've found either crack or find another pot." It was Kally's turn to lock Risa in place with her grip. "Seriously, I'm fine."

Risa, small in stature and recovering from hip surgery, held her ground like a soldier ready for battle. She was relentless. "What could it hurt to just meet the boy? He could use at least a friend. He's a good man. Loyal, steady and reliable, but he's had a rough go of it lately."

"I'm sorry to hear that." And Kally meant it. She was nothing if not sympathetic. "Maybe you should let him find his way when he's ready to. It might be a bit soon for him."

Risa sighed heavily. Pouting, she looked at Kally with sad eyes. "Okay. But if you happen to be in the same place, like, let's say, church, I'm going to introduce you."

"That's fine." Kally turned her attention away from Risa, facing the rest of the crowd. "Okay, everyone. It's been fun, but I have a little girl at home waiting for me to walk her."

After everyone had gone, Kally locked up and began to walk home. The street was unusually quiet; the only sound the clanging of ropes hitting the flagpole. The wind had picked up and she could sense change coming. The warm summer weather was about to depart, replaced by a damp chill. A storm of some sort was definitely brewing; Kally could feel it in her bones.

Blueberry Scones

Preheat oven to 425°

2 cups flour
⅓ cup sugar
1 tablespoon baking powder
½ teaspoon salt
7 tablespoons cold unsalted butter
1 ½ cups fresh blueberries
1 large egg
½ cup heavy cream
Zest from one small orange
2 teaspoons vanilla extract

*The secret to light, flakey scones is in not overworking the dough.

In a large bowl whisk the flour, sugar, baking powder and salt.

Cut butter into small pieces and drop into the flour mixture.

Use a pastry blender to coat the butter, cutting it up until the pieces are no larger than the size of peas. Stir in the blueberries. In a separate bowl, whisk the egg, heavy cream, zest and vanilla. Mix the wet ingredients into the flour/butter mixture until just moistened. Gently press into two balls. Place each ball of dough onto a floured surface and flatten to form a disc. Cut each disc into quarters or eighths, depending on how large you want your scones to be. Sprinkle with coarse sugar and place on a parchment lined cookie sheet. Bake until golden brown - about 14 minutes. Cool on a baking rack.

Chapter 3

Kally

The sound of heavy rain pelting the window panes woke Kally from a sound sleep. She rolled over with a moan, sprawling out on her stomach and covering her head with her pillow. If she didn't know any better, she'd think there was a family of angry woodpeckers tapping furiously against the glass. Through the cracks in the window blinds, evidence of another bleak day was clearly visible. For three dreary days, it had poured continuously. It would have been so easy to stay snuggled up under her comfy duvet, sleep in and not step outside to battle the elements.

Kally groaned. The longer she put it off, the less time she'd have to dress. A promise was a promise and Kally never disappointed. Her mother was expecting her in church with a supply of baked goods for the *Philoptochos* fundraising sale the ladies group was running during the coffee hour.

* * *

"You're late," Melina whispered a little too loudly when Kally slipped beside her into the seat closest to the aisle.

"I'm aware. I got here as soon as I could," Kally said. "I put the cookies in the community center."

Kally and her mother sat quietly through the remainder of the liturgy. When it was time for the priest to deliver his sermon, he signaled for the parish council members to come forth with the donation trays.

Rifling through her wallet, Kally found a wrinkled five-dollar bill. With a small frown, she attempted to smooth it out with her fingertips while waiting for the basket to come her way. When the usher handed her the red felt-lined wicker basket to pass along, she looked up to smile at him. But her pleasant expression was quickly replaced with one of shock and confusion as she stared into the equally surprised eyes of Max.

They both froze, each with their grip on the tray, until Kally dropped her bill into it before giving it a firm yank from his hands so she could pass it to her mother.

As Max moved on to the next pew, Melina elbowed Kally. "Who is he? Did you see the way he looked at you?"

Kally brought her fingers to her lips in a plea for her mother to be quiet. Oh, for the love of God, how long will it take for the real interrogation to begin, she wondered. But truth be told, Kally had questions of her own. This Max person seemed to have materialized out of thin air and now he was … everywhere.

"But I've never seen him before," Melina whispered. "And I'd remember him!"

"He's a police officer. I didn't know he was Greek," Kally whispered. "He stopped by my café the other day."

"And you didn't tell me?" she asked a little too loudly.

"Quiet! There's nothing to tell," Kally said, her exasperation building. "You really are a menace to be around." Kally tightened her lips and glared at her mother. The subject was closed. Melina's sigh of resignation confirmed that she had gotten the message. At least for the time being.

"Aren't you staying for coffee hour?" Melina asked after the liturgy was over.

"No, I have to get to work. I can't expect Egypt to cover for me all day."

Kally needed to leave quickly. There was no time for chit-chat or surprise run-ins.

"You should say hello to your new friend."

"Mom! I know what you're doing. He's not my friend." Kally crossed herself three times, kissed the icons in the narthex and swiftly headed for the double doors leading to the parking lot.

But she wasn't to escape that easily. Her mother followed behind. "Stay for a few minutes," she pleaded.

Kally whirled around. "Aren't you the one who told me to stay away from Greek men?" Kally pulled her keys from her bag. "Don't ever accuse me of not taking your advice."

"Why are you being so stubborn?"

"Family trait." Kally smirked. She knew she was driving her mother to madness. She turned back to her, kissing her briefly on the cheek. "I know you have my best interest at heart, but leave it be. Besides, he could have a girlfriend, a wife or …" Kally shrugged. "… a boyfriend. Don't waste your energy or brain power."

Chapter 4

Max

By the time the donation money had been counted and placed safely in the church office, liturgy was over and the parishioners were either heading to their cars or off to the community center for coffee hour.

Max walked briskly from the breezeway that connected the church to the community center, hoping to find Kally there. With his hands dug deep in his trouser pockets, he scanned the room. The woman he assumed was her mother was talking to a few of the other ladies but Kally was nowhere in sight. She wasn't by the dessert table, nor sitting by any of the chatty people. He even checked the kitchen as a last resort.

Thinking of when they had come face to face, he smiled. The expression on her face was as shocked as he imagined his had been. Only his surprise had been quickly followed with a hint of a smile and a jolt in his chest. Kally, on the other hand, seemed annoyed at the mere sight of him and had averted her eyes from his quickly.

This was the last place he'd expected to see her. It had never occurred to him that she might be Greek. Although the thick, dark hair; large, wide-set eyes the shade of dark maple syrup; and the olive complexion did hint at her ethnicity.

He figured, at some point, he'd run into her—a restaurant, the beach, or maybe even the Sunday Farmers' Market. And if he didn't, he could always go back to her café for coffee. But the Greek Orthodox Church of the Assumption? It had never entered his mind that he'd find her here.

Maybe he was better off leaving her alone. He had come back to his home town to sort himself out. The fast-paced life he'd led the past ten years had almost destroyed him. After what he'd gone through, getting involved so soon with anyone was the last thing that should be on his mind. He had to focus only on the priorities he'd set, to carve out this new life and then, maybe once he was settled, he could think about getting involved with the right person. Someone who would love and accept everything that came along with being involved with Maximos Vardaxis, reformed 'supreme royal screw-up.'

But as much as he kept telling himself that, there was something about Kally that he just couldn't stop thinking about. From that first moment when his finger had grazed hers as she handed over the license plate and looked up at him with that sweet, vulnerable smile, he'd felt a tightening in his chest each time he snuck a glance her way.

But speaking to her was like a game of tug-of-war. She'd be sweet and he'd suddenly clam up. He'd tried to make friendly small talk but then somehow manage to say something to put her off. He walked toward her; she backed away. She offered him a treat from her pastry case and he bolted from her place like he was running to catch a criminal. One part of him wanted to pursue her, but the other part knew he shouldn't. He understood his reason for this push and pull, but what was the cause for her equally contradictory behavior?

Max was roused from his thoughts when an energetic, golden-haired child ran over to him.

"Daddy!" the six-year-old called out. "Look what we got in Sunday School today." She handed her father a softcover textbook and a religious themed bookmark.

"Very nice, Athena!" Max watched as his daughter skipped off to join a friend. She was doing so well these days. It was evident she was happy here and he was grateful the turmoil of their lives over the past couple of years didn't seem to have a lasting effect on her.

About ten minutes later, Athena returned with Max's sister-in-law, Lena, accompanied by her ten-year-old son, John.

"Are you ready to head out?" Lena asked.

"Sure," Max said. "Hey, Lena," he said, an impulsive thought brewing in his mind. "Have you been to The Coffee Klatch?"

"No. I haven't gotten around to going yet, but I've heard good things," Lena replied. "Your dad goes there often. He likes the Greek *kafés.*"

"What do you say we take the kids there for a little treat?"

"That sounds like a good idea," Lena agreed. "Let's go!"

Lena dropped Max, Athena and John off in front of the café entrance, telling them to grab a table while she hunted for a parking spot. The café was bustling with chatty patrons indulging in tasty treats before lunchtime. Spotting a few vacant seats in the back, Max figured they were still in luck, excusing himself as he navigated toward the front counter.

"Wow!" Athena enthused, skipping to the counter and pressing her nose to the glass case. "Candy and cupcakes!" She stood on her tippy-toes for a better view of the countertop and the goodies adorning glass jars and cake stands.

Max edged over to his daughter's side and lifted her higher, his gaze shifting from the treats holding his daughter's attention to the woman pushing out of the kitchen door with a fresh tray of pastries. His eyes momentarily locked with Kally's until she shifted her focus to the two children in Max's care.

Smiling brightly, Kally asked, "And who do we have here?"

"This is Athena and John," Max answered.

"What's your name?" Athena asked.

"Me? I'm Kally." She extended her hand to shake the child's and then did the same for John.

"We were hoping for a table," Max said.

"Three?"

"Four. Thanks"

As Kally escorted them to their seats, Max leaned in and whispered, "I told you I knew a little lady who would love this place."

Kally nodded. "You did." He watched her as she shyly looked away, tucking a stray curl behind her ear.

"Athena, John, I think you might enjoy the special cupcake of the day. Rainbow cake with cotton candy frosting."

"Yes, please!" they both cried out in unison.

Chapter 5

Kally

"You got it! I'll be back in a flash," Kally said with a smile. Max had beautiful children and she wondered about their mother. At least now she could tell her own mother to put any crazy ideas she might have dreamt up to rest. And as for that little skip in her heart at the sight of him? Yeah, Kally would ignore that ever happened. After taking the rest of their order, she moved to greet another patron with a smile.

"Oh, I see my party, thanks. They've already been seated," the petite and very beautiful auburn-haired woman heading to Max's table said with a wave.

That answers that question then.

Kally handed one of her servers her order pad. "Nina, please fill this order for me at table nine. I'll be in the back if you need me," she said on a sigh.

Why was she so bothered? She knew he must have been unavailable, especially once she saw him with his children. And why should she care? After all, she was unavailable too. Well, emotionally unavailable; not actually tied to anyone. And Kally planned on keeping it that way.

Without realizing, she was pounding her fist a bit too hard into a disc of dough that would hopefully bake into lemon-poppy seed scones.

"Hey!" Luis scolded. "If you work over that dough anymore, they won't be flakey, they'll be hard as stone."

"Sorry, my mind drifted."

"To where? A boxing ring?" Luis joked. Hip to hip, he bumped her out of the way. "Go. I've got this."

Grabbing a platter of macarons, she took a deep, steadying breath, kept her head down and proceeded to the front counter. As she layered the pink and lavender macarons into a symmetrical pyramid, Athena came scampering over.

"Kally?"

"Yes, Athena. What can I do for you?"

"Daddy said I can have a piece of candy."

"He did?" She looked up for a split second and caught both Max and his wife looking directly at her. Maybe she was imagining it and they were simply keeping an eye on their daughter. Glancing discreetly up at them again, she saw them still gazing at her and she knew then that she wasn't mistaken. Well, whatever. It didn't matter, did it? Glancing back at the girl's eager eyes, she relented with a smile. "I'll tell you what. Come back here by me." Kally walked over to the counter opening to meet the girl, taking her by the hand. "I have a step stool back here. Step up onto it and you'll be able to see better and choose what you'd like."

Athena flashed her the widest grin, stepped up and examined each treat-filled jar carefully. After thoughtful consideration, she pointed to the rock candy lollipops. "I would like one of those, please."

"Which flavor? The pink ones are strawberry. Would you like to give one a try?"

Athena nodded eagerly.

As Kally reached for the sweet treat, Athena, still standing on the stepstool, reached up, sticking a finger through one of Kally's ringlets. "You have pretty hair."

"Thank you. So do you. Yours looks like it's been kissed by the sun." Kally handed her two lollipops. "Here, one for John, too."

It took the child no time at all to take the first lick of the crystalline confection. "I like your apron," Athena mumbled over her lolly. She ran her hand over the imprinted lavender cupcake.

"I have a whole collection of them."

Athena's eyes grew wide.

"You better bring John his candy now."

"Okay." She squeezed her arms around Kally, jumped off the stool and licked her lollipop as she made her way back to her table.

Not wanting to dwell on the sweetness of his child or the looks she could sense were peering in her direction, Kally busied herself. It struck her odd that instead of the attention being focused on their daughter, it had been on her and if her intuition was accurate, she was pretty sure they were talking about her. A few minutes later, she saw the woman leave with the two children, yet Max inexplicably remained. She tried to ignore him as he approached, busily wiping over a countertop, but a hand on hers caused her to look up into his smiling face. And once again, that nervous jolt of energy traveling through her entire being betrayed her effort to remain unaffected by him.

"Thanks. You were incredibly kind to my daughter."

"It was nothing," Kally said, pulling her hand away. "She's a very sweet child. And well-mannered. John too."

Max threw his head back and chuckled. "The kid barely lifted his eyes from his video game." Crossing his legs, he leaned against the counter. "You're Greek." It was more a statement than a question.

"That, I am. And apparently, you are as well."

"Your *karithopita* is the best I've ever had."

"High praise!"

"I'll have to see how your *galakteboureko* rates."

Max held her gaze for a brief moment until Kally self-consciously looked away. If she didn't know better, she'd think he was behaving a bit flirtatious with his hand over hers, that penetrating stare and the way he was lingering by the counter. She was about to offer him a sample of the pastry in question in a to-go container so there'd be no need for him to return when she heard a horn blow outside.

"That's for me. I'll see you around," Max said.

Whatever for, Kally wondered.

* * *

The next morning, Kally took Emma for a long walk. The sun had finally decided to return and the weather, in all its fickleness, felt as though the summer had just begun rather than ended. Cool in a lightweight ecru sundress that barely grazed her knees and her favorite metallic-colored sandals, Kally attached Emma to her bejeweled leash and headed out the door in the direction of the harbor.

From a distance, she could see the cars disembarking off the ferry, and a long line of others waiting to board. Emma trotted along as though she owned the town, knowing exactly where she wanted to go. Predictably, she stopped at every bush and each fire hydrant.

They walked the length of the pier, examining the boats still docked. Reading their clever names was an amusing pastime as she strolled by. 'Nauti-Buoy.' 'Ship Happens.' 'Codfather.'

"Come on, Emma," Kally urged, nudging her in the other direction. "Time to do a little shopping."

They crossed the road and headed down Main Street. Peeking out from behind the red, British-style telephone booth by the crosswalk were the backs of two village police officers. As one stepped into her line of view, Kally could tell by the thick, dark hair and commanding stance that it was Max.

In a split-second decision, she ducked into Gap, cutting her way to the back entrance to find another way to get to her destination.

An hour later, Kally walked out of Fame and Rebel with a large shopping bag of clothing for the upcoming season and headed back home.

"Kally!"

She turned when she heard her name and saw Max jogging toward her.

"Hey! Day off? I stopped by the café but it was closed."

"Yes. I'm closed on Mondays. Mondays and Tuesdays from January through April."

Max squatted down to pet Emma. "And who is this?"

"Emma."

"Hello, Emma." He looked up at Kally. "Can I pick her up?"

"Sure. She loves to be held."

"I know a little girl who would love to meet you, Emma. How did you come by that name for her anyway?"

Kally rocked back from one leg to another. "Jane Austen. You know, *Emma*, the novel and character."

"I'm not familiar."

"Ah, I'm not surprised," Kally said.

"What does that mean?"

"Nothing really. I suppose I take you more for a Baldacci fan."

"I tend to read biographies mostly, when I have the time."

Kally nodded, smiling politely. "Well, I have to go," she said, gesturing for Max to hand Emma back to her. "Take care."

"Wait. I'm about to go on lunch. Join me?"

"I don't think so," Kally said, the abruptness in her tone causing Max to frown.

"Have I done something to offend you?"

"No, not really. But I've learned to stay away from men like you."

Tight-lipped, Kally began to walk away. Turning, she observed his bewilderment as he stood, hands on hips with a dumbstruck look on his face. Just in case he needed further clarification, and by the look on his face he apparently did, she called out to him. "Oh, Max, don't hesitate to bring your wife and children back to the café. They're lovely."

Karithopita

Preheat oven to 350°

4 cups coarsely crushed walnuts
1½ cups sugar
3 cups flour
½ cup butter, softened
8 eggs, separated
2 teaspoons cinnamon
2 teaspoons baking powder

In a large bowl, beat the butter, sugar, egg yolks and cinnamon together. Set aside. In another bowl, beat the egg whites to a meringue. Fold into the butter mixture. Add the walnuts. Combine the flour and baking powder before adding it to the mixture. Stir until fully blended.

Butter and flour a 9 x 13 baking dish. Pour the batter into the pan. Bake for 40 minutes.

While the cake is baking, make the syrup.

5 cups sugar
5 cups water
2 cinnamon sticks

Add all the ingredients into a medium-sized saucepan. Bring to a boil. Lower the temperature to a simmer for 15 minutes.

Cut the cake into even-sized squares. Cool until warm or room temperature. Add the warm syrup, allowing the cake to fully absorb the liquid.

"Good communication is as stimulating as black coffee, and just as hard."
Anne Spencer

Chapter 6

Max

"My wife?" Max scratched along his furrowed brow, confounded. He watched her as she disappeared around the corner, shapely legs, trim waist and that gorgeous mane of curly hair swinging with the breeze. He stood, his feet frozen in place, racking his brain to figure out when he ever gave her the impression he had a wife. *I've learned to stay away from men like you.* Men like me? He played her words over and over in his mind. And then it hit him.

"I'm such an idiot!" he groaned out loud.

"For talking to yourself, or is there another reason?" a fellow officer asked, slapping him on the back good-naturedly.

"Maybe both. How's it going, Leo?"

"Better for me than for you, it seems. What gives?"

"Do you know Kally from The Coffee Klatch?" Max asked.

"Casually. I've been in there once or twice. Sweet girl."

"Yeah, well, she thinks I'm the devil or something. I asked her to have lunch with me and she almost stoned me for adultery."

"What?" Leo laughed.

Max's deep exhale was one of frustration. "Yesterday I came into the café with Athena and John and ... Lena. I introduced her to the kids, but Lena was parking the car and joined us a few minutes later."

"So?"

Max stared Leo down until he understood.

"Oh! She must have thought she was your—"

"Wife." Max sighed. "Now she thinks I'm the married man who hit on her."

"Fix it. It's easy enough to clear up," Leo said.

"Maybe it's for the best. I'm just getting my life in order. It's better I keep it simple for a while. Athena has had enough to adjust to."

"Bullshit!" Leo exclaimed. "Tomorrow morning, I'm taking your sorry ass to her place and I'll handcuff the both of you if that's what it takes for her to hear you out."

Later that evening, he called Lena and told her about Kally.

"Oh, crap! Why didn't I think of that? It's understandable how she could think such a thing," Lena said. "I should have introduced myself and this would never have happened."

"It's not your fault. There's no reason to clear things up. I told you I wasn't interested in her," Max said.

"But you are, right? Interested, I mean?"

With a deep exhale he reinforced, "I shouldn't be."

"Max, it's time. I don't mean to sound callous but it's been long enough and you deserve another chance."

"Maybe. Gotta go. Dad and I are going to watch a movie with Athena." He ended the call before she could argue further.

As Max sat with his daughter and father watching *Frozen* for probably the sixteenth time, his thoughts kept wandering to a puppy named Emma and her owner. He couldn't help but wonder how they were spending their evening.

Chapter 7

Kally

"Why all the questions tonight, Kalloype *mou*?" Melina asked. "What's weighing on your mind?"

Kally had gone to her mother's home. Her father was working, *Yiayiá* was with her cousin and Theo and Krystina were at the church youth group meeting, so this was a rare chance to catch her alone. Her mind had been spinning since she'd run into Max earlier that day and she desperately needed someone to talk to right now.

"Max asked me to lunch today."

"Who's Max?"

"From church. The one you kept pushing me to speak to."

"And that's making you sad?" Melina cupped her daughter's chin between her fingers.

"He's married." She looked up at her mother. "All men suck! Seriously. I saw her at the café. She's gorgeous, of course. What would possess any man to stray when he has such a perfect family?"

"I don't know, *koukla*. Forget him. Someday the right man will come along."

Kally ignored her mother's statement. The 'right man' was something she didn't pin her hopes on. "Why did you take Dad back after finding out he'd had an affair?" she asked suddenly. "How were you able to forgive him?"

"We were separated at the time. I thought that was understood." Melina frowned. "All these years, that's what you thought? That your father had been unfaithful?"

"You never talked about it, so I assumed."

"Your father and I weren't getting along. We fought constantly. He accused me of continually nagging him and I told him he was too controlling."

"And it's different today, how?" Kally asked.

"Very different," she admitted. "There was much more to it. He was staying out late, night after night … gambling. It became a problem. He put us into terrible debt," Melina explained. "I was furious. We had two little girls and my mother to support. He never wanted me to get a job of my own, meanwhile, he'd put us in a horrible situation."

"How did I not know any of this before?" Kally asked.

"I didn't want you to think badly of your father."

"So how did things change?"

"I took the civil service test and, it took a while, but I landed my job with the county. I had to do something to pay the bills. When your father found out, he lost his mind."

"I don't understand," Kally said.

"He didn't want me to work. And I think he recognized he had failed us and he couldn't deal with it." Melina got up from the kitchen table and poured herself a glass of wine. "Want one?"

"Definitely! I think I need it now more than I did before." She took the glass, savoring the first sip. "You got the job …" Kally waved her hand, urging her mother to continue.

"I said a lot of awful things to him. Truthful, but awful," Melina admitted. "I told him he was destroying our family and that if he kept it up, at this rate, we'd all end up on the streets. I told him I had to get a job because he wasn't supporting us."

Melina drew in a deep breath as if to steel herself. Kally sipped her wine, keeping her eyes trained on her mother, waiting to hear what she was hesitant to say.

"Then I asked him to leave and to not bother returning until he'd handled his addiction and settled his debts."

"That was gutsy."

"It sure was," Melina said. "I was scared shitless!"

"What happened? All I remember was Dad telling us he had to leave for a while and he'd be back when he could."

"He packed his things and slept at a friend's house. Two days later, he was on a plane to Athens. He called me from the airport to tell me he was about to board."

"Just like that?" Kally was astounded.

"Pretty much. He said he was going to work for his father and he'd send money home to us."

"He explained to me that his parents needed him and he'd be home as soon as he could," Kally remembered. "But he was away for what felt like a very long time."

"Over a year," Melina confirmed. "At the time, your *pappou* owned two jewelry stores. One in Monastiraki Square and the other at the Plaka. Your father went to work for him, partially on commission, and he did very well for himself."

"He kept in touch with you?" Kally asked.

"Yes, but I was so angry with him for leaving the way he did that I asked for a formal separation." Melina drained her wine glass. "I had told him to get his shit together, not to abandon his family by leaving the country. I never filed papers, but as far as we were concerned, we had split, and I wasn't sure if your father was ever coming back."

"And his answer was to have an affair?" To Kally, her mother's story only confirmed that men were not to be trusted.

"He said it happened when he read my letter telling him I wanted a separation. I never knew about the affair or Theo until your father and I had already reconciled and conceived Krystina."

"Are you kidding?" Kally's head was spinning.

"Nope. Open another bottle of wine," Melina said. "We're going to need it."

Chapter 8

Melina

2001

Melina stepped into an unusually quiet house after driving home from work. Normally, by five o'clock, music was blaring and George was yelling for the girls to turn the noise down. That is, if he had not yet left for the restaurant he'd opened the year after he and Melina had reconciled.

George had paid his debts, sent money home on a regular basis and had stopped gambling entirely. Once he'd proven himself and begged for forgiveness, Melina had conceded, telling her husband to finally come home. The children had missed their father and, although she didn't want to admit it, his absence had affected her as well.

"Girls? George? Where is everyone?" Melina stepped into the kitchen from the garage door. She dropped her keys in a metal bowl on the counter and shrugged off her raincoat.

Following the clinking sound of glass hitting glass, she walked into the living room and found her husband pouring a shot glass of *raki*. It was obvious by the way he missed the glass that this drink was far from his first. He was drunk. Or at least getting there.

"George?" Melina asked, her voice hesitant. She noticed a letter on the coffee table. Even from a distance she could see the envelope was stamped from overseas. "Did you get bad news? Is it your parents?"

George looked up at his wife, his eyes glazed over with a mixture of inebriation and tears. He covered his face with his hands and shook his head. "If I tell you, you'll leave me again."

"What is it?" Melina demanded. "Just tell me." She could feel her heart beating with such force, she thought it might rip her chest open. What could be so bad that he could think such a thing? What had he done?

"You can read for yourself," George said, picking up the letter with a shaky hand. He clung to it tightly. "But before you do, you have to know that I thought you would never take me back." He slapped his forehead. "You wouldn't talk to me. I was inconsolable and I eventually looked for comfort wherever I could find it."

"Give me the letter, *Yióryios*." Melina snatched it from his hands. "Comfort! You bastard. You never told me you had an affair."

"If I thought I had a chance with you I never would have."

"Fucking Greek men," she muttered under her breath. "Just like my own father. Abandoned my mother. Probably for a cheap piece of ass."

"I didn't abandon you!" George shouted. "I sent money. I asked you to let me come home. Don't compare me to your father; a father who sent you and your mother to a foreign country and never came for you!"

She didn't answer or make further comment. He was right. It was unfair to compare him to a man she never had the chance to know. Instead, she continued reading, gasping in shock as the details were revealed. Tears sprung to her eyes and she glanced back at George, mortified.

"You have a son," Melina's voice trembled.

"According to what Rovena told my parents," George said, his eyes peering at her regretfully. "The timeline works, but I can't know for sure."

"I need time to absorb all of this." Letter in hand, Melina turned and began to exit the room.

"Where are you going?"

"Out. I can't be near you right now. I need to be alone." She halted, pivoting to look at him. "Where are the girls? And my mother?"

"*Mamá* went to see Rhea. Kally was going to Egypt's house and I asked her to take Mia with her."

"I'll pick the girls up," Melina said coldly. "You're in no condition to go anywhere."

* * *

When Melina arrived home with the girls, George was passed out, sprawled on the floor between the coffee table and the couch, an empty bottle of *raki* in his hand. The girls looked at their father in horror and called out to him.

"He's okay, girls. He's just had too much to drink."

"Are you sure?" Kally asked, rushing to his side. She checked his pulse. "I was worried he'd had a heart attack."

Mia was frozen in place but for the tears streaming down her cheeks. At nine years old, she was still a child who felt more at ease clinging to her mother's apron strings.

"He's fine, *mikroúli mou*," Melina said, bending down to wipe away Mia's tears. "Your father received some surprising news and he drank a little too much. That's all. Go get into your pajamas and I'll come tuck you into bed."

Once Mia had disappeared, Melina asked Kally to help her get George up the stairs.

"I've never seen him like this, Mom."

"I'll explain when I can, but I need to speak to your father when his head is clear."

"Should I be worried?" Kally asked.

"No. As long as no one is ill or dying, just about every problem can be managed."

⋆ ⋆ ⋆

"Shut the blinds!" George groaned, shielding his face from the sun obnoxiously streaming in through the bedroom window.

Melina stood over him tight-lipped, one eyebrow raised and her hangover cure in hand—steaming lemon water with crushed *mastiha*, dry toast, two ibuprofen and tomato juice to wash the pills down.

He waved her off but she pushed the juice glass in his face and handed him the pills. "Drink," she ordered. She wasn't in the mood for his bullshit. They had too much to discuss.

After he'd showered and had something to eat, they locked themselves in their bedroom for privacy.

Melina broke the silence first. "Did you love her?" she asked stiffly, her back to him.

George came up behind her, turning her by the shoulders to face him. "I love you. No one else. It's always been you."

"Then why?"

"I was lonely. A little mad. Hopeless. I knew it was all my fault." The sincerity shone through his hazel eyes. "She was there and I was weak."

"And now there's a child." Melina sighed.

"Presumably so."

"We need to find out for sure," Melina said. "We obviously can't ask your mistress, poor thing."

"Rovena wasn't my mistress," George corrected.

"Don't split hairs with me, *Yióyios*," she scolded. "Whatever she was to you, she's gone now. And as much as I want to hate her, I can't. A brain aneurysm at thirty-two! Poor girl. It's truly tragic."

"It is. And I know this is the last thing you want to hear but she was a kind girl. She came from Albania to find work; my parents took her in and hired her."

"Did your parents know about the two of you?" Melina asked.

"No. I suppose she told them after Theo was born. They have him now."

Melina nodded. "That has to change. They've been talking about retirement, not starting a family."

"I know, but what am I to do?" George ran his fingers through his thick waves.

"What are you to do?" Melina repeated, aghast. "*Vre, Yióyios!* What do you think? We'll go to Athens and find out for ourselves if this child is yours."

"You'll come with me?" he asked.

"Of course." Melina planted her hands on her hips. "You'll need me."

George wrapped his arms around his wife, looking deeply into her eyes. "I thought I lost you again. Can you forgive me?"

She brushed away the curl falling over his forehead. "There's nothing to forgive. I was just as much at fault. I offered you no hope that I'd take you back." She brushed her lips against his. "Let's leave it all in the past. Whatever is to be now, we'll handle together."

George took his wife's face in his hands and kissed her. He moved from her lips to her neck, pushing away the strap of the camisole exposed under the slouchy shoulder top she wore. Grazing the silhouette of her shapely body, he roamed from her breasts to her hips and finally landed on her backside. With the palms of his hands, he pulled what he called her 'luscious Peloponnesian cheeks' toward his growing arousal and groaned.

Melina, equally turned on, freed her husband of the only garment he wore, a navy-colored pair of boxer briefs.

George, in caveman manner, picked her up over his shoulder, slapped her playfully on her ass and threw her onto the bed. He then proceeded to shed every bit of her clothing in little enough time to win a Guinness World Record.

"What happened to your hangover?" Melina giggled.

* * *

The week before Melina and George left for Athens had been stress-ful. So much had to be arranged and far too much explained. There was a strong possibility the girls would be gaining a brother when they returned home. To tell or not to tell. That was the question. What if the child didn't belong to George? Must the children know about their father's affair? Melina thought not. But if he was her chil-dren's brother, they couldn't bring a child into their home with no explanation.

In the end, they told all the necessary parties, took time off from work, arranged cover for the restaurant and additional help from her cousins with the children, should Melina's mother need it. As for the girls, all they needed to know for the moment was that their grand-parents needed their help.

With all of that out of the way, they were finally about to land in Athens. Despite the circumstances, Melina was excited. Many of her friends traveled to Greece on a regular basis, visiting family each year, but that had never been the case with the Andarakis family nor with Melina and her mother before she'd married George.

She and her mother struggled to make ends meet, but even if they hadn't, the thought of going back to Kalamata was painful. Melina's father, Panayiotis, had sent her and her mother to America ahead of himself with the promise that he would join them shortly. But that day never came, and as far as Melina knew he never wrote to them either. Kalliope, Melina's mother, had tried to track him down, but no one had any information. He had disappeared from their lives without a single word.

Once Melina married George, they only managed to get to Athens once to visit his family. But now, she was about to be ensconced in the land and culture of her heritage, something she hoped could happen more often. She wanted to expose her children to their culture, to experience Athens as she never could. Still, she had never expected to come under these circumstances.

Melina examined herself in the restroom mirror after landing. She had managed little sleep on the overnight flight. Coach wasn't the most comfortable way to fly on a nine-hour journey, especially coupled with inedible food and screaming children. Touching up her make-up and brushing her shoulder-length hair was the best she could do to make herself somewhat presentable.

The taxi ride was a whole other adventure. What should have taken thirty minutes grew close to an hour, even as the driver wove in and out of traffic, nearly ran a motorcycle off the road and practically took down an old man carrying a sack of groceries.

While Melina was gasping at every turn and jerk, the driver was unperturbed. She held her breath as he complained about the state of the economy and the politics of the nation, his cigarette bobbing up and down, dangling from the corner of his mouth. Every time his animated hands left the steering wheel, Melina dug her fingernails into her husband's leg.

George chuckled. "You're such an American."

"I'd like to be a living American."

When they finally pulled up in front of her in-laws' apartment, Melina's stomach felt jittery. "I think I lost ten pounds in sweat."

George took the bags from the taxi while Melina rang the door-bell. When the door opened, George's mother greeted her. But she was not alone. A child, the spitting image of her husband, stood by her side.

She had survived the cab ride, but would she survive this? The possibility that the child was George's was almost definite in her mind. But seeing him in the flesh was, to say the least, a bit earth shattering. Aside from the golden hair, he was her husband in miniature form—the wavy curls, hazel eyes and his facial bone structure. They didn't need a paternity test. There was no doubt. This was George's child.

Chapter 9

Kally

"And it wasn't long after we got home that I was blessed with another surprise," Melina said. "What I had assumed was airsickness during a rough ride home turned out to be pregnancy."

"With Krystina. Wow!" Kally exclaimed. "I never really thought about it, but in a matter of months you went from having two children to four."

"Unexpectedly on both counts."

"I give you a lot of credit, Mom," Kally said. She had her legs draped over her mother's lap as they sank into the sofa cushions. "Mia was little and it was easy to simply tell her Theo was her brother and leave it at that. But with me, it was different. You couldn't hide the truth from me."

While Melina massaged her daughter's feet with her free hand, the other was occupied with yet another glass of red wine. She took a long sip and set the glass down. "I did my best to explain it without shedding a bad light on your father."

"I don't think I could ever be that forgiving or put up with so much," Kally mused.

"For all his faults, he's a good man and he loves us." Melina pointed a finger at Kally. "I mean it. You need to understand that."

"I know, but you two have such a strange relationship. You're always bickering." Kally swung her legs around, sitting up and placing her empty wine glass on the table.

"It's healthier to argue than to not speak at all. You'll understand what I mean one day," Melina said. "There's two things you need to take away from what I've told you." Melina raised her forefinger. "One. Things aren't always what they seem, so don't jump to conclusions. And yes, I'm referring to that young man."

"He's inconsequential." Kally waved her mother off.

"Uh-huh. Inconsequential, yet you came to vent to me." Melina gave Kally that look she hated. The 'I'm your mother and I can see right through you,' look.

"What's the other thing?" Kally asked, biting back her annoyance.

"The second thing is that no matter what they think or say, we are the stronger sex. They might be physically stronger, but it's the females who do the heavy lifting. We fix the messes, soothe the souls and find the solutions. Remember that."

"So in other words, who needs them?" Kally joked. She knew that wasn't the point her mother was trying to make.

"Go home before I threaten to make a dating profile for you," Melina said.

"You wouldn't dare!"

* * *

After the unexpected dose of reality given by her mother, Kally decided it was time to snuggle up with Emma in bed and get lost in a new book—the fantasy romance kind. Regular girl meets hot billionaire. He has eyes only for her even though he's been with dozens of uber-gorgeous women. They jet off to faraway places and make mad, passionate love constantly. Let's forget that he runs an empire and she has a job. Unimportant details.

And that's the beauty and fun of romance fiction. There isn't a chance in heaven or hell that any of that could ever happen.

* * *

The next day, Kally woke up with a new attitude. Yes, her mother's confession surprised her. But she had also learned her father hadn't been unfaithful to her mother. Technically, maybe, but they had agreed to split, so they weren't together at the time. It certainly put a different light on how she viewed him.

Life was what you carved out for yourself and, this morning, she wore an apron stating that sentiment. A four-tiered cake on the bib of the apron was inscribed with curly letters, 'Life is what you bake of it.'

No earbuds today. Instead, she turned up the volume on her Bose player to the Barbra Streisand Pandora station. As though on a mission, Kally set out her ingredients while singing 'Don't Rain on My Parade' at the top of her lungs.

On her third chorus of 'Second hand Rose' there was a loud gurgling sound behind her. Whipping her head around, she saw Egypt holding the cord to the plug.

"Are you trying to deafen the entire neighborhood?" Egypt asked.

"It's just Barbra."

"Oh, it's not Barbra who sounds like a cow giving birth," Egypt retorted.

"Very funny." Kally held her head high, straightening her back. "I'm not going to let you spoil my mood."

"And what's put you in such a cheery mood?"

"I'm normally in a good mood, aren't I?"

"Normally, but lately you've been—"

"What?" Kally crossed her arms over her chest.

"A little all over the map. Almost like you were when—"

Kally raised her palm to Egypt, her smile dropping. "Stop."

* * *

With the weather still relatively pleasant, foot traffic along the main streets of the town was heavy. Patrons breezed in and out of the café, some searching for a specialty drink to sip as they shopped while others met with friends, settling in for a long visit in a seat by the window.

It was a little after two o'clock by the time a lull afforded the staff to slow down and take a break. Egypt rolled her eyes and huffed out her annoyance at the sound of the door chime alerting her of someone's arrival. As if her legs were made of lead, she dragged one and then the other off the stepstool she'd only just rested them on.

Standing up to greet the customers, she stared, her eyes widening. "Holy mother of God, there's two of them!" she muttered. Her gaze bounced from one to the other as they stood erectly by the door; Max, a bit paler than normal, the other slice of deliciousness, assessing her with a hint of a smile.

"Hi," Egypt said, barely breathing out a sound. She cleared her throat. "Can I help you, Officers?"

Delicious Man pushed Max forward. "Speak, man," he ordered.

"Is Kally here?" Max asked.

"Uh-huh," Egypt answered.

When neither Max nor Egypt said anything more, Delicious Man spoke up. "Would you ask her to come out front?"

Egypt bounced her head up and down like a bobblehead doll and scurried into the kitchen.

* * *

Kally stopped what she was doing and looked up at Egypt with amusement. Her friend had a flare for dramatic entrances, so Kally nonchalantly lifted her glass of iced tea and took a long draw from the straw.

The way in which Egypt was clutching her chest, someone would think the girl was having a heart attack. But her blazing green eyes spoke of something else.

"Spit it out, Egypt," Kally laughed. "What is it this time?"

Egypt came within whispering distance. Pointing toward the door, she burst out, "There is a hotter than fuck cop out there with another hotter than fuck cop—you know, license plate cop—asking you to come out front."

"Which one is asking?" Kally furrowed her brow.

"Who cares! Go out there."

"You don't know this other officer?" Kally asked.

"I've never seen him. Believe me, he's not someone I'd forget," Egypt swooned. "Skin as smooth as a milk chocolate Hershey kiss … powerful, grey eyes …" A sigh caught in her throat. "But never mind that!" She got behind Kally and pushed her out the door.

"Stop it! I can get there on my own two feet." Kally's stomach did a little flip. What did Max want now? Didn't he get the message that she wasn't the sort of woman who carried on with married men?

As the door to the kitchen swung open, Kally felt the constriction in her chest and the heat rise to her cheeks as their eyes met. This man should not be having this effect on her. Oddly, Max seemed nervous too. He stood and stared at her without a word until his partner … friend … whomever, nudged him in the shoulder.

Max cleared his throat. "Umm, can I have a minute of your time … please?" he stammered.

"Sure." Kally gestured with her hands for him to proceed.

"Maybe somewhere a little more private?" he asked.

"Is the corner table private enough?" Kally suggested more confidently than she felt.

He nodded and they wove their way through the other tables to get to the back of the room. He waited for Kally to sit first and then slid into his seat. Keeping his gaze averted from her, he ran his fingers over his forehead.

Kally furrowed her brow, speculating what he was trying to get to. "I really only have a couple of minutes," she prompted.

"Of course." Max inhaled and then exhaled nervously. His tension was evident. "I realized that you completely misunderstood my situation the other day and I want to clear it up."

"You don't owe me any explanations," Kally said sternly.

"But I do, especially if you think I'm a married man who would ask another woman out," Max insisted. "Lena, the woman I was with on Sunday, is not my wife. It never occurred to me you would even think that. I come from a big family. I'm one of four brothers. Lena is my sister-in-law. My brother's wife."

Kally put a hand to her mouth, aghast. "I'm so sorry for jumping to conclusions."

Max shook his head. "No, I see now how it must have looked. I never introduced the two of you. She came in after me and, I guess, you made the logical assumption."

"Oh my God, I am so sorry. You hit a nerve, that's all. And I took it out on you."

"Yes, something you said gave me that impression." Max looked into her eyes. "Anything you want to talk about? I'm a good listener?"

"No," Kally said abruptly. "But what about Athena and John? Where is their mother?"

"Lena is John's mother. He's my nephew. Athena is mine. Her mother is … no longer with us."

Kally could see the pain swimming in Max's eyes. She bit the inside of her lip to keep from shedding tears in front of him. How could she have been so wrong?

"I'm so sorry. I've said that a lot in the last five minutes," Kally apologized. "But it's so terribly tragic for you. And for Athena to have lost her at such a young age."

Max stiffened. Kally could see it in his jaw—his neck—his shoulders.

"It's not something I like to talk about."

Kally nodded, reaching out her hand to comfort him. "I understand perfectly." Max took hold of it and rubbed his thumb along the top of her hand but she gently pulled away. "We all have that one thing we avoid speaking of."

Max rubbed at the back of his neck. "So … we're good?"

Kally stood, smoothing out her apron as if it was her most important task of the day. "Of course. I should never have jumped to conclusions."

She was about to say goodbye but Max hastily rose from his seat. "Wait," he said. "Athena hasn't stopped talking about you, or this place."

Kally's face lit up. "I really enjoyed meeting her too. Bring her by any time." Awkwardly, they stared at one another until Kally broke the silence. "I … have to get back," she said, pointing toward the kitchen.

"I better get going too." Max turned to glance at Leo who was leaning over the counter, flirtatiously chatting with Egypt. "If I can pull him away that is."

Kally giggled, shaking her head. "Take care, Max. Tell Athena I will have an extra special cupcake waiting for her next time you bring her here."

Max waved goodbye and joined Leo, nudging him by the shoulders in the direction of the exit.

The officers had barely made it out the front door before Egypt shrieked her way over to Kally, her hands hanging onto the counter for support as if she was about to faint.

"I can't figure out if you're about to pass out or have a seizure," Kally said, pressing her lips together to hold back a smirk.

"Leo," Egypt choked out. "That's his name. Like a lion," she purred, swaying her hips. "And I'll gladly be his prey."

Her friend! She always kept Kally amused. Kally was like the Devonshire cream to a fruit-filled scone: a little sweet; a little plain. The sidekick of the pastry. Tastier accented with a dab of cream, but make no mistake, the scone was the star, oozing with flavor. Egypt was definitely the scone, Kally thought.

"Let's start to clean up and get ready to close for the day," Kally suggested.

"Hold on one minute, lady!" Egypt blocked her path. "I've been going on about Lee-oo," she stretched out his name, "but what did Max want?"

"We had a miscommunication and he wanted to clear it up. No big deal."

"Kally? Spill," she demanded.

Kally let out a frustrated breath. "He's not married, okay? Lena is his sister-in-law. Happy now?"

"I knew it!" Egypt exclaimed. "Divorced?"

"Widower."

"Oh, that's sad. How long?"

"I don't know," Kally said. "It wasn't something he wanted to discuss." She wet a clean rag and wiped down the counters where the baking trays had been stacked.

"Did he ask you out?"

"You're relentless. No." Kally walked over to the sink and rinsed out the rag. Turning, she added, "But he did tell me he planned on bringing his daughter back. She loved it here."

"What kid wouldn't?" Egypt asked. "But I bet her dad liked it even better."

Kally flung the sopping wet rag, hitting Egypt square on the back of the head.

"I'll get even with you for that when you least expect it," Egypt promised.

"I have no doubt! Come on, let's go home. I'm exhausted."

Chapter 10

Max

"I don't get you, man," Leo said. "You explained to her that you're not the lying, cheating bastard she thought you were, you're available and you like her. Yet you didn't ask her out?"

"First of all, you're assuming she'd say yes. And—"

"Wait! Assuming? The way the girls flirt with you on the street?" Leo scoffed.

"No different for you, bigshot," Max retorted. "Did you get Egypt to agree to a date?"

"Didn't ask her."

Max shot him a questioning look.

"Yet," Leo said with conviction. "I just met the girl. But she is one sweet little thing."

"She's very pretty, I'll agree." Max chuckled. "You must be a full foot taller than she is though."

"It doesn't make her any less intriguing," Leo admitted. "Especially with that fascinating line of tattoos running down from the base of her neck."

"You like that, huh?" Max asked. "Not my thing."

"If your thing is Kally, you better get a move on it."

"Every time I want to, something stops me. The last couple of years have been rough," Max admitted. "I need stability for Athena and for my own peace of mind. We're just getting there and I don't need to add anything to the equation. Not just yet."

"You can't live the life of a monk," Leo disagreed. "It's time to move forward. I'm not telling you to force it. But don't sabotage it either."

"There's nothing to sabotage," Max grumbled. "Just drop it."

* * *

Fallen leaves of orange, brown and gold crunched under the weight of Max's shoes as he paced the corner of the street waiting for Athena's school bus to arrive. Two weeks had passed since he had gone to speak to Kally. He hadn't taken his daughter back to The Coffee Klatch, even with her constant begging, always answering her in the same way; with 'another day,' or 'maybe next week.'

He was avoiding Kally and he knew it. But in this town, she was ubiquitous. She went to the same church, he spotted her walking her dog in town, snatched a view of her picking up food at the Mexican takeout on Main Street and he even saw her from a distance at the Farmer's Market in the village center. It was getting difficult to dodge her, but every time he was close, it was impossible to keep his mind on the priorities he set for himself.

Today, he would have to put his big boy boxer briefs on, suck it up and muster the willpower to walk into Kally's place. He sighed deeply. He had to do this for his daughter's sake. She'd been looking forward to it all week.

The bus pulled up and the door swung open. Athena was one of the first children to exit. She leapt from the bus and ran to Max.

"We have to hurry home!" she said with excitement. "The party starts at four-thirty and I have to change my clothes and you need to do my hair and we can't forget the gift and can you fix my hair and—"

"Hey, take a breath, Tinkerbell!" Max grinned. "And hello to you too!"

"Hi, Dad! I'm just so excited!"

"I would have never guessed," he joked. "Don't worry. We have plenty of time to get there."

An hour and a half later, a very eager Athena and her slightly hesitant father walked through the doors of the café for a birthday party. The Coffee Klatch had closed early that afternoon and was catering only to Jenna and her twenty-eight friends.

Tables covered with vinyl tablecloths were pushed together in long rows to seat the children together. Each place setting held two undecorated cookies for the partygoers to adorn. Pastry bags filled with icing, sprinkles and colored sugars were within arm's reach for all the children to get as creative as they wished.

Mothers sat at tables on the perimeter of the café, conversing and drinking coffee while staff guided and instructed the little guests on how to decorate.

Jenna, the birthday girl, ran to Athena when she saw her walk through the door.

"This is for you," Athena said with a grin from ear to ear. "Happy birthday."

"Thanks!" Jenna took the gift and placed it on a table with the others. "I saved you the seat next to mine."

And just like that, Athena left Max's side without a second thought. It made his heart swell to see his daughter thriving. He still had visions in his head of her tear-stained face and her frightened expression after each of her nightmares. Shaking his head, he dispelled the memories. He never wanted to see her like that again.

Max watched in awe at the complete control over what he thought should have been a chaotic disaster. More than two dozen six-year-old boys and girls were playing with frosting and sugar. Yet, the four women working with them ran the show like conductors guiding a symphony.

Kally had been busier than most. She'd barely taken her attention from the children for a second. When she came around to Athena's chair, Max saw his daughter stand to hug her around the waist. Kally returned the endearment, kissed her on the cheek and whispered something in her ear.

The exchange tugged at Max's heart. Turning, Kally looked up and caught his eye. Smiling, she waved to him.

Max waved back and mouthed, "Hi," feeling a little embarrassed that he hadn't so much as stopped by to see her in weeks and here she was being so kind to his child.

After the decorating was complete, the cookies were taken into the kitchen to dry and later wrapped in colored Cellophane to take home. The women bustled about the tables, clearing and setting them with Minion themed tableware. Jars of blue and yellow candy treats were spread out and each guest was given a clear bag to fill as their party favor.

Kally had created a two-tier cake with three dimensional Minions made from gumpaste sugar. Almost every child asked if they could have one of the slices with a little yellow figure on it.

Athena ran to Max. "Kally made that!" she squealed with delight, pointing to the cake. "Can she make mine when it's my birthday?"

"Whatever you want, Tink."

He watched as his daughter skipped away happily. But it was the woman with her hair tied up in a mass of curls and an apron that read, 'Baking is my superpower and my apron is my cape,' who had his attention.

Slowly, the party wound down and the guests began to leave. When just about everyone but Jenna and her mother had gone, Max lingered a little longer, offering to help Kally push the tables back to where they belonged.

"That's really nice of you, but Athena must be tired," Kally said. "We can handle it."

"I'm not tired," Athena chimed in.

"If Max is staying then I'm heading out," Egypt said. "I have a date tonight."

Max snuck a sly glance at Egypt. He didn't need to guess her date was with Leo.

"Don't look at me that way," she whispered, patting him on the shoulder as she walked out the door. "You might want to take a lesson or two from your friend."

"You can go too, Julie. Krystina and I will finish up," Kally said.

"Thanks. You were great with the kids."

"Can I help?" Athena asked, her eyes shining with enthusiasm.

Kally looked to Max for approval and he nodded. "Sure, sweetie. Why don't you help my sister take the candy from the jars and put them back in the boxes?"

"You have a sister?"

"I have two sisters and a brother," Kally said. "This is Krystina, my little sister."

"I'd like to have a sister," Athena said.

The table Max was pushing in place slammed into the wall. Kally looked over to him quickly before turning her attention back to his daughter.

"I'll tell you what, if Krystina agrees, you can borrow her."

Athena giggled. "You can't borrow a sister."

"I have a secret for you. Something my *yiayiá* told me," Kally said, bending down to her level.

"You have a *yiayiá*?" Athena asked, wide-eyed and impressed.

"Yes, I do. She lives with us."

"I don't have one," she said with resounding disappointment. "I don't have a mother either." A small sob escaped her.

Kally latched onto the child and held her while Krystina stroked her hair. Max would have snatched her from them and squeezed all his love into her if his heart hadn't cracked liked dry clay hitting cement.

"Each family is made up a little differently, but the children in it are loved all the same," Kally murmured to her.

"I know," Athena said in a low voice. "What's the secret?" she asked, looking up at Kally with glassy eyes.

"Secret? Oh! You said you can't borrow a sister but you can. You know why?"

Athena shook her head.

"Because you can't tell a Greek woman she can't do something. That's why. We come from a long line of strong women going back thousands of years," Kally said. "And you! You're named after a goddess. The goddess of wisdom. And if that wasn't enough, she was also a warrior. No one wanted to mess with her."

Max watched on as his daughter began to laugh. She looped her arms around Kally's neck.

"No one better mess with me," Athena giggled.

"Or they'll have to answer to me," Max said firmly. "Time to go home. I think Kally and Krystina have had enough for one day."

"Can I come back and bake with you another day?"

"Athena, this was a party," Max reminded her.

Kally held her palm up to Max to silence him. "You are welcome any time. As a matter of fact, my *yiayiá* is coming here tomorrow to bake something very special. Would you like to help?"

"Can I, Daddy? Please?"

"If you're sure it's not too much trouble," Max said uncertainly.

"Not at all. We are making *artoklasia* to bring to church on Sunday. Our family is making the offering."

"What is that?" Athena asked.

"Sometimes when we go to church at the end of liturgy the priest gives us large pieces of sweet bread. Have you ever had that?" Kally asked.

Athena nodded. "I like that one."

"That's good, but it's not just to eat something that tastes good. We bring it to thank God for all the blessings in our lives."

"I'm coming too," Krystina added. "We can learn how to make it together."

"Okay," Athena agreed. "And you can be my sister tomorrow."

"That's a deal." Krystina outstretched her arm to shake on it. "I'm the youngest in our family. I always wanted a little sister."

Athena's smile could have illuminated a darkened planet. Krystina took her by the hand and led her into the kitchen.

Max shuffled his feet awkwardly. To think he was once an over-confident, cocky bastard and here he was now, not knowing how to behave in front of the most genuine person he'd met in years. "Thanks for all of this," he mumbled. "You've been more than generous with Athena."

"It's nothing."

"But it is and I'm sorry," he said.

"Sorry for what?" Kally asked in surprise.

"For not coming around the last couple of weeks."

"You're apologizing for not wanting coffee and cake?"

"Are you going to make this harder on me than it needs to be?" Max asked.

"There's nothing to make more difficult, is there?"

He hesitated. "No," he said with a deep sigh.

"What time can you drop Athena off?"

"Is two-thirty okay? My shift starts at three. I'll see who I can get to pick her up when you're done."

"What time do you get off?" Kally asked.

"Eleven."

"I can take her home with me and you can pick her up from there."

"That would be imposing too much on you," Max said.

"Not at all."

Athena and Krystina came back from the kitchen.

"Okay then. Thanks. She'd love that," Max conceded with a glance at his daughter's expression. "Ready?" He took his daughter's hand and headed for the door. "Goodnight. See you tomorrow."

"If baking is any labor at all, it's a labor of love. A love that gets passed from generation to generation." Regina Brett

Chapter 11

Kally

Athena bounced her way into the café kitchen. "Hi, Kally," she said. "Krystina said I could come back here."

"Only bakers allowed," Kally said seriously, bending down to hug the child.

"Hey, Kal," Krystina called out, cracking the door open. "Max would like to speak to you for a second."

"Send him on back," Kally answered. "Athena, I have someone I want you to meet."

Kally waved her *yiayiá* over. The tiny woman emerged from the pantry closet carrying a sack of flour that had to be almost as heavy as she was.

"Athena, this is my *yiayiá.*"

Athena politely extended her hand but the old woman grabbed the child's face instead, kissing her on both cheeks. "*Póso ómorfi eísai. Ftou sou, ftou sou.* Beautiful girl!" *Yiayiá* said, rapidly making the sign of the cross three times.

Kally turned at the sound of heavy footsteps to find Max, brows raised, grinning. She walked over to him. "You think that's funny? Wait. Or better yet, run."

But it was too late, Kally caught the mischievous gleam in her grandmother's eyes. "*Yiayiá*, this is Athena's father, Max."

She lifted her hands as if calling to the heavens. "*Po, po!*" she declared with rapt admiration. She reached up and held Max's face in her hands. He bent down reluctantly to give the old woman easier access and Kally covered her face with her hands, embarrassed.

"Beautiful boy! You Greek?"

"Yes, Ma'am," Max said, lifting back to his full height.

"My Kallyope is—"

"Okay, *Yiayiá*," Kally interrupted. "Max will be late for his shift if you take any more of his time."

"*Éla, Athená.*" *Yiayiá* took the eager girl by the hand, leading her further into the kitchen. "I have something for you."

"Thanks again for this," Max said to Kally. "She's been asking just about every hour if it was time to head over here."

"I'm not sure who will have more fun, Athena or my grandmother." Kally cocked her head in their direction.

Athena skipped over. "Look at me! Look at me, Daddy!" She spun around, giving him full view of her apron.

"That was mine when I was just about your age," Kally informed her.

"I know! *Yiayiá* said I could wear it."

"You can keep it." Kally said, playfully poking her in the belly.

"Can I, Daddy?" She puffed out her chest. "Read what it says!"

A white stork carrying a baby bundled in a Greek flag was imprinted on the Robin's egg-blue apron. Captioned underneath the image was 'Made in the USA with Greek ingredients.'

Max read it out loud. "Just like you. I guess that means it's yours." He tapped a finger to her nose. "Have fun." He turned to Kally. "I'll pick her up a little after eleven. Thanks again for this," Max said, brushing his hand lightly across her arm.

"Any time," Kally said as their eyes held for a brief moment. The graze of his fingertips sent a jolt straight to her heart. And it wasn't even a lingering brush of his hand; it was a tap. Nonetheless, her heart ceased to beat for a second or two.

"So … later then," he said.

"Yup." Could she be any more awkward? Not knowing what else to do with Max still planted in one spot, staring at her, Kally turned and padded over to Athena and her grandmother. Doing her best to ignore the unnerving energy she felt every time he was near, relief washed over her when she finally heard the creak of the swinging door. Kally exhaled slowly and went back to the task at hand.

Fisting her hands on her hips, Kally jokingly stamped her feet in protest. "Hey, did you start without me?"

"I'm beating the eggs!" Athena said.

"I can see that. That's a job fit only for a big girl." Kally could see Athena was taking her assignment seriously and she wondered if the child had ever done anything like this with her own mother. Max hadn't elaborated on the circumstances of her death. Was it recent or so long ago that Athena had no recollection of her mother at all?

As they kneaded the dough, *Yiayiá* explained to Athena the symbolism behind the offering of the *artoklasia*. Not only was it a gesture of thanksgiving for all of God's blessings, but it was also a representation of the miracle when Christ had multiplied five loaves of bread to feed five thousand people.

Mesmerized, Athena didn't take her eyes off the animated, heavily-accented woman as she spoke. Meanwhile, Kally separated the dough into five mounds, handing one to Athena to form into a ball. After they placed each round loaf on a greased baking sheet, covered them with a cloth and set them aside to rise, it was time for a break.

"How would you like a mug of hot cocoa?" Kally asked Athena.

Her eyes widened as she nodded enthusiastically. "And a cupcake? Please?"

"Absolutely!" She took her by the hand and they walked to the front counter.

Sitting at a table by the window, the remnants of fading sunlight cast a pink reflection off Athena's golden tresses. "Don't move!" Kally said as she pulled her iPhone from her apron pocket. She snapped a photo and turned the screen to show her. "Look! You have pink hair."

Athena laughed. "Let me take your picture."

Kally handed her the phone and made a silly face for the camera.

"Not pink," Athena said, disappointed.

"My hair is too dark," Kally replied. "But your pretty hair is like a canvas for the setting sun."

They chatted away together as they sipped their drinks. When Athena had consumed the last morsel of her caramel cupcake and every last drop of the cinnamon cocoa, they went back into the kitchen to see what *Yiayiá* was up to. With the bread now risen, together they baked it, packed it up to bring to church in the morning and headed for home.

Chapter 12

Max

The quaint village of Port Jefferson wasn't quite as serene as it seemed once the sun had set. The area known as 'Upper Port,' a respectable distance from the waterfront, had its occasional problems—a bar fight, gang related vandalism or a domestic dispute.

Weeks could pass with nothing remarkable to report, but not tonight. A brawl had broken out on Main Street about a block away from the train station. Max responded to the call but as soon as he'd arrived at the chaotic scene, it was clear he'd need a good amount of back up. Glass shattered not too far from his squad car as a gunshot blew out a store window. Max knew that alone, he'd never have a chance to restore order. Alone, he'd be going into the belly of a beast. And he was also certain that one man in a uniform would not deter the rage between these angry men. Fighting ceased only when the sound of blaring sirens and flashing lights warned of law enforcement as four additional police vehicles arrived. The offenders were instructed to drop their weapons and raise their arms above their heads. Max and the other officers handcuffed the brawlers, read them their Miranda rights and pushed them into squad cars. In the midst of all the turmoil, a few managed to disappear into the darkness and avoid arrest. It was a miracle that no one had been killed, although one man, who looked to be in his late twenties, had been stabbed. He had been taken away by ambulance along with several others who had sustained minor injuries.

Max was bone tired when he finally stepped onto Kally's front porch— mentally as well as physically. He was all his daughter had— the only parent on which she could rely. Sure, they lived with a houseful of family and he always had Lena for support, but without a mother in the picture, he was solely responsible for her. The thought weighed heavily on his mind. If something were to happen to him …

Max rapped on the door.

"Hi," Kally greeted as she swung the door open. "Come on in."

He looked around the space as he entered. It had a surprisingly open floorplan for an old home. The walls were painted in a pale lavender, a color he noted she seemed partial to. Pistachio accent pillows complimented a white slipcovered sofa and her distressed coffee table was adorned with a low-sitting vase of white hydrangeas.

As if she sensed the question he was about to ask, Kally explained, "Athena fell asleep in my bedroom." She motioned for him to follow her down the narrow hallway. Light from the television illuminated his daughter's angelic face and he smiled softly. She slept like a little princess in her pink nightgown, her hair French braided, the ends reaching below her waist. Emma was curled up at her side, sleeping as peacefully as the child.

"We were watching *Tangled*. I told her she looked exactly like Rapunzel and she asked me to do her hair."

"I really appreciate this," Max said. "I hope she wasn't too much trouble."

"Not at all. I think I had as much fun as she did." Kally put her finger to her lips. "Let her sleep," she whispered. "Can I offer you something to drink."

Max sucked in a deep breath. "I could use a beer."

Kally pouted. "Don't have any. Sorry. I hate beer. I have wine though."

"That'll do it."

"Rough night?" she asked.

"Yeah." He sighed, following her into the kitchen. "Let me do that," he offered, taking the wine bottle from her. Inserting the opener into the cork, he twisted. "I moved here to be with family for Athena's sake."

Kally handed Max two wine glasses and he began to pour.

"I wanted a safe environment for her, far away from the chaos of our life before. Now I'm questioning if becoming a cop was the right thing to do."

"There's no guarantee no matter what you do with your life." Kally shrugged. "Anyone can be in the wrong place at the wrong time. We must have faith that our decisions are for the best."

Leaning his elbows on the granite top of her small kitchen island, he ran his fingers across his brow. "Take it from me, most of my decisions have not been for the best."

"You're very hard on yourself," Kally said firmly. She rested her hand on his bicep. The warmth of her touch immediately drew his eyes up to her kind, brown eyes. "I see a man who has done everything to protect his child and surround her with people who love her."

Kally lifted the wine glasses from the counter, motioning for Max to follow her. They took a seat on the sofa, her at one end, him at the other. He didn't want to get into all of his failings with her. She was everything he had once hoped for in a woman but, now, how would someone like her feel about the life he had led for the last several years? He himself was ashamed to think about it. Kally was kind and sweet. A bit mercurial at times, although he suspected there was something yet to be discovered behind that. Max needed to shake his self-deprecating mood. He decided to change the subject.

"How was it that you were free to watch my little one tonight? I'm sure there was something more interesting you could have been doing."

"Not really. I'm a bit of a homebody." She shrugged. "I don't have this compulsion to be out all the time."

"Like Egypt?" Max asked.

"She is an extrovert. If it wasn't for her I probably would never leave the house," Kally joked.

"Leo is really into her."

"She feels the same," Kally laughed. "Egypt is a free spirit. She always was but her parents' expectations were too confining. Once she stomped all over their dreams for her, there was no stopping her." Kally took a sip of her wine and set the glass down. "She never stayed with any one thing for too long. Except me. We've been friends forever. But boyfriends? They came and went. But now she's really put forth a dedicated effort into her jewelry line. And I probably shouldn't tell you this since you're his friend, but her attitude about Leo is different than I've seen with any other man. She really likes him."

"And what about you?" Max asked. He knew he shouldn't go there but he wanted to know more about Kally. And as much as he knew he shouldn't be, he was drawn to her.

"Me? I think Leo is great. Perfect for her."

"I meant you with a … significant other," he laughed.

Kally picked up her glass and gulped down her wine, nearly choking. "No. No one," she said. "I'm not exactly a … dude magnet." She laughed nervously.

"No, of course not," he mocked. "Men are never on the lookout for beautiful, successful and interesting women like yourself." Is she for real? he wondered. "I'm surprised you're not already married with a couple of kids. I watched you at the party. You were a natural with those children and Athena hasn't stopped talking about you."

Max had said too much. It was obvious he'd made her uncomfortable and that wasn't his intention. An awkward silence filled the air as they both sipped their wine. Both Max and Kally began to speak at the same moment and then they both excused themselves … at the same time. Could this get any more embarrassing? Max thought.

"Go ahead," he said, encouraging her to begin. "I'm sorry if I spoke out of line." He slid in a little closer to her, brushing his hand over hers in apology.

Kally took in a deep breath, her shoulders slumping as she began to speak. "I can't even count how many years I've been barraged with advice on how to live my life. My mother, who continually complains about my father, tells me to be an independent woman one minute and in the next, asks if I've found anyone marriage worthy yet."

She threw her hands up in resignation and Max grinned.

"Oh, and while most Greek mothers want their daughters to marry other Greeks, she warns me away from them. Yet, my *yiayiá*, who as far as we know was abandoned by her husband when my mother was a little girl, has nothing but loving things to say about him. My mother's cousin thinks I'm getting older and I should consider freezing my eggs, but not before talking to our priest to make sure it's allowed by the church."

Kally drained the rest of the wine in her glass. "And let's not even mention my father. He thinks I should still live at home, work at his business and marry a Greek and only a Greek."

"I can see how all those opinions can get to you," Max said quietly. "I have enough advice flying my way too, but not quite as much as that."

"What they don't understand is that our lives aren't stamped out and shaped like identical cookies. A woman can be successful, interesting and even ... beautiful, as you said, but sometimes an ingredient is missing that makes her desirable. Once I understood and accepted that, I created the life I now have and I'm content. I just wish my family would accept it too."

Max stared at her, trying to process what she had just said. Not desirable?

"No, you're wrong. You're the one that needs to accept that you are not only desirable but damn irresistible." Max knew he'd said too much but he couldn't hold back anymore. "Any man who made you feel undesirable was simply not ready for what you had to offer," he whispered, edging closer to her.

He had to touch her, feel the softness of her skin and the warmth he was sure emanated from her. Cupping her cheek in his hand, he brushed his fingertips down her jawbone. He looked into eyes swimming with uncertainty, forcing her to hold his gaze. "You have to know how beautiful you are."

Kally lowered her eyes down to her lap.

Lifting her chin with his forefinger, he reiterated, "On the outside but also where it counts the most, on the inside." His heart hammered in his chest. Never in his life had he wanted to kiss anyone more than right now. *Oh, fuck it! Damn the risk.*

Kally's breath hitched as he closed what little space was between them. Lightly, he pressed his lips to hers. They were soft and welcoming and he gently urged her mouth open to let him deepen the kiss. Kally sighed softly, rendering him completely out of his mind for her.

An involuntary groan came from deep within his chest as he broke the kiss. Half desire. Half conscience. Hesitation flickered through his mind without warning and he frowned. He didn't want to land her in the middle of his messy past. A past that a woman like her could never begin to understand or forgive.

He held her face in his hands, rubbed his nose tenderly down the length of hers and kissed her softly once more. "You're too good for me," Max said softly.

She looked at him as though she didn't understand his meaning, her brow furrowing.

Max leaned back on the sofa and ruffled his fingers though his hair. "What I should have said was that I'm no good for you."

"Why would you say that about yourself?" Kally asked slightly more loudly than she intended. "I've watched you with your daughter and I can see the type of man you are."

Max stood, facing away from her. "There is a lot you don't know and I don't want you to know," he said briskly. "I need to get Athena home."

"Okay," Kally agreed, confused by the sudden shift in his attitude.

Silently, they walked to the bedroom. Kally collected Athena's belongings while Max picked his daughter up carefully so as not to wake her.

At the front door, they said their goodbyes. "Thanks again for everything," Max said. Bending, he kissed her on the cheek and, without another word, he walked away.

Max placed Athena in the car and looked up to wave to Kally one last time but, regrettably, she'd already shut the door.

Chapter 13

Kally

2009

There were those people who, for some mysterious and inexplicable reason, radiated a magnetism that had others clamoring for their attention. Kally had never been one of those girls that drew others to her like butterflies to daylilies. It wasn't that they were prettier or smarter, or even that the possessions they owned might have added to their appeal. But there was something—an air or an attitude Kally couldn't quite put her finger on, and although she wasn't an envious girl, she couldn't help but wonder what she lacked that made her all but invisible save for the few she could call true friends.

Kally, in fact, had turned out quite pretty. But not before she had suffered the awkward pre-teen years when her uncontrollable curls, braces and gangly body convinced her she would always be ugly.

In high school, she had a small group of friends, stayed involved in school activities, if not just on the fringes, and joined the GOYA—the church youth group. But as her friends began to date and pair off, the same just never happened for her. No one ever asked her out on a date and no boy seemed to pay her much mind. Egypt said she was too timid and not outgoing enough. And her friend was most likely correct, because Kally was a bundle of nerves that had nothing much to say to the unapproachable male species.

That is pretty much how her track record went with boys and continued on with men as she matured. Kally had finally begun to date by the tail end of her senior year of high school. She and a boy from school went to prom together but the guy ended up ditching her halfway through the after party for a girl who was willing to put out for him.

In college, she dated a boy seriously for two years. They were practically inseparable, but when school ended, so did their relationship. Basically, he told her they were great together during their school years but he couldn't imagine being with her for the rest of his life. She just wasn't the one for him and he wasn't looking to be tied down right now anyway.

That was two years ago and she hadn't been out with anyone since. It didn't matter how many of her mother's friends told her how pretty she was and suggested a set up with their son or a nephew. She was done. She had come to the conclusion that she was one of those girls who was simply not appealing to men and, she in turn, had not met one single person she was interested in.

So when Kally heard a rap on her car window after she found herself stuck on the side of the road on the Long Island Expressway, she was startled to come face to face with the most arresting set of eyes she'd ever seen—icy blue ones that could both seduce and destroy with a single glance.

A ghost of a smile formed on his lips, his expression one of mocking amusement. Her heart skipped a beat. Kally was instantly intimidated by this man.

"You need some help?" His voice was deep, the slight rasp making him sound almost as dangerous as he looked. Deep, golden, sun-kissed skin contrasted with the color of his eyes. His long, dirty blond hair looked windblown and a bit disheveled, yet there was a commanding air of authority about him.

Kally reluctantly rolled down her window. It was a hot, August day. She had pulled her hair partially off her face, the rest flowing down her back in a mass of silky, dark ringlets. Her pale pink camisole revealed her delicate neck and shoulders.

"No, thank you," she answered. "I called roadside assistance."

Exhaling a low rumble of laughter, he said, "Princess, you could be waiting for hours." Cocking an eyebrow, he motioned for her to get out of the car.

Hesitantly, she complied. Her shorts showed off her long, lean legs and she felt his stare sear into her. He moved into the driver's seat and turned the key over.

Kally eyed the inked muscles on his forearms. They were impressively toned. His whole body was, from what she could tell. His black t-shirt clung to him, accentuating the broad shoulders and narrow waist. Popping the hood, he got out from behind the wheel and sauntered to the front of the car.

Even his ass was perfect, she mused. He wasn't GQ model worthy but perhaps an aspiring rock star on the cover of *Rolling Stone.* Or a construction worker who was too lazy to get a haircut. His body had obviously been created from hard labor and his face had been designed by the devil himself. There was a raw sexuality about him that she had never encountered before, and when he lifted his head from the engine to look at her, she felt weak in the knees.

"I'm pretty sure it's the alternator," he said. "I have a friend who has a shop close by." He pulled his cell phone from his back pocket. "I'll call him and he'll send a tow over ASAP."

"That's very nice of you but I can wait for—"

But his ear was already to his phone. Holding up a finger, he silenced her, before turning his back to her while he spoke, giving directions to the receiver on the other end as to the car's location.

Killing the call, he returned it to his back pocket. "He'll be here in less than ten minutes." He eyed her up and down, the corner of his mouth curling up in a smirk. "Unless you want to wait in the heat for roadside to show up."

"No. I appreciate it. Thank you," Kally mumbled.

Leaning back against her car, he crossed his arms over his chest, his gaze following her as she paced back and forth.

"Are you in a rush to get somewhere?" he asked.

"No, why?"

"You seem awfully jittery."

Of course, she was jittery. The hottest and scariest man she'd ever stood face to face with was staring at her and she didn't know what to do with herself.

"I don't want to hold you up, that's all," Kally said. "I'm taking too much of your time as it is."

"No worries. I'm relaxed about it." He crooked his forefinger, beckoning her over.

She stepped into his line of view but remained a good distance away. Not far enough though for her not to notice the biceps peeking from his sleeves or the intricate design on his Celtic cross tattoo branded onto his right arm.

"You have a name, Princess?" he asked.

"Kally."

"Is that the whole name?"

"It's Kallyope." She waited for him to give his name but he stayed quiet, eyeing her as though he was deciding if her name fit. "Do *you* have a name?" she asked, bouncing the question back at him.

"Jax."

"Is that the whole name?" she asked, tilting her head to one side.

He huffed out a laugh. "Funny," he said humorlessly. "Jaxon." Moving into her space, he extended his hand to her. "Nice to meet you."

She accepted the offer, gently slipping her hand in his. Gripping her firmly, he pulled her close, their bodies merely inches apart. An involuntary gasp ripped from Kally's chest as she averted her eyes from him.

Lifting her chin, Jax forced her to meet his gaze. The heat of his stare burned a hole right through her. Her cheeks were flush and the back of her neck was on fire.

"Maybe we can do a little better than just nice." Jaxon released her at the sound of the tow truck coming to a halt beside them. "Hey, Frank! Thanks for coming right away, man."

"Anything for you," Frank said. "I'll hook her up and meet you at the shop."

Jaxon nodded, waving off his friend as he walked to his vehicle. "Come on," he said to Kally. "I'll give you a ride over to the repair shop."

Kally hadn't even noticed the motorcycle parked behind her broken down car. She stood in place, her mouth agape, shaking her head. "You expect me to get on that?"

"How else are you going to get to the shop?" Jaxon muttered under his breath. "Put this on," he demanded as he walked toward her.

When she didn't reach for the helmet, he placed it on her head himself, secured the strap and pulled her over to his bike.

"No, no. I—I can't get on that thing."

"Sure you can, Princess." Jaxon picked her up as if she weighed only a few ounces and seated her on the bike before mounting it himself. Turning, he glared at her impatiently. "You're sure to fall off if you don't wrap your arms around my waist."

Kally did as she was told, her front to his back, her arms secured around him. She could feel every ripple of muscle on his hard body. Nervous didn't even cover what she was feeling, but she was exhilarated too, and as Jax revved up the engine, her grip on him tightened.

"Relax. I'll take it slow," he promised.

The repair shop was only a few miles away and Jax had kept his word, not tearing off as she had expected him to. Even so, Kally was a bundle of nerves. As he drove off the expressway exit and into commercial traffic, she loosened her death grip on him and relaxed into his back.

He'd acknowledged the abandonment of her tension by reaching back and patting her bare thigh and, oh my God! The electrical spark that coursed through her veins in a matter of seconds was one she had never experienced before.

"That wasn't so bad, was it?" Jax asked as they pulled into the repair station.

"No," Kally said in a whisper.

After she gave Frank the information he required, Jaxon offered to drive her home. They were now standing outside the shop alongside Jaxon's bike. As much as her heart skipped a beat at the thought of riding with him again, she hesitated.

"My parents will kill me if I drive up on that."

"You live at home … with your parents?" he asked.

"I do, yes."

"How old are you, Princess?"

"Twenty-three, and why do you keep calling me that?"

"It seems to fit," he said, matter-of-factly.

From the moment she'd met him, it felt as though he was constantly analyzing her. It was unnerving the way he looked right through her.

"Twenty-three's a good age."

"I'm happy you approve." Kally's voice dripped with sarcasm.

"You hungry? Let's get something to eat."

"I don't know," she said nervously. "I should get home. I can call a friend."

"Have lunch with me and then I'll drive you home." He raked his hands through his hair, brushing back the strands that had fallen across his face. "I'll leave you a block up the road so no one will see."

"Okay." She was in so much trouble with this intriguing man. She couldn't seem to say no to him. Not to mention, if anyone she knew saw them together, the 'Greek hotline' would be alerted faster than the speed of lightning.

She climbed back onto his bike, this time with more ease than before. Her hold on him lacked the death grip it had on the way there. When Jax dared to pick up speed, weaving in and out of traffic, Kally laughed and screamed, enjoying herself as though she were on a carnival ride.

They stopped on the side of the road for Mexican food at a little place that was more of a rundown snack bar than a restaurant, but the food was fresh and authentic. Orange market umbrellas shielded the outdoor picnic tables from the heat of the sun and Kally claimed a couple of unoccupied seats while Jaxon ordered food. After waiting for their order at the pickup counter, Jaxon slid onto the bench next to her rather than sitting across the table as Kally had expected.

"Other than breaking down on expressways, what do you do with your time?"

"You didn't have to stop for me, you know," she retorted. "You make it sound like I make a habit of it."

"Don't have much of a sense of humor, do you?" He took a bite of his burrito, staring intently at her.

"I work at my father's restaurant as a pastry chef," she said. "That's what I do with my time." She inched her body down the bench so her thigh was no longer touching his. "It's what I went to school for. I'm hoping to open my own café one day."

"A cook. I like a girl who knows how to heat things up." Jaxon made no attempt to hide his overconfident grin as his eyes roamed her body.

"Pastry chef," Kally corrected. "And must everything you say have a sexual undertone?"

He closed the gap that she had widened between them, leaning in to whisper in her ear. Kally could feel his warm breath tease the flesh on her neck.

"I'm a very sexual man." He played with a stray curl from her hair and she instinctively pulled away.

"I shouldn't have come with you," she said, looking down into her lap as her heart thumped in her chest. "I don't want you to get the wrong idea. I'm not *that* girl."

Leaning his elbow on the table, Jax rested his chin on his hand. "What girl would that be?"

Kally didn't know how to handle a man like this. The only thing she knew for sure was that she sensed trouble and she had to get away from him. He was hotter than a bonfire and way out of her league. It scared the hell out of her.

"I'm not the type of girl that picks up men or lets them pick me up. And I'm not a girl that guys like you are into," she said, stiffening.

"I didn't pick you up," he corrected. "I gave you a ride. I believe I saved you from sitting in a hot car waiting for help to come for fuck knows how long."

"And I appreciate that," Kally said politely. She stood up to throw her food wrapper in the trash.

Jax stood with her, grabbing hold of her arm and drawing her around so they stood chest to chest. "I'm not done," he said firmly. Kally detected irritation in his tone. "Not the girl guys are into? What asshole put that in your head?" His voice was low and throaty. He looked at her as though he was searching for the truth in her eyes.

Kally felt as if she were a specimen under a microscope. Any moment now and he'd figure out that upon further inspection she wasn't worth the bother.

"You don't get it, do you?" Suddenly he dropped his hold on her. "I'll take you home," he said, shaking his head.

Kally followed him to his bike, mounted it and wrapped her arms around him once more. Gone was the feeling of exhilaration. Tears stung her eyes as they drove toward her home. She was afraid of this man, yet at the same time, captivated by him.

She tapped him on the shoulder. "You can pull up here. It's only a block from my house," she said.

Jax pulled over to the side of the road by a wooded area. "I really don't want to leave you here alone," he said.

"It's safe. I jog by here almost every day."

He killed the engine and dismounted. "Princess," he said, turning her around by the shoulders. He let his hands linger up and down the length of her arms. "Let's get one thing straight. From the second you rolled down your window, I was into you."

Kally's breath caught in her throat. A shiver crawled up her spine and her face took on a frightened, vulnerable expression.

He regarded her for a moment. "Do I make you nervous? Jax asked finally.

"A little."

"I can fix that," he said.

"By getting out of my personal space?" Kally asked quietly.

Jax shook his head imperceptibly. "No. By making it non-existent."

He lowered his head until his lips touched hers. The kiss wasn't sweet or gentle, but rough and powerful—meant to claim and possess. It was like no other kiss she had known, not that there had been many. From the few boys she had dated, their kisses lacked experience and care. Jaxon took her mouth with determination and skill, taking what he desired without apology.

"I'll be seeing you, Princess," he said, breaking the kiss.

Kally watched him as he sauntered over to his bike, hopped on and drove away without a backward glance.

Cherry Chocolate Chunk Cookies

Preheat oven to 350°

2 cups flour

1 teaspoon baking soda

1 teaspoon baking powder

½ teaspoon salt

2 sticks unsalted butter, softened

1¼ cup sugar

1 large egg

2 teaspoons vanilla extract

½ cup cherry liquor

4 ounces dried cherries

10 ounces dark or semi-sweet chocolate chunks

Line two cookie sheets with parchment paper. Soak the dried cherries in the cherry liquor and set aside. Combine flour, baking soda, baking powder and salt in a bowl. In a large bowl, cream the butter and sugar with an electric mixer. Add the egg, vanilla extract and 1 tablespoon of the cherry liquor. Slowly, add the flour mixture. When the flour is fully mixed through, add the chocolate chunks. Drain the dried cherries and add to the mixture. Fold until the chunks and cherries are evenly distributed. Use a small ice cream scoop to form the cookies, placing them directly onto the parchment-lined cookie sheet. Bake for approximately 12 minutes. Cool on a wire rack.

Chapter 14

Kally

2018

If Kally could have stayed home Sunday morning, she would have. But she'd promised Athena she would be in church when they offered the *artoklasia* and she wasn't about to go back on her word. This time though, she made sure she sat four persons deep in the middle of a pew so she wouldn't come face to face with Max when he passed around the donation tray.

When the children filed into the church from Sunday School, Athena left her line of classmates and slipped into the pew with Kally's family. "*Yiayiá* said she would let me go up with her to get our bread," Athena whispered excitedly. She inched her way over to Kally's grandmother. The old woman peppered her with tiny kisses as though she hadn't seen her in years.

After the priest concluded the liturgy and the blessing of the *artoklasia*, he asked that a member of the family making the offering come forward to receive one of the blessed loaves. Athena beamed as she skipped up to the altar hand in hand with *Yiayiá*.

Kally smiled as she watched how happy the sweet girl was, probably more for the female attention she'd received and the pride she felt in taking part in this tradition with them. She couldn't help but notice the proud look on Max's face as he observed his daughter, but when he glanced in her direction, she swiftly looked away.

Athena carried the loaf back to the pew, taking her seat between Krystina and Kally.

"You did a great job," Kally congratulated her. "I'm so happy we did this together. But now I have to go."

"Why?" Athena asked with a pout. "You're not staying after?"

"I have to get to the café," Kally explained. It was an excuse, but a true one. "I'll see you soon, okay?"

Athena nodded, trying to smile through her disappointment.

"How about if I take you to meet your dad at the community center instead?" Krystina asked.

"It's all settled then," Kally said as the excitement rushed back to Athena's face.

With a hurried goodbye, Kally fled the church as if a fire drill had alarmed. She knew she couldn't avoid Max forever, but for now she needed a little space. She kept reminding herself it was only one kiss. One incredible, toe-curling, feel-it-to-the-core kiss. But still, just one kiss. And, as Kally's luck usually ran, she thought morosely, the man bolted from her door as fast as he could soon after it.

She just needed a little time to place him right back in the friend zone where all men belonged. Maybe then, she could see him around town without her heart fluttering or feeling as though it had dropped to her knees. Setting herself up for rejection was not an option. It was much easier this way. And this was exactly how she explained it to Egypt when she arrived at the café and told her what had happened the night before.

"So let me get this straight," Egypt said. "The man kisses you. And not just a stingy peck. A mind blowing, full impact kiss, and then he tells you he's no good for you?"

"Pretty much," Kally said.

"What happened when you saw him this morning?" Egypt inquired.

"You must have seen him. You said Athena sat with you."

"I left before the service was over."

"Coward."

"Damn straight!" Kally said. "You think I wanted to deal with all that awkwardness in front of so many scrutinizing eyes?"

"Don't you want to know what Max meant?" Egypt bobbed her head excitedly, circling a pointed finger. "If a man said that to me after planting a hot one on me, I'd demand an explanation."

"But I'm not you," Kally reminded her. "And what does it matter anyway. It's not like it could ever go anywhere."

Egypt opened her mouth to argue but Kally shoved a tray of cherry chocolate chunk cookies in her hand and pushed her toward the door. "Discussion over! Stack these in the glass cookie jar."

For a late October Sunday, it had been unusually crowded at the café all afternoon. If not for the brisk chill every time the front door opened, Kally would have thought it a typical summer day. With only one party of four left lingering over *cappuccinos*, she flipped the sign in the window from open to closed.

Twilight came early these days, reminding Kally that shorter and colder days were about to make an unwelcome appearance. If there was one thing she could change about where she lived it would be the length of the warmer months. She needed more of them.

Anxious to wrap up the day, Kally pulled the money drawer from the cash register and pushed through the kitchen doors. Toward the back, by the exit, a room barely larger than a closet was set up as a makeshift office. She had only moments before taken a seat behind her desk to count her receipts when she heard a rap on the door. Kally looked up expecting to see Egypt or Luis.

"You left," Max stated. He leaned against the doorframe and crossed his arms over his chest. There was accusation in his tone.

"What are you talking about?" Kally asked dryly.

"This morning. You left before I could thank you for everything you did for my daughter."

"I have a café to run," Kally retorted, rising from her seat. She gripped the wooden surface for support. "Besides, there was no need for you to thank me. You already did that last night." She stared at him for a beat. "Why are you here, Max?" she asked in frustration.

"Egypt said I could come out back."

Kally massaged her forehead. "Why are you here at all?" she clarified.

"I ... I wanted to speak to you."

"I think you said everything you had to last night." She locked her gaze with his. "You're no good for me, remember?"

"Kally ..." He sighed, ruffling his hand through his hair.

Lifting her hand, she blocked him from saying any more. "Stop! I'm way past dealing with anyone's mixed signals." Dismissively, she returned to her chair to resume her task. "It was no worries, really," she reiterated, shuffling the papers in front of her. "Feel free to bring Athena around any time she wants another baking lesson." Kally moved the mouse along the rubber pad, bringing her computer to life. "I need to get back to work now."

Max stood stony faced and defeated. He dug his hands into his front pockets and exhaled a frustrated breath. Nodding once, he turned and strode out the door.

As the latch clicked shut, Kally leaned back in her chair, covering her face with her hands. She hated that he had the ability to get under her skin. Hated that he affected her in any way at all. Long ago she had promised herself to never open herself up to be hurt again, and she was doing just fine until he had to spoil it by kissing her the night before.

Kally's eyes snapped open when she heard Max suddenly re-enter her office.

"No!" he exclaimed. Three swift strides had him hovering over her chair, his hands braced on its arms, trapping her in her seat.

Chapter 15

Max

Damn it to hell! Max had come back to his home town in order to straighten out his life and give his daughter some semblance of stability. Meeting Kally had thrown all hopes of that into turmoil. His mind was constantly consumed with thoughts of her, when the only thing that should occupy him was the welfare of his daughter. Athena had already been a victim of one parent's selfishness and neglect and Max, in no manner whatsoever, wanted to place his child second to his own desires.

Yet, he couldn't help but see how taken Athena was with Kally. The sight of the two of them baking side by side never ceased to bring a smile to his face, and this morning, as Athena was sitting beside Kally's family in church, his heart had swelled with joy. This female interaction, an essential lacking in her day-to-day routine, was good for her, and Kally's interest in his daughter seemed to be genuine.

Seemed to be. That is what scared Max. He feared for Athena. She had already suffered the absence of a mother. The last thing she needed was to become attached to Kally only for her to disappear as well. Surely, she would want no part of him once she learned who he really was and what he'd done these past years.

Confessing he was no good for her was the truth, yet she was exactly what he wanted—what he needed. When she abruptly left the church before the service was over, Max inwardly groaned. He'd hoped for a chance to clear the air from the night before—a chance to explain he wasn't an asshole playing mind games. As the day progressed, Max grew restless, and it all weighed heavily on his mind. Not at the unconditional kindness and generosity Kally and her family extended to Athena. No. It was her—Kally—and the idea that he might have wounded her; the knot in his stomach churning with worry that she probably harbored ill feelings toward him due to his confusing behavior. He had to make everything right with her. He just had to.

Max waited until closing time before heading over to The Coffee Klatch. When he stepped through the front door, he noticed only one table was still occupied but it looked as though they were getting set to leave. He spotted Egypt wiping down the counters. As he walked toward her, she raised her head, smirking at him. Just as he was about to ask where Kally was, she beat him to it, cocking her head toward the kitchen door and sizing him up with a knowing grin.

"She's in the office. In the very back," Egypt directed.

"Thanks."

Easily finding his way to the small office, Max leaned against the door frame and watched her shuffling papers before he rapped on the door. Her expression was unreadable—was it one of puzzlement or annoyance?

He didn't mean for his statement to come off as accusatory, but by her defensive response, that was the way it must have sounded. Oh yeah, she was pissed. Impenetrable. But even now, after all the doubt and anger he'd caused her, she was still offering to extend herself to his daughter.

"I need to get back to work now," Kally finished, dismissing him.

Max stood defeated, dug his hands into his front pockets, exhaling in frustration. Nodding, he turned and strode out the door. What else could he do? *Man the fuck up! That's what.*

With determination, he swung around and marched back into her office.

"No!" he exclaimed. Three swift strides had him hovering over her chair, his hands braced on its arms, trapping her in her seat.

"No, what?" Kally asked, rattled by his close proximity.

"No, I'm not leaving until I say what I need to," Max affirmed. "Because no, I didn't say all I should have last night. No, I wasn't lying when I said I'm no good for you. But I can't stop thinking about you and it's time I let you know why I said what I did. And when I'm done, it will be your turn to say no and tell me to leave you alone, but not before I've explained exactly who I was then, who I am now and how I feel about you."

Max looked deep into eyes swimming with trepidation. Her next words confirmed his suspicion.

"You're frightening me."

His lip curled up into a lopsided smile. Max ran his finger tenderly along her cheek. "I'm not an axe murder and I'm not using an alias or anything," he said softly.

"An alias by the name Maximos Vardaxis?" Kally cocked her head to one side. "That wouldn't be conspicuous in the least!"

Max mentally exhaled. She was letting her guard down, hopefully enough for an honest conversation. A difficult one, but a necessary one.

"So? What do you say? Will you give me a chance?" He pulled himself away from her personal space and sat in the chair across from her.

Kally stared at him pensively, as though grappling with her decision. Before she could answer, Egypt came bouncing in the door.

"Hey! You all right, Kal?" she asked. "Need me to stick around?"

"No, you go on," Kally answered. "Thanks for everything. It's all good here."

"Okay, have a good night you two." She put her hands together, bowing slightly. "Namaste." And as quickly as she appeared, she was gone again.

"She's something," Max said with a puzzled smile.

"She is! The ying to my yang, I suppose," Kally said. "She's the fun, daring adventurous one. I'm the practical homebody who only dares to dream through the pages of the novels I read."

"There's something to be said for that though," Max said, rubbing the back of his neck. "My wife liked to live on the edge. Which brings me to much of what I have to discuss with you."

Kally nodded. "Okay. Do you want to stay here? I could make you a cup of coffee or something. Or would you prefer a glass of wine? We could go to my place if that's more comfortable for you."

"A glass of wine would be perfect." Max blew out a heavy breath— half from relief, the other half tinged with nerves. "Thank you."

Kally powered down her computer, stood and removed the camel wrap coat she had draped over her office chair. Shrugging into it, she then retrieved her bag from the bottom desk drawer.

"Ready?" she asked.

"That's up for debate," Max mumbled.

Chapter 16

Kally

This man! He was going to drive Kally to drink this entire bottle of wine by herself. The forceful man who had stormed her office demanding her to hear him out hadn't said a word to her on the thankfully short walk to her home. Now he was sitting on her couch, his elbows resting on his knees, rubbing his forehead with his fingertips.

Max looked as though the entire future of the world rested upon him. Kally observed him quizzically as she entered her living room holding two glasses of Merlot. Clearing her throat to break him from his thoughts, he immediately looked up at her and stood politely. Kally handed Max one of the wine goblets and they both sat awkwardly on the sofa, Kally seating herself at the furthest corner away from him.

"So?" Kally prompted after silence filled the room.

"So." Max placed his wine glass on the coffee table, clasped his hands together and tapped his chin. "Where do I begin?"

"The beginning is a good place," Kally advised. "I could ask you questions but I think it's better you tell me only what you choose to."

Max nodded in agreement. "The beginning. Okay, well, it was always expected I'd go into the family business—real estate or construction. If not, maybe politics like my uncle and cousins."

Kally gulped her wine before placing her glass down. "Wait! You're part of that Vardaxis family? The ones with their names on just about every building site on this island?"

Max looked at her, bewildered. "Yeah, how many families are there with that name? I thought you knew."

"It never crossed my mind."

"Anyway … I wanted to make my own way in the world. I was ambitious. I graduated high school a year early, did my undergrad at Georgetown in finance with a double major in computer science. I landed my first job in the city as a stock trader and took classes for my MBA at night."

"That's interesting," Kally mused. "My first impression of you was that you didn't fit the uniform."

Max screwed his face up, looking almost insulted. Kally chuckled.

"Don't give me that face!" she teased. "What I mean is that you looked like you belonged in a well-cut suit. You just didn't look like the typical police officer, that's all."

"Well, I suppose your instincts were correct," he conceded with a shake of his head. "A police officer was never in my plan, but shit happens and plans change."

"That's a huge change in career from stock trader to village police officer."

"That's not even the half of it." Max grimaced.

It was getting chilly. Kally rose from her seat and went over to the brick fireplace on the adjacent wall. The bricks had been painted over in white and a wreath of greenery hung over the mantle. The wood was already in place. Kally added a fire starter, lit a match and returned to the sofa.

"I have a feeling it's going to be a long night," she said. "So you got your first job on Wall Street."

"Yes, and considering I was taking night classes and trying to fit some time in to go out with my buddies, I did really well and was pulling in some serious money." Max leaned back against the sofa cushions, rubbing his eyes with the heels of his hands. Sighing, he continued, "In between all of that I met Bridget." He looked up at Kally with an unreadable expression. "My wife."

"Oh. How old were you when you met?"

"Twenty-five. She was twenty-three," Max said. "We were out one night on Stone Street. Have you ever been there?"

"No, I haven't but my sister, Mia, has mentioned it." Kally sipped her wine before continuing, "She goes there after work sometimes with friends and coworkers."

"So you get the idea—mostly young professionals hanging out by a cluster of bars after work. It was very chill, especially after a stressful day," Max explained. "Bridget was hanging out with a group of her friends at a nearby table and we started talking to them and she and I clicked. She was very beautiful with long, blonde hair, sea blue eyes and delicate features. Back then, she was such a sweet girl. She had just moved from Ohio to work in the 'big city.'" Max laughed sardonically. "The big dream," he added bitterly.

Kally drank a large gulp of her wine. Max's walk down memory lane was not a happy one from the expression on his face and it made her uneasy.

"We started dating and things got serious quickly. We both weren't strangers to hard work and long days," Max said. "She was an assistant buyer for Bloomingdales which sounds impressive but it was actually an entry level position with way more hours than the typical nine-to-five job."

"It sounds like you barely saw each other."

"We managed. Once I got my MBA I had a little more free time. Then I got this incredible offer to work as a junior analyst at a hedge fund," he continued enthusiastically. "I had no idea I could do better than I already was so early in my career but I had graduated from the right schools and had the education and background they were looking for. Plus, I had an excellent track record with the company I was with. That was the golden ticket. The more money I made for the clients and the company, the more desirable I became. I pulled down almost four hundred thousand dollars in that first year alone at the hedge fund."

"Are you serious?" Kally was dumbstruck. He must have only been about twenty-six years old and he was making nearly half a million dollars?

"No joke. I bought an apartment in the city and an impressive-sized rock for Bridget and we soon moved in together."

"It sounds like the idea of what the big city could hold came true for both of you," Kally said.

"You know what they say, all that glitters is not gold," Max said. "After we got married I slowly saw a change in Bridget. She became more and more materialistic. At first, I didn't mind because we had the money to spend but it soon became her main focus. The second she became pregnant with Athena she quit her job. Her days were spent at spas and shopping."

Kally kicked off her shoes and tucked her feet underneath her. "Why don't you put your feet up too?" She gestured at his posture. "You look so tense," she told him.

He waved her off. "I'm fine. Reliving all of this isn't very pleasant."

"Then don't. You don't owe me any explanation of your past," Kally said. The truth was that she had so many questions but pressing him was not the way to get answers.

Max slid from the end to the middle cushion on the sofa. He took Kally's hands in his. "Yes, I do owe it to you to tell you everything because I want you in my life. I thought I made that clear, but the only way I can do that is by being honest. Once you know everything, you can draw your own conclusions and decide if I'm worth it to you."

"What could you have possibly done to make me think less of you?" Kally tried to read the answers hidden behind his wounded eyes.

"My whole life spun out of control." Max looked up at her, tears brimming his eyes. "Once Athena was born, I thought our lives would settle down a bit. Bridget would stay home and raise our daughter—clearly, she had no intention of going back to work. But she hired a nanny and spent very little time with her. She was always off with friends for the day. The weekends were better but it seemed like I did more of the diapering and feeding than Bridget did. I didn't mind though because often Athena would be asleep by the time I got home from work so it was my way of bonding with her."

"So far, I'm hearing you were the same caring father I know you to be today."

"Until we started getting invited to parties and yachting weekends hosted by clients and company heads. Not going wasn't an option if I wanted to maintain my position," Max explained. "And it could have been nice. But Bridget got carried away with the glamour of it all and, before I knew it, I was sucked in too. Too much drinking and eventually … drugs." His eyes flew to hers and Kally could see he was looking for her reaction. "Recreational mostly, at least on my part. Cocaine more often than not."

"Where was the baby through all this?" Kally asked, concerned.

"With the nanny if we were out for the evening. At my parents if it was for a weekend or more." Max ran a hand through his hair. "I'm not proud of having to tell you this, but you have the right to know. The truth is, luckily, I kept it to a minimum, not that I should have done it at all, but Bridget got caught up in the whole thing. She became addicted. Not just to the drugs, but to the whole lifestyle. That's when everything started falling apart." He closed his eyes as if picturing it in his mind. "I'd walk into a crowded room and find her flirting with a client or, worse, catch one groping her. She'd beckon me over like she was doing nothing wrong and tell me how she was entertaining so and so on my behalf for the sake of my career."

"Oh, Max!" Kally exclaimed. "Was she cheating on you?"

He laughed humorlessly. "Nooo," he said with exaggerated sarcasm. "She was doing me a favor," he bit out. "And the expensive baubles she somehow ended up with were for my sake, too."

"I'm so sorry," Kally said with sincerity. "I'm not sure how you reason with someone who doesn't think she's doing anything wrong."

"You don't. There is no reasoning. I tried to hold it together and attempted to pull her away from that scene and back into our family life, but she was too far gone."

His eyes swam with regret, guilt and a laden responsibility. Obviously, he blamed himself for much of what had happened.

"It was all my fault. I introduced her to that world," he choked out.

Instinctively, Kally reached out for Max and wrapped her arms around him. He buried his face in the crook of her neck and sighed deeply.

"Max, everyone is responsible for their own actions," she soothed. "You didn't force her to take the drugs, or to be with other men. Yes, she was caught in the lure of what she thought was a glamorous lifestyle, but that was all on her." Kally took his face in her hands, forcing him to meet her eyes. "You gave her everything. Love, a comfortable life, the freedom to make her own choices. But she destroyed everything you built together."

"But I couldn't save her. She wasn't the same girl I had met and fallen in love with."

"Am I to assume it never turned around for the two of you?"

"No. It only got worse," Max said. "I really was a dick myself, you know? I was working all the time and at first had no clue she was as far gone as she was. Finally, the nanny quit, but before she left she pulled me aside and told me that Bridget was always high and that she never paid any mind to Athena."

"She quit and left the child with a continuously stoned woman?"

"It wasn't her problem and I don't blame her." Max sighed. "It was my mess to fix. I hired someone else because it was clear I couldn't trust Bridget alone with our daughter. Meanwhile, we did nothing but fight. I tried to get her help with her addiction but she wanted no part of it."

Abruptly, Max stood. "I need a glass of water."

Kally got up but Max stopped her. "I'll get it. I just need a minute."

When he returned he had two glasses in his hand and offered one to Kally. She took it and motioned for him to sit next to her.

Max gulped down half the glassful. "I came home early one afternoon. I'm sure Bridget wouldn't have expected me. I rarely came home before seven o'clock. When I walked in, I heard Athena crying—screaming really. I ran to her bedroom and the door was locked from the outside. I was furious. When I unlocked the door, Athena lunged into my arms, tears pouring down her little face." Max clenched his fists at the memory.

"How old was she," Kally asked, horrified at the thought.

"A little over four years old," he replied. "I calmed her down as best I could. Once she seemed better, I ripped through the apartment, looking for my wife." Max groaned. "I found her strung out in our bedroom, remnants of cocaine on the dresser alongside empty liquor bottles. She was barely conscious and she wasn't alone."

Max murmured under his breath. Kally didn't dare ask him to repeat himself. She didn't have to. A string of expletives had fallen from his lips.

"Low-life, immoral, back-stabbing bastards," Max growled.

Kally's eyes grew wide.

"My boss and a potential client he'd been courting were sprawled out on my bed with her. If I didn't get out of there I might have killed them all. I didn't even bother to see if my wife was okay. I shoved a few things in Athena's overnight bag and got her the hell out of there."

"Poor baby!" Kally cried. "Does she have any memory of that day?"

"Only through occasional nightmares." He braced his hand on top of his head. "Damn it! In the car, she told me her mother locked her in the room sometimes when her friends came over. I had no idea!"

"Oh my God! It wasn't a one-time occurrence?"

"No," he said through gritted teeth. "I may as well finish off. If you haven't lost respect for me by now then you're about to. I got a call the next day that Bridget had overdosed. And you know what? I didn't give a shit. I had taken Athena to my parents' home and I decided right then and there Bridget could no longer be part of our lives."

"Tragically, it seems fate took care of that for you."

Max opened his mouth to say something, but then shook his head as though thinking the better of it.

"Hey," Kally said softly, rubbing her hands gently up and down the length of his forearms to comfort him, "that's enough for tonight. You must feel stripped raw."

"What I need to know is what you're thinking. You must want nothing to do with me for ruining a woman's life and jeopardizing the safety of my child."

He sounded so close to breaking point and Kally could feel her heart going out to this broken man sitting beside her.

"Bridget made her own choices. She neglected her child while you were working hard to support your family. She was the one who put Athena in an unsafe situation, not you." Kally touched her palm to his cheek. "You've been carrying heavy burdens. It's time to let go of them."

Max extricated himself from her, walked over to the front window and leaned his hands on the sill, facing away from her. Abruptly, he turned.

"Don't delude yourself into thinking I was innocent in all of that."

Kally flinched at his harsh tone. He wanted her to see the worst in him. But why?

"I was just as much seduced by the money and the lifestyle as she was until I saw what it was doing to us. When I didn't even recognize myself anymore or the girl I married, I knew something had to change."

"And you made that happen." Kally stood and joined Max on the other side of the room. "I'm sure there is so much more I could ask you that would fill in the blanks, but for tonight, I'd like to digest all of this."

"I understand," Max said. His shoulders dropped imperceptibly, but Kally caught the slight shift in his posture.

"Max, it's okay," she assured him. "You're a good man and an amazing father. Can I ask you one last thing though?"

"Anything," he replied.

"Are you recovering from any kind of substance abuse?"

"No. I meant it when I said I used it only recreationally. I never let it get out of hand." He dug his hands in his front jean pockets and sighed deeply. "I should go."

Kally walked Max to her front door and handed him his jacket off the coat rack. Standing on her tippy-toes, she reached up and kissed him on the cheek. "Thank you for trusting me with such a personal part of your life," she whispered.

As Kally began to pull back, Max wrapped his arm around her waist, keeping her close to him. Time stopped as they stared at one another—eye to eye, lips a breath away from a plea. Kally felt a charge run through her entire body as he gently, but determinedly, kissed her. When Max finally broke the kiss, what she saw on his face was uncertainty and resignation.

"We all have demons," she said, more to reassure him than herself. "There are parts of my past I'm not proud of either."

Kally opened the front door. Before Max stepped out into the brisk night air, she gave him one last peck on the cheek.

"Can I call you tomorrow?" he asked.

"I need a day or two, okay?" Kally was mentally exhausted and she suspected what she hadn't learned yet was equally if not more draining. And she couldn't help thinking, now, after all he had just shared with her, was she expected to share her past with him? Kally wasn't sure she wanted to.

Chapter 17

Kally

2009

Two days after her car had broken down, Frank from the repair shop called to tell Kally her car was ready and that he had arranged for someone to drive it to her home.

"Oh, please don't go out of your way. I can get a ride to pick it up myself," Kally said.

"It's too late," Frank said. "He's already on his way."

"That's very kind of you. How much do I owe you?" she asked. "I can give you my credit card over the phone."

"There's no charge. I owed Jax a favor."

"No, please! This is my responsibility."

"Sorry, miss, I can't take your money."

Just when Frank ended the call, Kally heard a knock at the front door. Anxiety built at the thought that she would have to find a way to repay Jax. Just the memory of his parting kiss had her in knots.

Kally opened the door and was stunned motionless when she saw who was standing before her.

"Good morning, Princess," Jax said, smiling a little too brightly. He held out her car key and dropped it into the palm of her hand.

"I've come to deliver your car."

Kally, her mouth agape, was speechless. Thank God she was the only one left at home this morning. Everyone else was either off at school or work.

"Of course, now I'll need a ride back to Frank's shop," he said slyly.

He looked like a different man today. Gone were the ripped jeans and body-hugging t-shirt that had accentuated his six-pack. Today he wore a suit—a suit! Was he going to a funeral or something? His long, blond hair was neatly combed back and secured with an elastic band at the nape of his neck. And there were those eyes, staring straight through her soul it seemed. Glacially blue, yet a fire burned behind them. He unnerved her and she knew, without a doubt, with him, she would be like a ship fatally slamming into an iceberg.

"I appreciate all the trouble you went through to help me, but your random act of kindness was more than enough the other day," Kally said. "I wish you hadn't called in a favor on my behalf. I'm perfectly capable of paying my bill."

Stepping in to erase the space between them, Jax brushed his knuckle along her jawline. "I'm sure you're capable of many things."

Kally could feel his breath tickling her delicate neck. This man was irresistibly dangerous and she was barely equipped to resist him. Her snarky replies were her only defense yet he never seemed fazed or deterred by them.

"I am," she said sharply as she strode past him. "I have an innate talent for resisting men like you." Descending the porch steps, she turned, planting a hand on her hip. "I'll drive you back to Frank's and then you can go off to wherever it is you're going in *that* ..." She swirled a finger in his direction.

"What? My suit?" Jax teased, pretending offense and smiling with impish satisfaction. "I'll have you know it's a Fioravanti." He followed her around to the driver's side of the car and opened the door for her.

"And that's supposed to mean something to me, bigshot?" Kally slid into the car.

Jax shut the door and ambled to the passenger side. "It's bespoke!" he exclaimed, adjusting the seat back to fit comfortably.

Kally pressed her fingers to her temples, exhibiting frustration or the beginning of a headache, or possibly both. "And where are you going in that *bespoke*?"

"To work," he said matter-of-factly. "I have a meeting."

Kally shifted the car into drive and tore off.

"Slow down, Princess. You're in a residential area."

"I want to get you to work on time," she said, glancing his way. "What exactly is it you do?"

"I'm an attorney. I'm headed out to East Hampton to meet with a client."

"You? You're a lawyer?"

Jax leaned in, wrapped a ringlet of her hair around his finger and whispered, "Tell me what you had me pegged for, Princess. What has that beautiful head been thinking?"

"I haven't given you a single thought." Kally jerked her head away from him.

"You're a terrible liar," he chuckled. "I practice entertainment law. I can get away with a less conservative look most of the time."

"How are you going to drive out to the Hamptons on your motorcycle and not ruin that … what did you call it? A Fabio?"

Jax threw his head back and laughed.

Kally pulled into the repair shop parking lot.

"Those are my wheels," he pointed out.

Kally pulled up next to a black Mercedes SL 450 Roadster convertible. She wasn't a person who swooned over cars. To her, they were simply vehicles to get you safely from one place to another. But she'd never laid eyes on a piece of machinery more intoxicating than this, and it looked every bit as alluring as the owner himself.

"Thank you again, for all your help," Kally asserted as she pulled up next to his car.

"Are you brushing me off?" Jax asked with a wicked grin.

"No, I … um … want to thank you. You've gone out of your way and now you've done your quota of good deeds for the year."

"If you really want to thank me, have dinner with me tonight."

"I … I don't think that's a good idea." Kally averted her eyes from him. Suddenly the chip on her polished nails had become her focus of interest.

Jaxon lifted her chin, forcing her to look straight into his penetrating stare. "I do. Give me one valid reason why not and I'll walk away."

"You're much older than me, I don't know you and you don't know how to take no for an answer," Kally rattled off.

"One," Jax raised a finger. "True, you don't know how old I am. Thirty-two, by the way." Raising another finger, he said, "You know more about me than you realize. You've had your arms wrapped around me." Jax surprised her by running his finger along the seam of her parted lips. "I've had my mouth on yours. I'd say we were beginning to know each other intimately," he murmured. He shot up a third finger. "And lastly, I don't take no for an answer because I go after what I want, but I'd never force myself on you." He nuzzled the underside of her earlobe, breathing out his words. "Tell me you don't want me and I'll walk away and you'll never see me again."

Every part of Kally tingled with nervous energy. Her heart thundered in her chest and her breathing became shallow. He grazed her neck with his lips and took her face in his hands, brushing his thumbs over her cheeks. When she turned her face toward his, Jax took that as an invitation to claim her lips. The sensation was dizzying. In that millisecond, all thoughts of reluctance fled her rational brain.

"I thought so," he said smugly when he broke the kiss. "I'll pick you up at seven."

"No! I'll meet you," Kally was quick to reply.

"I have to meet them sometime, Princess."

"Not happening," she said. "My dad will throw you out on your ass if he doesn't murder you first!"

"I'll text you the time and place then," Jax said, exiting the car.

Kally watched from her car as Jax peeled out of the parking lot. White-knuckling the steering wheel, she rested her head against it. She was in way over her head with this guy, yet something within her couldn't let him walk away.

* * *

Jax was leaning against his car in the parking lot of La Plage when Kally pulled up. He was still in the same suit he'd been wearing that morning but looked as fresh as if he'd just showered and dressed.

La Plage was an intimate, pricey restaurant, written up in the local newspaper as being one of the most romantic dining experiences on Long Island. Situated only steps away from the Long Island Sound, the outdoor seating and string lighting made for an enchanting atmosphere.

Although Kally lived less than fifteen miles from the establishment, not only had she never dined there, she had never even seen the place. Egypt, who nearly lost her mind over Kally's encounter with the mystery man, as she referred to him, insisted on choosing Kally's ensemble for the evening.

The next thing she knew, Egypt was dragging Kally to the mall because, in her words, she had nothing fit for a date with the hot dude Kally had described.

Of course, she would take her to BeBe, where the garments were meant for the more shapely, voluptuous figure—for the bold woman who flaunts her assets.

"Trust me, you'll look amazing in this," Egypt insisted, and before she knew it, Kally was at the cash register paying for a dress she wasn't sure she could pull off.

Kally's eyes met his, as Jax drank in the sight of her when she emerged from her car. She had pinned some hair up off her face, the rest flowing down her bare back. The ebony, body-hugging dress showed off a hint of cleavage and her matching strappy, high-heeled sandals brought her equal to his height.

Slowly, she walked to him, the sheer material of the train on the back of her above-the-knee length dress billowing in the breeze.

Jax reached out to take her hand, looking at her with admiration. "You look like an angel," he stated. "Maybe a fallen one in all that seductive black."

Kally smiled shyly, looking down at her feet. No one had ever thought of her as seductive. She certainly never thought of herself in that way.

Jax lifted her chin. "That was a compliment. You must know how fucking hot you look."

"Your eloquence is astounding," she joked.

Jax took Kally by the hand and they walked toward the entrance to the restaurant. "Do you always do that?" Jax asked.

"Do what?"

"Make snide comments to conceal your insecurities?"

She didn't know how to answer him. "I apologize for being impolite."

"You didn't answer my question," Jax said. He halted just shy of the door and faced her.

Kally closed her eyes and sighed. "You make me uneasy," she conceded. "I've never met anyone quite like you."

"Good. And you never will again if I have anything to say about it." He held both of her hands and brought them to his lips, kissing her on the knuckles. "I haven't stopped thinking about you from the minute you rolled down your window and looked at me with those expressive, brown eyes. You have nothing to be uneasy about." He turned one of her hands, palm up, and kissed the inside of it. "If anyone should lack his usual ease, it's me. I always get the sense you're about a second away from bolting on me."

Jax placed his hand on the small of her back and escorted her into the restaurant. Moments later, they were led to an outdoor table overlooking the water.

Jax requested a bottle of Chateau Grand-Puy-Lacoste and the hostess who had seated them, wide-eyed and willing to jump at his every request, now seemed more eager to please than ever.

"I hope you like red wine," he said.

"Yes, but what had her so impressed?" Kally asked. "She looked like she was about to trip over herself."

"It's a fine bottle," he shrugged. "I don't suppose it's requested too often." Jax had taken the seat beside her rather than across from Kally. He draped his arm over the back of her chair, allowing his fingertips to tease her bare back.

"So explain to me again why it is that I couldn't pick you up?" he asked. "You said something about murder?" he laughed.

"It's complicated." Kally was interrupted when the sommelier presented Jax with the bottle of French wine he'd requested. He nodded his approval before the bottle was uncorked. Kally watched as the wine was poured. Jax swirled and sniffed—sipped and savored. Finally, he offered his approval and the wine was poured into Kally's glass.

This was the same man who strode up with ripped jeans and wind-blown hair, tattoo clad, riding on a Harley. How was he even the same person? So worldly and sophisticated. Yet, she could see the truth behind those pools of blue. He was not born into a life of luxury with a monogrammed silver spoon. He'd clawed his way to privilege. She sensed it. It took effort for Jax to maintain this controlled, mannered behavior. Simmering underneath was an untamed maverick and Kally wasn't sure if it terrified or enthralled her.

"You were saying?" Jax urged Kally to continue. "Spit it out, Princess. You ashamed of me?"

"No, it's not that!"

"I've been there before and I've proven them all wrong." His tone held an edge of bitterness. "They all thought I'd never make anything of myself. I'd be lucky to make it through one year of college, they all said. Laughed at me when I applied. My father wanted me to get into the plumbers' union, but I had different ideas. Stupid ideas, according to him."

Kally didn't know what to make of this. Obviously, it was a sore spot. His own family had no faith in him.

"Didn't your parents read your report cards? Surely they would have realized you were college material?"

Jax brought his wine glass to his lips, assessing Kally as he sipped. "Let's get back to you."

A gentle breeze drifted over Kally's skin. Crossing her arms over her chest, she rubbed away the momentary chill.

"Are you cold?"

"No." Kally smiled. "It's a beautiful night," she said, looking up at the bright moon suspended above. "It's just … I'm sure I'm not like the other girls you've brought to places like this." Nervously, she sipped her wine, peeking over the glass. "I'm not sure I can keep up."

"Keep up?" Jax repeated incredulously. "You have nothing to keep up with, Princess. Just be straight with me and tell me what's on your mind."

Just then, the waiter came to their table. Jax rattled off their orders quickly, dismissing him abruptly before turning his attention back to Kally.

"I live at home," she said, hoping that was enough for him to understand.

"I'm aware. And …"

"There's a lot of restrictions. Curfews, interrogations … It's my dad mostly. I haven't dated a lot and anyone I did date had to be approved by him and he prefers—insists—they be Greek."

"Greek? So you're Greek?" he asked, regarding her curiously as though she were from a different planet. "And your father is like the one in that movie? What about your mother?"

"She's Greek too but she tells me to run as fast as I can when a Greek man is within earshot."

Jax threw his head back in laughter. "So who do you listen to?"

"I take it as it comes. I've only had a couple of boyfriends and none of them worked out—Greek or otherwise."

"So what's the problem?"

"He'll take one look at you and throw you out. 'He's too old for you, Kally, not Greek, his hair is too long hair, and what do we know about him?'" Kally mimicked in her father's accented voice. "And if he, by some miracle, does allow it, he'll probably insist on chaperoning us. It won't be worth the trouble to you."

"That bad?" He rubbed his forefinger over his bottom lip.

"Worse. In my home, I'll forever be a twelve-year-old, or at least feel like one."

"But you're not. You're an adult. Move out," he whispered in her ear, grazing it with his lips.

Kally shuddered. "You don't get it," she said, shaking her head.

Their entrées were placed in front of them. "We'll have to revisit this at a later date," he said.

A later date? He still wanted to see her after tonight? She couldn't figure out what he'd want with a girl who was saddled with so many limitations when he could be with any woman of his choosing. Obviously far more sophisticated women than herself.

After Kally and Jax finished their meal, they lingered over dessert. Enjoying the warmth of the night and the illumination from the moonlight, they took their time walking back to their respective vehicles.

Jax, bracketing Kally against her car, leaned in to deliver a long-lasting kiss, one she felt to her very core as it awakened every cell and nerve ending in her body.

"You know what I want?" he asked huskily as he broke from her lips. He shook his head. "Never mind, it doesn't matter. Tonight, I'm going to be a gentleman. Tomorrow though," he growled in a hushed tone, "might be a different story."

"Tomorrow?" Kally asked, breathless.

"Yes. Say you'll see me tomorrow."

"I don't know," she said.

"Yes, you do." Jax withdrew his Blackberry from his breast pocket. He began to tap out a text. "You would have given me a definite no if you didn't want to or if you had other plans." After a few more taps at the keyboard, he returned the phone to his pocket. "Check your phone." He smirked. "I'll be waiting for you at that address at seven p.m. tomorrow."

"And what if I don't show up?" Kally asked. "I haven't agreed."

"Then I'll have to come looking for you. Do you think your father will be home? I'd love to meet him."

"You wouldn't!" Kally felt every muscle in her body tighten. "That's blackmail."

Jax dug his hands into her hair and brought her face to his. He planted a punishing kiss to her lips—one that told her he meant what he said—one that made it clear to her that this was only the beginning.

Chapter 18

Kally

2009

What in Hell was she thinking? Kally was panicking. Jax was so far out of her league that, although he lived in a nearby town, he may as well have been from a different universe. Yet, here she was, standing on the doorstep of a townhouse in one of the most exclusive complexes in the area.

Jax was obviously wealthy, mingled with the rich and famous, and could have any woman he wanted falling at his feet. He was intense, confident and exuded a raw sexuality that made her so nervous she wanted to run to the far corners of the Earth where no one would ever find her.

Egypt, naturally, tried to slap some sense into Kally, insisting she call her parents and say she was staying over at Egypt's for the night while they rummaged through her things for something to loan her.

Egypt pulled a garment from the overstuffed closet. "This will get his attention."

"It sure will!" Kally exclaimed. "I'm a good four inches taller than you. That dress is already too short on you."

But Egypt would hear none of it. "Put it on!" she insisted.

Kally had to admit, if only silently, that the scarlet skater dress did compliment her complexion. The strapless bodice and the flare in the skirt accentuated her figure in all the right places, and her legs looked as though they went on for days.

Forcing her mind back to the present, Kally ghosted her finger over the doorbell. If she rang it, there would be no turning back, but if she walked away, Jax would be none the wiser. She'd call him later and make an excuse. But before she could make the decision whether to press the button or turn and run, the front door swung open.

Jax, planted in a firm stance with his arms crossed asked, "Have you made up your mind yet, Princess?"

"My mind?" Kally's mind was a blur. Her focus, what little she had at the moment anyway, went straight to the biceps flexing behind the sleeves of his t-shirt.

He raised an eyebrow. "Are you coming in?"

"I … Yes, I'm here." *Oh, God, what an idiot I am!* "Here, I brought you this." She held out a gift bag. "It's *ouzo*. I thought you might like to try it."

"Thanks." Instead of taking the bag from her, he pulled her in by the waist, dropping his head down to meet hers. "I've sampled the flavors of Greece before. I have a feeling it will become my new favorite," he growled softly. "You look like a goddess."

Commanding and hypnotic, his kiss was spellbinding. If this was the way the evening was beginning then she didn't stand a chance of holding her head above water. This man was going to drown her in seduction and Kally didn't know how to navigate those waters. She'd only known boys before. Boys in comparison to Jax. He, on the other hand, was all man, skilled and experienced, carnal in a way that both frightened and exhilarated her, and she was sure he came with expectations she could never begin to meet.

Jax lifted Kally off her feet, eliciting a squeal of surprise. He carried her into his home. As he set her down, he grazed his fingers teasingly up her leg from her calf to the upper part of her thigh.

"You're killing me," he groaned. "I cooked dinner, but fuck if I don't want to dump it in the garbage right about now."

"Don't do that! I could definitely eat," Kally lied, her stomach a tangle of nervous knots.

Jax took her by the hand, leading her from the two-story tall foyer to an elegant kitchen that looked as though it had never been used. The glass dining table with the pewter base was not set for a meal though.

Kally frowned in confusion until Jax took her by the elbow.

"This way," he said, guiding her to French doors that opened onto a secluded fenced-in patio.

Overhead, lighting softly illuminated the small space. Jax had set a table suitable for outside dining. The aroma of grilled steaks brushed with garlic butter awakened Kally's appetite.

"Have a seat while I flip the steaks." Jax pulled a chair out for her before checking the food on the grill.

The man was a paradox. A complete enigma to her. When she'd first met him, she'd taken him for a man with simple needs. But here he was with all this wealth and standing. Who was the real Jax? she wondered. This man in the ripped jeans and t-shirt standing before her or the man in the five-thousand-dollar designer suit she'd dined with the night prior?

He was both, Kally decided upon learning more about him over dinner. He was real and down-to-earth, never forgetting where he came from and how he had achieved success. But he knew how to play the game when he needed to. Polish and taste was a learned necessity yet, when he was off the clock, Jax preferred his natural, relaxed state of being.

Kally helped to carry the dirty dishes into the kitchen. She turned the faucet on, found a sponge and began to rinse the dishes.

"Leave it," Jax insisted, coming up behind her.

"At least let me put away the leftover food." She went to open the refrigerator door but Jax slammed it shut, taking Kally by surprise when he pressed her up against the cool stainless surface.

"I'm done waiting for you."

The sexy rasp of his voice and his close proximity caused her to unconsciously suck in a gasp of breath, holding it in anticipation. Kally's heart hammered in her chest to the point of embarrassment.

Jax ran his lips down the length of her neck, trailing kisses to her bare shoulders and finally finding his way to the hollow of her cleavage. Lifting the skirt of her dress, he grabbed the firm mounds of her shapely backside as he ground himself into her.

Kally was rendered helpless. Her defenses were lost to him, reduced to a pile of putty, breathless and wanting.

"I'm giving you one chance to back out," Jax panted. "After that, I can't be responsible for what I do next."

He was giving her an out. She could leave right now. All she had to do was walk away. But did she want to? No. If she was honest with herself, she didn't want to. This man made her feel what she never had before. Lust and longing clashed within her, begging to be released. But there was so much more. There were stories to be unearthed deep within his eyes, secrets in his soul to be discovered. Kally tenderly brushed back the strands of hair falling across his face. Reaching for the nape of his neck, she pulled him to her, bringing his lips to hers.

Jax, needing no further permission, suddenly turned primal. He tugged roughly at the zipper on the back of her dress until it fell in a puddle on the floor. A feral growl rumbled from deep within his chest as he soaked in the sight of her in red lace.

Kally's body reacted to him in a way it had never before with any man. The intensity of her arousal overruled her inhibitions and insecurities. She pulled desperately at the t-shirt tucked into his jeans and Jax quickly shed himself from it altogether.

"Fuck, I want you, Kally," he growled. "Right now."

The sound of foil ripping surprised Kally. She'd lost her head and hadn't thought anything through, other than the sensual thrum coursing through her veins. Thankfully, he had.

Jax unclasped her bra, letting it drop in the pile with the rest of her garments. Circling his thumbs over her erect nipples, he admired her beauty. Greedily, he took one breast in his mouth, suckling and teasing her to a greater arousal with his tongue. Kally closed her eyes, panting, her head spinning at the sensation of his touch. Grabbing a fistful of his hair as he kissed his way down her belly, Kally shuddered at each sensation, the feeling intensifying as her need grew. With a slow sensual tease, Jax slowly shimmied her panties down her slender legs but then entered her without warning, inciting involuntary gasps born from deep within her core. Gentle caresses changed to desperate hunger. He lifted her off the floor, her back supported against the cold, steel surface of the refrigerator. Wrapping her legs around him, Jax voraciously moved in and out of her with a raw carnality she had never experienced. Erotic, lustful grunts came from deep within Jax as he met his crest. Kally, riding on the coattails of his climax, chased her own release. Boneless, she collapsed onto his shoulder, spent, sated and bewildered.

Jax lifted her over his shoulder.

"What are you doing?" Kally said with what little breath was left in her body. "I need my clothes."

"No, you don't," he disagreed, carrying her out of the kitchen. "We're just getting started. You won't be needing them for a while."

✳ ✳ ✳

Slivers of light filtered in from the window blinds. Disoriented, Kally blinked, trying to awaken her mind from slumber. The clock on the nightstand indicated it was well past three a.m. It hadn't been her intention to spend the night, but after doing whatever it was they had done for the better part of the night, she was too exhausted to move.

In truth, Kally didn't know how to label what they had done. The first time, pushed up against a kitchen appliance, wasn't what she could call lovemaking. Later, in his bed, Jax was slower, more deliberate, yet there was still a possessive forcefulness to his every movement, as though he was claiming or branding her as his.

She turned her head, regarding the man beside her. A stream of light striped his face. Kally propped her elbow on the pillow to support her head with her hand. She watched Jax as he slept peacefully—the even, steady breaths, the rise and fall of his chest, the relaxed expression on his face. Another ray of light sneaking through the blinds caught his bare abdomen. The crisp, white sheets narrowly covered his muscular form. There was much to admire here: the eight-pack abs, a faint line of hair traveling down from his navel and the panty-melting V bracketing his hips.

Kally furrowed her brow with concern and, she had to admit, a good dose of curiosity. She noticed a fairly large, violent looking, jagged scar on his right side just below his waist and another alongside it that seemed more surgical in nature. With an urge to kiss away the memory of pain it must have inflicted, she restrained herself. Instead, Kally ghosted her fingers above the raised skin. Jax chose that very moment to open his eyes and snatch her wrist before she made contact with the injury.

Kally yelped as he dragged her body on top of his.

"Can't keep your hands off of me, can you, Princess?" His words teased, but his eyes darkened with an emotion she couldn't make out. Before she could answer, he growled a response for her. "Same."

Daring to run her fingers over the telltale area, Kally asked, "What happened?"

Jax brushed her hand away. "It's nothing to concern yourself with," he said sharply, averting his eyes from hers.

Kally chewed at the inside of her lip. "I didn't mean to upset you. It's evident that it's an old injury. I just want to get to know you better."

"That's not going to teach you anything you need to know, trust me." He rolled over, pinning her body under his. "This is all you need to know." He kissed her as he lowered himself onto her. "I can't get enough of you."

The smell of coffee wafting through the room finally roused Kally from her sleep—that, as well as the ray of sunlight warming her bare skin; a reminder of the day's obligations. She picked up the t-shirt Jax had shed the night before, bringing it to her nose to breathe in his scent. Bergamot and amber. She closed her eyes, committing the smell and the man to memory. She slipped the shirt over her head and padded in the direction of the rattling of dishes and pans.

"I should get going," Kally said. "My dad is expecting me at his restaurant by ten-thirty."

Jax glanced at the clock on the microwave. "That's two hours from now. I made you breakfast." As if he did it for a living, he flipped an omelet with precision before returning the pan to the stove. "Sit," he ordered.

"Bossy much?" Kally said, complying to his demand.

"I like you better this way," she said as he set a plate down in front of her.

"Better than what?"

"Better than in a suit and tie." She threaded her fingers through his hair when he bent to kiss her. "The way you looked when I met you." She ran her hands down his chest and over the contours of his muscles. "Ripped jeans and a band t-shirt," Kally purred.

"Same. But I like you even better in nothing but my client's shirt. I'll have a fresh one ready for you when you return tonight."

"Tonight? I can't see you tonight."

Jax grimaced. He had that intense look on his face that unnerved Kally. She could actually see the muscles in his jaw jumping.

"Tomorrow then, and if you have any other plans that don't include me, cancel them."

Chapter 19

Kally

2018

"Big deal!" Egypt exclaimed. "So he has a past. Just about everyone's done some sort of drug at one point or another."

"I haven't," Kally said. "He claims addiction was never an issue for him, but how do I know for certain?"

Kally turned the store sign around and unlocked the door, opening the shop for the day. She didn't bother to drag the sidewalk chalkboard easel out. The strong gusts of wind would have only knocked it down. A banner day for business it would not be, that was one thing she was sure of.

"You know this is just another excuse for you to keep from getting involved with someone," Egypt said, challenging her.

"It's more complicated than that." Kally, sitting on a high-top stool, lowered her head, resting it on the countertop in defeat. Hiding her face with her hands, she mumbled, "How do you think Max will feel about me when he finds out I had an affair with a married man? That would have to be a deal breaker after what his wife did to him."

"Girl, I love you but you are so damn infuriating," Egypt scolded.

"You did not have an affair. You had a relationship with a man you thought was single."

"A technicality doesn't change the facts."

"Look, I'm sorry Jax died before you could get the answers you needed from him. I'm also sorry he isn't here so I can personally kick his ass from here to China," Egypt said. "But you didn't do anything wrong and you need to move on—from the grief, from the pain, and especially from the goddamned unwarranted guilt. It's been eight years already! Let it go!"

Kally looked up when she heard the door chime. "Saved by the bell! It looks like some of our regulars can't stay away even when the weather is nasty."

"This discussion isn't over." Egypt glared at her.

"Yes, it is," Kally said through a forced smile. "Mr. and Mrs. Lawson! How are you? Welcome home."

Kally seated the older couple as they shared with her the details of their visit to Mrs. Lawson's family home in France to attend a wedding.

"Now that you've been reminded of the perfection that is an authentic French croissant, I'll hold my breath that mine won't disappoint."

Kally waved to a familiar patron standing by the takeout counter when she spotted Milton and Spyro walking in.

"*Kaliméra*, Kallyope," Milton greeted her.

"Ba!" Spyro argued. "It's more like *Kakiméra*."

Kally shook her head. Clamping her teeth over her lips, she tried to suppress a smile. The two elderly men bantered over everything: politics, religion, sports, and even their favorite foods. Given the chance, they would probably argue over the name of the color painted on her walls. None of it was spoken with any malice; they were the best of friends and had been for many years.

"I'll be over with your *kafés* in a few minutes," Kally told the elderly men as they found their way to their usual table.

"Kally turned her attention back to the Lawsons. "Croissant?"

"No, dear, not today," Mrs. Lawson said as she perused the menu. "The pistachio madeleines sound mouth-watering. I'll have that with a cup of English Breakfast tea please."

"I'll have the same," Mr. Lawson said. "But make mine an Earl Grey."

Kally asked Egypt to prepare the Lawsons' order while stirring together finely granulated coffee grounds and water into a *briki* hovering over a low fire. Kally stood over the small pot, waiting for the foam to rise. After she removed the coffee from the heat, she carefully poured it equally into two demitasse cups.

"*Skétos?*" Spyros asked when Kally set the cups down in front of them.

"*Vevaios!*" After all this time, she knew better than to taint their *Ellinikos Kafés* with sugar. Even though Kally herself preferred it *glyko* - very sweet.

"How many times do you need to tell the girl? She knows, *vre mori!*" Milton scolded.

"No worries." Kally wanted to circumvent at least one argument. "I made *galakteboureko* today." Kally was treated to exclamations of approval.

"*Bravo*, Kallyope *mou*," Milton exclaimed. He laid a hand over hers. "You stick with my boy. He could use a good girl like you."

Kally crinkled her nose. What and who was he talking about? "Your boy?"

"My grandson. Maximos," he emphasized as though it were obvious.

Kally's eyes widened in surprise. "Max? Max is your grandson?" She looked at Milton with fresh eyes, trying to search for the resemblance. "He mentioned that he moved back home with his father and that Athena had to put up with a houseful of men."

Milton chuckled. "True, but we spoil her. Me, my son, Peter, Maximos and my other grandson, Stefanos."

"That poor child," Kally laughed. "That's a lot of testosterone for a six-year-old girl."

"That's okay. They're back where they belong. Away from that life," he added in his heavily accented voice. Milton shook his head. "She seemed nice at first, his wife, but she had us all fooled. Or maybe she changed. I don't know." He lifted his shoulders. Making a very typical Greek circular gesture with his hand, he continued, "What did we know of her? *Xeni!* But you! You, we know for certain who you are."

"Milton." Kally patted his arm. "Max and I are not together. We are just acquaintances." Kally could almost taste the lie in her mouth. He was becoming so much more, but she wasn't yet sure where it would lead or if it would even last. "I have to get back to the kitchen."

"Just remember," Milton said with a knowing grin, "it all begins with acquaintance."

Hours later, Kally was still dwelling on Milton's words. She wondered what Max had told his grandfather. He hadn't called or texted her since their talk the other night. Every time the door chimed, she looked up to see if it was the handsome constable entering her premises. A pang of disappointment washed over each time her hope was dashed.

"Seriously? Kal, decide what you want to do and go for it," Egypt asserted untying her apron when Krystina walked in the door to relieve her. She retrieved her bag from under the counter, fished for her car keys, jiggling them in triumph when she finally found them.

The door chimed and Kally's eyes flew once more in the direction of the entrance.

"Call him!" Egypt insisted. "The ball's in your court. He's not going to call you."

"Hi, Loukas!" Kally's face brightened at the sight of the boy entering. He was from her family's neighborhood and also happened to be one of Krystina's classmates—one she outwardly tried to avoid. For what reason, Kally couldn't understand. He was adorable—tall and lean, yet muscular. His mop of silky black hair hung over his forehead revealing rather than concealing a stunning set of eyes the color of blue topaz.

"Hey, Kally. Do you have a minute?" he asked.

"Sure. What's up?"

"I was wondering if you had any job openings?" Loukas asked.

"Don't you already work for my dad?"

Loukas stared down at the floor. "I could use more hours."

Kally looked at him with concern. "Hey," she said to get his attention. "Come to my office so we can talk."

She escorted him through the kitchen doors, leading him to her small office space. Shutting the door behind her, she turned to face Loukas. "Talk to me. Is everything okay?"

"It's just better when I'm out of the house. Besides, I need to save money for college."

"There are other ways to get out of the house," Kally advised. "You can go out with friends or spend time at one of their homes. You know my mother would be happy to have you for dinner any time."

"Is that a no then?"

The boy looked forlorn. Kally wanted nothing more than to reach out and hug him. God knows he could use one. "No, of course not. You can start by bussing tables and in time I might be able to give you other responsibilities. I don't have a lot of hours to offer you though."

"Whatever you can give me, I'll take," Loukas said with enthusiasm. "Thank you."

"No need to thank me," Kally said. "I've got you. Anything you need, okay?"

He nodded soberly as they exited the office.

"What are you doing here?" Krystina asked as she caught sight of him, a look of disgust on her face.

"Loukas is going to be working here two days a week," Kally explained.

"Is this your latest way to annoy and stalk me?" Krystina asked, bumping his shoulder as she stormed past him.

"Krystina!" Kally was furious. "Get over here and apologize for your rudeness."

"It's okay," he said quietly. "I'll see you tomorrow. Thanks again."

When Loukas left, Kally marched over to her sister. "What's the matter with you!" she shouted. "What did Loukas ever do to you for you to treat him that way?"

Krystina rolled her eyes, offering her sister nothing but a, 'Don't lecture me,' glare. "It's Luke. At school, he wants to be called Luke."

"Oh, so you're considerate enough on his behalf to correct me on his name, yet it's somehow okay for you to make him feel unwelcome here?"

"He's a pain in my ass," Krystina said. "Always has been since we were little."

"He likes you," Kally said, trying to conceal a smile. Her sister could be so stubborn sometimes. "Be nice. He's going through a rough time. And honestly, would it kill you to give him a chance?"

Cocking her head to one side, Krystina pointed accusingly at her sister. "Maybe you should take your own advice."

"Get back to work," Kally commanded.

* * *

Work occupied Kally, but thoughts of Max consumed her. It had been three days of dwelling, pondering and obsessing. Three days of no decision-making. Three days of wearing out her carpet at night, walking Emma twice as far as she normally did and binge watching *I Love Lucy* episodes while eating chocolate chip ice cream out of the carton.

By now, Max had probably given up on her. He may have even moved on to someone else. A spark of panic shot through her at the thought. She could do absolutely nothing and lose him for sure, or she could tell him about Jaxon and, in the end, she wouldn't be any worse off.

With her fingers hovering over the face of her iPhone, Kally hesitated before tapping out the text.

Can we talk?

"Press the send button, Kally," she muttered under her breath.

Finally, she hit the button, dropping the phone as though it had singed her skin. Sitting on the floor in her living room, she draped herself over her coffee table, obsessing. An hour passed, then two. It was almost eleven p.m. when her phone signaled an incoming text.

Max: I'm just getting off work. Heading home.

Kally: Oh. I thought maybe you could come by. It's late though. I understand.

Max: No, I don't think you do. Three days of doubting tells me all I need to know.

Kally: It's not you I doubt, it's me.

Max: That's original.

Kally: I mean it. I told you I have a past also. And trust issues.

Max: Me, too. Opening up to you was a huge leap of faith for me.

Kally: Was? Give me a chance to leap with you. Please.

Nothing. No reply. Kally had her answer. She had dragged her feet and now it was too late. After another ten minutes of staring at her phone, she gave up and turned the bedsheets down. She was about to slip under the covers when she heard a rap at her front door.

Alarmed, Kally looked out the window, her concern assuaged when she saw Max standing on her front porch.

"You didn't answer my last text," she accused as she opened the door, relieved to see him.

"Can I come in?"

She could just imagine what he was thinking as he swept his eyes over her body, clad in lavender cupcake sleep shorts and an old, mint green camisole. Her hair was bunched in a loose knot at the top of her head and her face was completely bare of cosmetics. Kally swallowed nervously, cracking the door open wider to let him in.

They stood unmoving in the doorway, Kally self-consciously rubbing her hands over her crossed arms, Max jiggling the keys in his pocket.

Simultaneously, they both began to speak and abruptly halted.

Clamping her mouth shut in a tight line, she indicated for him to go first.

"Kally," Max began, "I can't do this with you. We're either all in or all out. I have Athena to think of. As it is, she's already getting more attached to you and your family than she should."

He scratched his forehead, pausing before verbalizing his next thought. Kally didn't dare say a word. She owed it to him to at least let him say what he needed to.

"When I came back to town, I had no intention of becoming involved with anyone for quite some time. At least not until I felt Athena had settled into her new life here."

"You're not giving your daughter or yourself enough credit, Max," Kally said. "She's happy and thriving and it's all because of you." She said this with sincerity regardless of what was to happen or not happen between them.

"I know," he said with a sigh, rubbing a hand over his face. "But it's not just because of me. Every time she's with you or your grandmother, she lights up."

"That makes me happy to hear." Kally smiled encouragingly up at him. "Are you staying a while or making a mad dash to your car?" They were still lingering by the front door and she gestured for Max to come inside. "Beer?"

"You have one?" He looked surprised.

"Just for you," she said shyly.

Kally went into the kitchen, took a deep breath and shook out her nerves. *Get with it, Kally.* When she returned to the living room, she found Max sitting on the couch, his forearms resting on his thighs and his head hung low. He looked up at her when she tapped him on the shoulder with the neck of the beer bottle.

"A nickel for your thoughts," Kally said.

"What happened to the penny?"

"I think what's on your mind is worth more than that." Kally wanted to reach out and touch him but she refrained herself. The tightness of his shoulders and the forlorn expression on his face didn't erase her attraction to him though.

Max returned his gaze to his lap. "The first time I saw you, I knew I was in trouble. I knew that as much as I was determined to focus solely on my daughter and her wellbeing, I was pretty much screwed."

Kally's heart constricted at his words. All those mixed signals. All the push and pull. He had been dealing with his own doubts as much as she had.

"I tried to stay away from you but it was no use." Max met Kally's watchful stare. "The day I brought Athena to the café, I saw how genuinely sweet you were with her and how taken she was with you. It made me realize that it was okay for me to care about you—to bring you into our fold—to allow you into the protective cocoon I had created for her."

"And for you," Kally pointed out.

He nodded. "And for me," he agreed.

Kally took his hands in hers, looking Max directly in the eyes to emphasize her honesty. "I would never, ever do anything to hurt either you or Athena. I care for both of you more than I want to admit. More than I've allowed myself to care about anyone for a long time."

Kally pulled her hands from his, placing them in her lap. "That's why I've pulled away these last few days. Once you hear what I have to tell you, you won't want me anymore. I'm no better than your late wife."

Max winced. Anger swiftly replaced the anguish. "Never compare yourself to her." His tone held such vehemence that Kally was afraid to reveal her truth. "You're nothing like her," he snapped.

"That's not entirely true. You need to know my past before you consider becoming more involved with me." Kally sucked in a deep breath as though the air filling her lungs would grant her courage. *Here goes ...* "I had a relationship with a married man," she blurted out. "Once you told me what Bridget did to you, I didn't think you could be with someone who did virtually the same thing."

Max looked at Kally as if it was the first time he'd ever laid eyes on her. It was as though she was a stranger to him. The minutes dragged by in silence. Finally, he spoke. "Wow!" He shook his head in disbelief. "That does change things." Disgust coated his words, causing Kally to flinch. "I guess my judgment hasn't improved after all." He chuckled but the sound held no humor. "You intentionally fucked another woman's husband?" he asked accusingly, his reprehension evident.

Kally blanched at his uncharacteristically vulgar choice of words. Tears blurred her vision. "I didn't know he was married," she said quietly.

"Care to explain?" he asked harshly.

"I met Jaxon purely by accident. He was very different from anyone I had ever known. Commanding and determined," Kally began, wiping a tear from her cheek. He pursued me and it didn't take much for me to give in. He was mesmerizing, older than I was, and I was flattered."

"When did you find out he was married?" Max asked, watching her closely.

Kally closed her eyes. Tears dripped like raindrops from her lashes. "When he died," she whispered. Wiping the flood from her face with her fingertips, she choked out, "I found out at his funeral. Imagine my surprise when the funeral director led me to a room and pointed out his parents and his very pregnant wife."

"Oh, Kal," Max said, his tone shifting to convey sympathy. He took her in his arms and let her cry into his chest. "You've been carrying this guilt that wasn't yours to bear. That wasn't on you." He pulled her back to look at her. "You had no inkling at all?"

"No. His behavior never led me to believe there was someone else. If anything, he was growing impatient with me because I wouldn't introduce him to my family."

"Why not?"

"He wasn't the kind of guy I'd ever dare bring home. I was always afraid of how my parents would receive him and he wasn't a man about to take any bullshit," Kally explained. "He'd decided I was his and he would have had no qualms in telling them so. Let's just say he wasn't the clean-cut, polite boy my parents would have approved of."

"And you liked this guy?"

"I was in love with him—or so I thought," Kally mused. "You have to understand that my track record with boyfriends was off the charts awful. No one had paid that kind of attention to me. Certainly not anyone like him. And … I have to admit, there was a bit of rebellion sparking in me at the thought. My father was always trying to push me toward one of his friend's sons. The idea of being with the bad boy was alluring."

"You don't seem like the rebellious type," Max said, looking at her with interest.

"I'm not—never was," Kally admitted. "I don't know what came over me. It was as though I had stepped into a secret, private world far away from my father's expectations and the limitations I'd set for myself."

"So you were not only left grieving, you were broken-hearted by the betrayal." Max stated this as a fact he well understood.

"It left me with more than that. A lack of trust most of all," Kally confessed. "Love must be mutual. Whatever I felt for Jax had to be a delusion. I was merely infatuated with the attention, I suppose. After that, I came to the conclusion that some people just weren't meant for love and I was simply one of them. That's when I decided to create the life I have now with my own home and a business I'm passionate about. That was all I needed. It was enough."

Kally was afraid she might have sounded cold or closed off, but this was her story and she was being as honest as she could. "Don't get me wrong, I'm a sucker for a good love story. But I get my romance fix off the pages of ridiculously unrealistic novels. The idea that a woman isn't whole unless she's connected to a man is archaic and simply not so."

Kally tried to read Max's expression. She watched as he ran his fingers though his hair and sank back against the sofa cushion, deep in thought. She was laying it all out for him. This had been her mindset after Jax. It had to be, after all that had happened. Now something within her had changed, and she admitted to herself it was because of the man before her. But did she have the courage to take that step? To truly leap?

"Max, look at me," she implored. "When I said that was all I needed, it was true, until the day you stepped into my café to recover a license plate."

With that simple statement, Kally saw hope spring to his eyes.

"You weren't the only one trying to fight your feelings," she admitted. "I was too afraid to trust them. So very afraid of unlocking the door to my heart only to have it shattered again."

Max cupped her face in his hands. "I would never do anything to hurt you. Never," he added emphatically. "I know what it's like to have your entire world implode—to have the one person you built your life around obliterate everything you worked for without a single apology."

"Or an explanation," Kally added. "I can't get answers from someone who's gone for good—from a man whose death I may have caused."

"What?" The creases in Max's brow deepened as his incredulity grew. "How is that possible?"

"I told him something that I thought he was happy about. At least he told me he was," Kally explained. Her mind drifted off, remembering that moment so long ago, and her words came out slowly as if she was still trying to make sense of it all. "The delight on his face was short-lived. Suddenly he seemed lost in his thoughts and burdened by them."

"What was it that you told him?"

A soft groan escaped Kally's lips. "I'd rather not say right now." She looked up at Max apologetically. "But he left in a hurry, saying he had something he needed to resolve and that he'd be back." Kally rose and walked to the window. The moon hung low and the midnight sky allowed for the stars to shine brightly. On another occasion, she would have deemed it a setting for romance. Tonight, the twinkling luminous balls of gas were mocking her.

Kally whipped around to see Max staring at her, waiting for the rest of the pieces to unfold. "He never made it back. He was killed in a fatal motorcycle accident."

Max immediately dashed to her side, cuffing his hands over her shoulders. "That's tragic but not your fault."

"I was told he was going over ninety miles per hour. His bike spun out of control and hit the concrete wall of an overpass," she cried. "Don't you see? What I told him drove him to ride at that speed."

"What did you tell him?" Max asked. Silence fell between them. "Kally, we need to be completely honest with each other if we're to have a chance. You can trust me."

Turning away from his penetrating stare, Kally looked out beyond the stars, into the blackness. "I told him I was pregnant with his child." A great sadness crept into her voice. Instinctively, she laid her hands over her abdomen. "I don't even have to look at you to know what your expression must be right now." She was certain he was about to walk out of her life at any moment. "I lost the baby shortly after his death."

Max wrapped his arms around her, drawing Kally back around to face him. He nuzzled the underside of her neck, gently pressing his lips to her soft flesh.

"We've both had more shit thrown at us than either of us deserve," he whispered in her ear. "But it's in the past. It's over and all that matters now is that we found each other." He cupped her face. "I want you, Kallyope Andarakis. I want to be with you and see what we can build together."

Max bent down to kiss her, pouring every ounce of emotion into each brush of his lips and stroke of his tongue. Kally wanted to melt into a puddle—one where all the murkiness muddling her brain washed away.

"So I'm going to ask you one more time." Max smirked, breaking the kiss, "Are you in or are you out?"

Kally tugged on the collar of his uniform, pulling him to her lips. Smiling through the kiss she murmured, "In. I'm so in."

Pistachio Madeleines

Preheat oven to 375°

1 cup sifted cake flour
6 ounces raw, unsalted pistachios, very finely ground
½ teaspoon baking powder
¼ teaspoon salt
1¾ sticks unsalted butter (14 tablespoons), softened
3 large eggs
1 large egg yolk
1 cup sugar
2 teaspoons vanilla
confectioners' sugar

Sift together the flour, pistachios, baking powder and salt. Return mixture to the sifter and set aside.

In a medium bowl, mash the softened butter with the back of a spoon or spatula until creamy.

In a large bowl, beat the eggs, yolk, sugar and vanilla on high speed for two minutes.

Sift the flour mixture into the beaten egg mixture and mix on low speed. Add the butter mixture and continue to mix until all is combined.

Fill two greased madeleine pans three-quarters full. Bake until the cakes are slightly golden on top and golden-brown on the edges, approximately 12 minutes.

Remove from the pans immediately and cool on a wire rack.
Dust with confectioners' sugar. Yields approximately 32 - 36.

"He was my cream, and I was his coffee - And when you poured us together, it was something." Josephine Baker

Chapter 20

Kally

2010

"I have to fly out to LA again," Jax said. "Come with me."

Kally and Jax were snuggled under a cozy, gray fleece blanket watching *He's Just Not That into You*. Though Jax preferred action films to her rom-coms and oldie classics, he suffered through it since one of the actors was his client.

"I can't, you know that," she answered.

"No, I don't know," Jax said, feigning ignorance.

He looked at Kally blankly but she saw his exasperation and impatience hidden behind the calm façade.

"You're a grown woman. You can do whatever you want." He dislodged himself from her embrace, pulling his body upright to lean up against the armrest.

Kally sighed inwardly. They were going to have one of those discussions. They had been seeing each other for ten months and Jax was still Kally's secret. Only Egypt knew about them and she had used her friend as a cover more than once. Sneaking around and lying to her parents was uncharacteristic behavior for her, but she didn't see how it could be any other way.

"In my home, I may as well be a twelve-year-old."

"But you're not. You're twenty-four, old enough to date who you want, work where you want to and make your own life decisions."

Jax held his arms out to her, wiggling his fingers in her direction. "Come here." Kally reached for him, lacing her fingers with his.

"Can't you see that every aspect of your life is driven by what your family expects. Your job, living arrangements, even your relationship with me because you're hiding the truth." He lifted her hand and kissed her knuckles. "You're a sexy, smart and talented woman. Own it. Rule it."

"I know it's hard for you to understand. You were raised in a completely different world than I was." Kally inched closer to him, running her hand down the stubble of his jawline.

Jax grasped her wrist, yanking her into his lap. "I don't give a fuck about parents." His eyes bore into hers like blue flames turning wood to ash. "You and me. That's what matters. We're the only thing that matters."

"And that's the problem right there." She sighed. "My parents do matter and you're a loose cannon. All I need is for you and my dad to get into it. He'll throw your ass out of his house and that will be that."

"How do you feel about me, Kal?" He kept his eyes trained on hers but she picked up on his well-concealed vulnerability hidden by the ever-present confidence and gruff exterior.

Kally brushed the falling strands of dirty blond hair from his face and kissed him. "I love you. More than anything. You know that. You're the most unexpected person to enter my life."

Jax looked down at her, eyes smoldering, lips curled into a menacing grin. "Same. It's the same for me."

"Why do you always say that?" Kally asked, pushing back, her brow furrowing.

"What?"

"Same," she answered. "You never say the words."

"I don't need to," he said. "I'd rather show you every damn day."

He grabbed the hem of his Henley, pulling the shirt up over his head.

Kally ran her hand over his bare biceps, tracing her fingers along the designs inked over his muscular form. Tattoos on a man had never appealed to her before but on him they were so much hotter. Every part of him made her crave him, love him. She'd wondered many times what the meaning was behind the winged, caped figure, trampling the grim reaper. The indelible marking was drawn on his left pectoral, rippling imperceptibly with the beat of his heart as though it breathed a life of its own.

Jax took her hand, guiding her fingers to run down the length of his ribcage. When she saw what he'd brought her attention to, she was astonished. Written vertically, in Greek letters, was Kally's name—her full name—permanently branded on his body. And in his heart, she realized. No man would do that unless he truly loved her.

"I don't know what to say." Her eyes glistened with emotion.

"Tell me you don't need to hear the words," he growled, moving her hand over his heart. "It's what's in here that counts. I pledged my commitment to you on my body. Show me how you'll do the same for me."

"I will. I promise," Kally vowed. "You're the only man I'm ever going to want."

Now if she could only find a way to break it to her father.

Chapter 21

Kally

2018

Kally entered her parents' home with an armful of boxed pastries. It was Sunday afternoon and the aroma wafting from the kitchen was divine. The combination of lamb, garlic and oregano made her mouth water. A cold snap and a hike in precipitation blanketed the island with its first dusting of snow for the season. Patrons had flooded The Coffee Klatch with orders for hot chocolate and steaming cups of coffee. So much so that Kally hadn't touched a morsel of food except to serve it to someone else. The rumbling in her stomach verified her level of hunger.

"Kallyope *mou*," *Yiayiá* greeted her. "Let me take those from you."

Kally handed her the boxes and shrugged her coat off. "It's freezing out there!" she exclaimed, hanging it in the closet and stamping up and down to ward off the cold.

"What did you bring?" *Yiayiá* opened the top box. "Ah! *Tolumbakia! Poleé oraía*." She planted a peck on each of Kally's cheeks.

"And *karithopita*. And for Athena, I made her favorite, s'mores cupcakes."

"So, you and Maximos?" *Yiayiá* smiled knowingly, a glint of mischief twinkling behind her eyes.

"Yup, me and Max."

"It's about time!" she exclaimed, smacking Kally lightly on the cheek. "You've been alone too long."

Kally agreed with a sad smile, remembering how she'd confided in her so long ago, at a time when no one besides Egypt knew about Jaxon. Her grandmother had promised to be by her side when she told her parents about him, hoping they'd accept him, but that day had never come. Tragedy struck instead. It wasn't until she'd landed in the hospital that her own mother found out what Kally had been up to and with whom. After she lost the baby, she confessed everything to Melina, however, her father was, and is to this day, still in the dark. He had no idea she'd had a life-threatening ectopic pregnancy. Instead, Melina kept her daughter's confidence, telling her husband Kally had a large cyst that ruptured.

"*Ela.*" *Yiayiá* took Kally by the hand. Before they entered the kitchen, the old woman turned to regard her seriously. "No secrets this time, eh?"

"No," Kally laughed. "Besides, he's Greek. Dad should be performing a victory dance right about now." She shook herself free of her *yiayiá's* concern and walked in.

The whole family crowded the room, hovering over the kitchen island. But this was nothing new, nor were her mother's mumblings that everyone was in her way.

"Mia!" Kally exclaimed at the sight of her sister popping a chunk of *kasseri* cheese into her mouth. "I'm so happy you came. I miss you."

"You've been busy, I've been busy. You know how it is," Mia said, filling a small plate with *mezethes*. "But if you really missed me you'd get off this island for a day and come see me."

"I'll come!" Krystina chimed in. "Can I stay over and go out with you and your friends?"

"No." George found that exact moment to step into the kitchen.

"You're not old enough."

"I don't go out much anyway," Mia admitted. "I mostly work. My deadlines are insane at the magazine and I've taken on some freelance work in my spare time."

"Don't overdo it," Kally suggested. "You need to make some room for socializing."

"Look who's talking," Mia retorted. "All you do is work."

"I've been making more time for myself lately," Kally said.

"Time for Max, you mean," Krystina teased.

Melina waved her wooden spoon at her youngest. "*Skase!*" she scolded just as the doorbell rang. "Behave yourself."

Kally scooted out of the kitchen to answer the door.

"Hi!" she said enthusiastically. She gave Max a quick kiss and then wrapped Athena in a bear hug. "I'm so happy you're here!"

"Me, too!" Athena said. "Daddy said you have another sister."

"It seems she can't be surrounded by enough women these days." Max shrugged, grinning in defeat.

Kally helped Athena shrug off her coat and took her by the hand. "I do have another sister, and a brother, too. Everyone's in the kitchen. Come and meet them."

After introductions were made, Melina announced that dinner was ready. As they all began to file into the dining room, Loukas barreled in through the side door.

"Sorry I'm late," he apologized.

"What's he doing here?" Krystina asked her mother in a low, yet clearly agitated tone. If the volume of her voice didn't give away her annoyance, her sour expression surely did.

Melina grabbed hold of Krystina's arm and pinched the flesh between her fingers.

"Ouch," she shrieked. "What was that for?"

"A warning to be nice." Melina gave her daughter 'the look.' She meant business.

"Athena, do you want to sit next to me?" Krystina asked.

"I think I'll claim her tonight," Mia said, taking the little girl by the hand. "You can see her any time. We need to have a girl chat."

Athena beamed at the attention.

"She's loving this." Max came up behind Kally and wrapped his arms around her waist. They were interrupted by the gruff sound of George clearing his throat as he glared at Max, particularly focusing on the pair of hands flattened over his daughter's torso. Letting go of her without hesitation, Max escorted Kally to the dining room.

"He has a way of reducing me to a child in two seconds flat," Kally whispered in Max's ear. "He forgets I'm thirty-two."

"Remember that feeling in school when you knew you were about to get detention?" Max whispered back.

"No." Kally stifled a laugh. "I was never in trouble in school."

"Well, I was," Max admitted. "And that sinking feeling is all starting to come back to me."

"He's all bark and no bite. You'll be fine … I think."

"What are the two of you whispering about?" George asked.

"Nothing, *Baba.*" Kally sighed.

George remained standing and lifted his wine-filled glass. "*Kalós irthate Maximos kai Athená*—welcome to our home.

"*Efharistó, Kyrios Andarakis,*" Max replied.

Kally's expression revealed her surprise. She was impressed. He had never given her any indication that he spoke Greek.

"What did you just say, Daddy?" Athena asked.

"I was thanking Kally's father in Greek for having us in his home."

"The child doesn't speak Greek?" George asked as though a crime had been committed.

"No," Max answered. "I'm afraid not."

"Well that has to change! The church offers Greek school for children, you know," George informed him.

"*Yióryios,*" Melina interjected. "It's not your business."

"Here's an idea," Kally said. "Let's eat dinner and have no more discussion on how to raise other people's children," she said, barely retaining her composure. She was beginning to wonder why she thought it was a good idea to invite Max over.

Simultaneously, the family crossed themselves three times in prayer before quietly digging into their food.

"Theo," Max began, "Kally tells me you're attending the community college. Do you plan to continue on to a four-year school?"

"Yes, but I work with Dad at the restaurant so I'm going to attend locally and major in business."

"What are your plans, Max?" George interrupted.

"My plans?" Max looked bewildered by the question. "I just moved back fairly recently and plan on staying here. I think my position with the village police department is pretty solid."

George pointed a forkful of lamb at him. "Yes, yes, but what is your plan for my daughter? Your intentions?"

Kally wanted to crawl under the table. Oh my God. He wasn't doing this! Oh, but he was, and she wanted to die. She just might from embarrassment alone.

"*Baba*, that's not an appropriate question," Kally dared to reprimand. She shot daggers at him. "I didn't bring Max here for an interrogation."

"It's okay, Kally," Max said. "I have a daughter and I imagine I'll be just as protective of her when she arrives at the dating age."

"I have no doubt about that," Kally laughed. "But I'm way beyond those first years of teenage dating."

"Nonetheless, fathers worry." Max turned his attention back to George. "Kally and I have just begun officially dating, but my hope is that it will become much more. That's all I can say for now since our relationship is still so new."

"Fair enough," George grumbled. "But she's not getting any younger."

"*Baba!*" Kally shouted, hiding her eyes with the tips of her fingers.

"Just don't take too long to decide, *pethia*. That's all I have to say."

"You've said enough, *Yióryios*," Melina said. "*Ásto*."

"I'm sorry," Kally mouthed to Max, but he didn't seem deterred. Under the table, he took Kally's hand, threading her fingers through his as he offered her a warm smile.

* * *

"I'm glad this night is over," Kally groaned with relief after Max stepped through her front door. He had taken Athena home after dining with the Andarakis family, settled her into bed and waited for her to fall asleep before leaving her in the care of his father and brother.

Max pulled Kally in for a deep kiss. "I was hoping the night was just beginning," he said, his voice low and seductive.

Kally gave his arm a playful slap. "You know what I mean." She groaned. "That was painful."

Max brushed the curls from her face. "I didn't think it was so bad." He trailed tiny kisses down her neck. "I was honest with your father," Max said bringing his focus to her troubled expression. "I do want this to be the start of something greater."

"Me, too."

"Then stop worrying!" He chuckled. "Trust me, your father won't chase me off." He skimmed the length of her body with his finger-tips, settling his hands firmly on her curvaceous bottom. Kally was tall and lean, but she had a shape men could admire and Max was certainly doing just that as he slowly backed her up against the wall.

"No?" she asked flirtatiously. "Not even when he finds out you're about to have sex with his daughter?"

"Is that what's happening here?" he teased, but the rumble coming from his chest let Kally know exactly where his mind was at.

"Oh, I guess I was mistaken." She pushed free of him, feigning embarrassment. "Thank you for stopping by." She kissed him on the cheek and headed to the door to let him out. Out from Max's line of vision, Kally concealed her playfully impish grin. But before she could cross the room, he took her by surprise, whisking her up and effortlessly throwing her over his shoulder.

Kally let out a yelp. Gripping Max's arms for support, he carried her into the bedroom as though she weighed less than a pound. He dropped her onto the bed, caging her in as he hung over her, his chestnut eyes darkening with desire.

Kally shuddered—partly from yearning for this man, partly out of nervousness. She had not been with anyone since Jax, and even before him, there had only been one other.

"You're wrong, you know?" Max said, the texture of his voice taking on a tender quality. "I'm not about to have sex with you."

Kally looked up at him, bewildered. "No?" The word came through a wisp of breath.

"No. I'm about to make love to you."

Kally closed her eyes and smiled. No one had ever said those words to her before. Max kissed her, his body pressing down on hers, the evidence of his desire for her undeniable as tongues collided and hands explored.

Max took his time undressing Kally. He admired each inch of flesh he uncovered as though he was granted a long-awaited gift. And she, in turn, unbuttoned his shirt slowly, sliding it off his broad shoulders. She ran her lips down his chest until her hand rested on the top button of his jeans. With unsure fingers, Kally unzipped his fly and slipped the denim down his legs. Her breath hitched as she took in his form—the defined pectorals, the tight abs and that irresistible trail of hair leading from his navel to below his boxer briefs.

He aroused her with his touch—gentle yet passionate—every movement intentional yet, somehow, equally, unbridled. He moaned out his pleasure as he ran his tongue around the peaks of her breasts, and when she put her hand intimately on him, circling and stroking, his moan turned to a feral groan.

"Hold on, sweetheart," Max instructed, his voice strained. "I need a second." He reached for his discarded jeans, pulled out a foil packet and sheathed himself. "You're driving me to the point of no return. This isn't how I wanted it to go tonight."

Kally reached up, locking her hands around his neck and pulling him down to meet her lips. He kissed her softly, attempting to control the frenzy that was building between them. Gently, he entered her, and Kally let out a deep moan of contentment. Rhythmically, Max moved in and out of her. Like the even rocking of a boat, they found their pace together. It was sweet and serene—as euphoric as floating away on an errant cloud. Her soft cries as she hit her peak was all Max needed to drive his own release over the edge. Grunting her name into the crook of her neck, he collapsed, rolled onto his back, dragging Kally on top of him.

"That was ..." At a loss for words, Max ran his fingers up and down her bare spine.

"Yeah, it was ..." she agreed, shivering from his feather-like caresses.

"I've waited a long time for you." Max rolled onto his side, never breaking their embrace. "I came home only to discover what I've missed all my life."

"Max." Kally sighed, their bodies pressed together, their lips stealing kisses between tender words. "You've brought to my life what I never thought was within my reach." She cupped his cheek. "You unlocked something within me that I thought was hidden away permanently."

They stayed joined together in a blissful state until Max had no choice but to leave. "I hate this. I don't want to go."

"I don't want that either but Athena needs to see her daddy in the morning," Kally said. "She comes first. Always. I understand that and I wouldn't want it any other way."

Max picked up his discarded garments and began to dress. "You're an incredibly special woman."

Kally slipped on her robe and walked him to the door. They lingered in the foyer sharing long, passionate, nearly desperate kisses.

Kally didn't want to say goodnight and, from the way Max clung to her, neither did he. Finally, they broke away from each other.

"Go," she urged. "I'll speak to you tomorrow." But by the time she shut the door, Kally had already begun to miss him.

Chapter 22

Max

Each year for as long as Max could recall, Port Jefferson transformed itself back in time to the early nineteenth century for its annual Dickens Festival. Women clad in full-skirted modest garments, wool capes and bonnets paraded the streets escorted by men sporting waistcoats and top hats. Along Main Street entertainers acted out dramatic skits or performed magic shows, while others appeared in restaurant after restaurant, caroling for the diners.

Max had almost forgotten how festive the Dickens weekend was, having been away from it for so long. At one time, when he'd left it all behind, he would have thought of it as provincial in comparison to the fast-paced life he led in the city. He had been so very wrong. Here, there was a sense of community. The streets were filled with eager, smiling faces while people of all ages joined in, dressing in period costume or sharing a bag of roasted chestnuts with friends as they headed from event to event.

It was a work day for Max though. Just about every officer was on duty, but as he patrolled the streets, he kept an eye out for Kally and Athena. He'd ducked into The Coffee Klatch earlier to catch a glimpse of the two of them. Kally wore a simple dress indicative of the garments a servant from that era would have worn. She'd had a duplicate frock made in Athena's size and allowed his daughter to help her in the café, greeting guests with a tray of Christmas cookies. The proud smile on his daughter's face when he walked through the door would be branded in his memory forever. She was happy, and that's all he'd ever hoped for. It's why he'd come back to his home town and it had proved to be the best decision he'd ever made. For both their sakes.

* * *

Max sent Kally a text to let her know he was looking for her. He waited a moment for her response and, when it didn't come, he continued to search for her. Through the continuous caroling, the chatter of pedestrians and the clippity-clop of the horses pulling the carriage down Main Street, somehow Max still managed to hear his name shouted above the din. Turning, he spotted Kally and Athena seated in a horse-drawn buggy, furiously waving to get his attention. He smiled from ear to ear at the sight of them.

"Hop on!" Kally shouted. She tapped the driver on the shoulder and he pulled on the reins. Max ran to them and jumped on.

"This is the best day ever, Daddy!"

"Yes, it is," he agreed. He pulled Athena onto his lap and kissed Kally. Draping his arm around her, he whispered in her ear, "Thank you."

"Kally took me ice skating!" Athena's eyes grew wide with excitement. "I didn't even fall once."

"She's a natural," Kally said, grinning. "Look!" She pointed. "It's the ghost of Christmas past!"

The large bearded man dressed in a red robe marched along regally carrying a staff and commanding a cast of characters to follow him.

"And there's Jacob Marley and Tiny Tim. You see, Athena?" Kally pointed them out.

It occurred to Max that his daughter might not know who Kally was talking about. "She's not familiar with the story," Max whispered.

Kally's mouth formed an O. "Really? Well, I suppose she's still young." She turned to Athena. "I just happen to have tickets for us to see *A Christmas Carol* at Theatre Three tomorrow. It's tradition here. You'll love it."

Athena clapped her hands, giggling at the excitement around her. His daughter was soaking in every new experience—experiences that he had taken for granted for far too long.

When the carriage ride was over, Max reluctantly parted, returning to his post. He would meet them at the tree lighting and later his family, together with Kally's, would dine at Danfords.

Max hadn't expected his life to fall into place so seamlessly, yet surprisingly, it had. After all the drama, the chaos and the fear for how his and his wife's actions might have permanently affected their daughter, he was overcome by a sense of serenity—a feeling that had eluded him for years. More importantly, his daughter was now surrounded by loving, supportive people and from here on in he vowed to provide her with nothing but stability.

Chapter 23

Kally

Kally's eyes shone with emotion as she huddled by Max and Athena, looking on as colorful lights illuminated the large tree dominating the square by Danford's Restaurant and Marina. Glancing around, she spotted everyone she loved—her parents and *Yiayiá*, Krystina, who, as usual, was trying to shake off Loukas and his buddy, and Mia. Even she came out for this unmissable weekend. Max's father, who was normally inundated with business, had also made an appearance, along with his own father, Milton, who was pushing beads back and forth with his thumb on a small string of *komboloi*—Greek worry beads. Lena and her son, John, approached, handing Athena and Kally a mug of hot chocolate. Her husband, Paul, Max's brother, was still in line waiting for the rest of their order.

Had Kally not opened her heart, she would have missed out on all of this. She'd shut down any idea of falling in love for so long that she never even entertained the possibility on what she could be losing out on. Her skin heated at the realization. *I love him.* She repeated the words in her mind, as if trying to make sense of it all—as if assuring herself it was real. What's more, she wasn't just in love with Max, she loved Athena too. She couldn't have loved the child more even if she was her very own.

Kally snuck a glance at Max in profile as he sang along to 'Here We Come A-wassailing.' A large crowd still gathered around the tree, but Kally barely noticed. Her head was spinning in reaction to her revelation. Max turned to look at her and furrowed his brow in an expression of concern. He must have seen the contemplative look on her face and the flush across her cheeks.

"Are you feeling okay?" Max asked.

Kally forced a smile that didn't quite reach her eyes. "I'm fine." She loved him, but she wasn't sure how deeply his feelings ran for her and that scared her. 'All in or all out,' that's what he'd said. So what was she worried about?

"Are you ready to head into the restaurant?" Mia bounced over, dragging Kally from her thoughts. "I'm starved!"

"Yes," Kally answered. "Have you seen Egypt?"

"She's down by the docks with Leo," Mia said. "I saw her earlier. She and her mother will meet us inside the restaurant."

"This is nice," Max said. With the lightest of touches, he caressed the nape of her neck.

Kally's skin tingled from the contact. "It is." She sighed. A group of Dickens carolers approached their large table and began to sing, urging everyone to join in. When they had moved on to the next table, Milton approached.

"I'm going home," the elderly man announced. Kally rose from her seat and Milton engulfed her in an affectionate hug, whispering in her ear, "You listened to the old man. I knew you were good for each other."

Kally chuckled. She'd had a soft spot for him as one of her favorite patrons at the café, but once she'd learned he was Max's *pappou*, her affection for him had deepened.

Slowly, everyone began to depart. Egypt and her mother, Dr. Alvita Basu, were saying their goodbyes and weaved through the jovial group to Kally.

"It was lovely of your family to invite us to join them," Egypt's mother said, with sincerity, taking Kally's hands in her own. "Vijay sends his apologies but he was on call tonight."

The woman had a commanding sophistication about her. The combination of her Jamaican accent and exotic beauty only enhanced her elegant demeanor.

"We'll see you both for Christmas Eve, I hope," Kally said.

"As it stands right now, we will both be there." She turned her attention to Max. Athena had fallen asleep on his shoulder. "It was so nice to meet you, Max."

"It was," he agreed. "Forgive me for not getting up."

"Don't be silly." Alvita patted the child's head. "She's precious."

"I'll see you tomorrow morning in my knickers and bonnet," Egypt said in her best attempt at a cockney accent.

"I hope you'll be wearing more than that!" Kally laughed. "You'll scare away the customers."

"Or bring in new ones." Egypt wiggled her eyebrows and, with that last thought, she shimmied out the door.

"I think you better get this little one home," Kally suggested, rubbing gentle circles on Athena's back. Just about everyone had gone. It was late but it had been a wonderful day sharing in Athena's enthusiasm. Her heart swelled as her love grew for this sweet child and her devoted father.

"If you really want to make a friend, go to someone's house and eat with him...the people who give you their food give you their heart." Cesar Chavez

Chapter 24

Kally

Theo, stumbling slightly as he struggled to hold onto a galvanized steel wine tub loaded with ice, asked, "Where do you want this, Kal?"

"On the long table by the front window," she answered, pointing to the spot. "Thanks, Theo."

It was New Year's Eve and Kally had enlisted her siblings to help her pull together a celebration in typical Greek fashion: food, drinks and card games. What better place to throw a private party than in her own café? She and Krystina had rearranged the floorplan, joining tables together to accommodate a larger group. One table set for six had a deck of cards, ready for a poker game, while another was set for a game of bridge, and on the remaining smaller tables, backgammon boards were placed. Card games and even a bit of gambling was a Greek New Year's ritual, and so Kally placed a basket of scratch off lottery tickets at the counter closest to the front door for each guest to take upon entering.

Mia, stunning in a body-hugging black dress, emerged from the kitchen with a case of stemware.

"Let me help you with that," Kally offered.

"I have it." Mia set down the box and began to line up the glasses evenly.

Scanning the room, Kally scrutinized each detail, biting unconsciously on a thumbnail as she mentally ran a checklist through her mind.

"Kally," Mia admonished, "it's all under control. Go change into your dress."

"What about the—"

"Done!" Mia said firmly.

"You don't even know what I was about to say."

"Whatever it was, it's been taken care of." Mia waved her off. "Now go! Everyone will be arriving at any minute."

Kally retreated to her tiny office. She'd left her dress draped over her desk. She removed her jeans and the lightweight sweater she'd worn all day. Wishing she had time to go home and freshen up, Kally resigned herself to settling for a change of clothing and a quick touchup on her makeup. Although tonight would be a holiday celebration, the hours leading up to it had been a normal workday, and an exhausting one at that.

Yawning, she took a moment to collapse in her chair. Tempted to lay her head on the desk to rest her eyes for a moment, Kally resisted the urge. There was no time to indulge in a nap, not even the briefest of ones.

After she applied ruby red lipstick to match the shade of her dress, she slipped the garment on, struggling to clasp the tiny hook at the top of the zipper.

"Who is it?" Kally asked when she heard a rap on the door.

"It's me," Max said, entering.

It was a rare occasion to see Max out of either his uniform or a pair of faded jeans. Tonight, he looked every bit the handsome businessman she imagined he'd been at one time. In a charcoal pair of designer slacks and a crisp white cufflinked shirt, a wide-eyed Max was rendered speechless at the sight of her. Kally shyly sank her teeth into her bottom lip as their eyes locked.

"You're breathtaking," he whispered, assessing her from the raven locks cascading past her delicate shoulders in soft waves to the ruffled scoop neckline teasing him with just a hint of cleavage. His gaze drifted down to a form-fitting scarlet dress and a pair of black, platform stiletto pumps that accentuated her long, lean legs.

"I could say the same about you." Kally held her hand out to him. "Are you going to kiss me hello or do you plan on standing in the doorway for a while?" Kally joked.

It only took two steps into the cramped room for Max to evaporate the air between them. He circled her waist with his hands, drawing her close enough to press his lips to hers. "What's this?" he asked. He slid his hands down the length of her back only to find her dress partially unzipped and the hook undone.

"I couldn't reach it." Kally turned and lifted her curls off her back. "Can you help me out?"

"I'd love nothing more," Max murmured. He began to trail feather-like kisses from the hollow of her shoulder down, unzipping the dress further as his lips traveled to the small of her back.

Goosebumps pebbled Kally's skin. His touch was electrifying yet gentle. Kally could easily get lost in Max's heat and the sensation he elicited from her. "You're supposed to be zipping me up," Kally said, her voice a strained whisper.

"Oh, but this is so much more fun."

Kally turned to face him but remained in his arms. Nose to nose, lips a breath away, she agreed. She wanted nothing more than to linger deliciously in the moment.

Resigned, she sighed, pulling away. "We have guests. Please?" Kally turned around once more, gathering her hair up and off her back.

"O-kay," he drew out in mock disappointment. "Just as long as you grant me the first kiss at midnight."

"It looks like the party has begun without us!" Kally announced as she and Max emerged from the back of the café. George, Milton and some of the other men had already begun a poker game. Melina had gathered the children by a table of board games and Mia and Krystina were serving drinks.

"*Tsipouro?*" *Yiayiá* asked, offering them a pair of shot glasses.

"Yuck." Kally scrunched her nose. "That stuff is vile."

"No, it's good," *Yiayiá* claimed. "It makes you, how they say? Horny!"

"*Yiayiá!*" She loved the woman with all her heart but, God, sometimes Kally wished her grandmother was one of those old women who wore black from head to toe and quietly nodded, only pretending to understand the chatter around them.

Max took the proffered glass from her, immediately knocking back the drink. "I'm with you." He winked at *Yiayiá* mischievously.

"Don't encourage her." Kally grinned, shaking her head. Her attention was drawn to a far corner of the café, away from the rest of the guests.

"What is it?" Max asked, taking notice of Kally's worried expression.

"Nothing," she answered with a bite in her tone. "At least nothing new." It was her parents. They were arguing and she wondered what it was about this time. Pointed fingers and flailing arms told the story. She couldn't make out any of the evidently harsh words thrown back and forth over the music though.

"They fight often?" Max asked.

"They bicker all the time and have the occasional blowout," Kally said. "Watch this. Dad will storm off any minute, pour himself a drink, light up a cigarette and go back to his game with a sour face."

As Kally began to explain the sequence of events to Max, her father did just as she predicted. "Now my mother will smooth her hair, plaster a smile on her face and join her friends."

Max raised an eyebrow and smirked. "You're either a psychic or reading from a well-rehearsed script," he joked, watching her mother walk back to the guests. "Any prediction on how this charade ends?"

Before she could answer, Krystina knocked into her as she whizzed by with Loukas on her tail.

"Come on, Minnie! I'm not asking for much," Loukas pleaded almost desperately, but Kally witnessed a glint of mischief in his eyes.

"Stop calling me that!" Krystina stopped dead in her tracks, whirling around to chastise Loukas. "You're the last guy on Earth I'd kiss at midnight, so fuck off!"

"What is in the liquor tonight?" Max asked, holding out his glass with a playful frown.

Kally pointed her forefinger back and forth between the two of them. "That battle has been raging since they were eight."

"Why? What could have possibly happened at that age to cause so much contempt?" Max asked. "Loukas seems like a good kid."

"He is." Kally's eyes held sympathy for the boy. Her sister had stormed off into the kitchen, practically slamming the door in his face. Now he just stood, leaning his elbows on the pastry counter, his chin resting on his fists, his expression a bit forlorn but not completely defeated. He was used to Krystina's angry dismissals.

"Our parents were very close friends but everything has changed since his mother died," Kally explained. "His father isn't the same man he once was. He drinks way too much and when he's drunk he's verbally—and we suspect, occasionally physically—abusive to Loukas. We do our best to give him the affection he's missed since his mother passed away."

"Everyone but Krystina, it appears," Max said. "Poor kid."

"To her, he's that annoying boy in school you can't shake off."

"Why'd he call her Minnie?"

"The short story is that he got a peek of her Minnie Mouse underwear when they were little."

Max threw his head back in laughter. "That'll do it! Don't forget, I come from a household of boys. We were experts in torturing our female counterparts."

Time passed quickly as guests amused themselves with the games Kally had set out. She stood back, observing the party while sipping on a cocktail. The children happily entertained themselves, family and friends devoured the food she'd prepared while some of the men in the group seemed absorbed in deep concentration over a high stakes card game.

"It's almost midnight," Mia announced, gliding over with a tray of champagne.

"Max, go get Athena. She should be by our side for the count-down," Kally suggested.

"I'd leave her," Mia said. "She's having a blast with the other kids. I should find Krystina though. My little sister will have to do for my New Year's kiss."

"I find it hard to believe that men all over the city aren't drooling over you," Max said. "You didn't want to bring a date?"

Mia screwed up her face as though what Max had said was prepos-terous. "You lived in the city, right?"

Max nodded.

"Then you know it's not the easiest place to meet people. And the few who are worthwhile are either unavailable or unobtainable." She sighed.

Kally narrowed her eyes, a knowing grin forming as she read her sister's expression. "You have your eye on someone." It was a state-ment that came out sounding more of suspicion than fact.

"Just an eye," Mia confirmed. "I've only seen him, never actually spoken to him or been properly introduced." She took a nervous gulp from her champagne glass. "He's way out of my league anyway."

"I find that hard to believe," Max said.

"Trust me!" Mia exclaimed. "I joined a community for creatives in the publishing industry and he heads the whole thing. I've only seen him speaking in a room filled with dozens of people."

"You're a resourceful girl," Kally said. "Find a reason to speak to him after one of the meetings."

"Like you would do that, Kal. Not!"

Mia was right, Kally supposed. But she'd had a period in time where she took chances and was bolder than she ever thought she could be. Mia never had.

"You know I'd rather hide behind my computer," Mia admitted. "I'm not good in new situations. Joining the CCP, the Community of Creative Professionals," she explained, "was a leap for me."

"Mia!" Melina scolded. "Stop the gabbing and pass the champagne. There's only two minutes to go!" Kally's mother handed each of them a packet of paper streamers before moving on from person to person distributing the rest.

Max drew Kally in by the small of her back, his fingers teasing along the edge of the low-cut V on the back of her dress. When the countdown began, he looked deeply into her eyes, the heat between them intensifying as each number was shouted by the loved ones surrounding them. 3 … 2 … 1 … As excited screams sounded around them, Max leaned close.

"Happy New Year," Max said, his voice low and gravelly.

"Happy New Year," Kally echoed. She lifted her glass to clink with his, but he took it from her, setting both flutes down.

"Now about that Happy New Year," he said, his eyes darkening with mystery. Max brushed his thumbs affectionately over Kally's cheeks. In the moment before he kissed her, Kally felt a charge run through her entire being. The thumping of her heart warned that something momentous was about to happen.

"Kally, Kallyope, these past months have been the best I can remember," Max said. "I came back here to start over, but I never dreamed I'd find you."

Kally cupped his cheek tenderly. "I feel the same. You came to me, unexpected, opening doors I'd long since slammed shut."

She read a myriad of emotions flickering across his face—hesitation, uncertainty, relief, and finally something else. Contentment perhaps? "A quarter for your thoughts," Kally whispered.

"A quarter?" Max feigned confusion. "Last time it was a nickel."

"Something tells me what's on your mind is worth more than a nickel."

"It is," he confirmed. "More than even a silver dollar. I'm falling in love with you, Kally." His expression held a great amount of seriousness.

Kally's sudden intake of breath left her dizzy. Or was it Max's declaration? No one had ever said those words to her. There was no offhanded agreement stating a lackadaisical 'me, too' only because she'd confessed it first. Here her admission wasn't being dittoed with a one-word confirmation. His revelation left her breathless. Suddenly, any awareness that her café was lively with guests was lost to her. The children blowing horns and rattling noisemakers fell on deaf ears. Kally heard and saw nothing past the sparkling eyes before her as they waited for her response.

"Max, Maximos," she breathed, adding seriousness to what she was about to say. "You make me feel alive again. You've given me what I thought, for me, was unobtainable. I'm falling in love with you, too."

The relief was evident on his face. "Given what you've shared with me, I wasn't sure if my words would be welcome or cause you to run."

"Only into your arms," she assured. "I won't lie. The stronger my feelings grew, the more terrified I became. But I trust you. I trust you not to hurt me."

"Never," Max confirmed. "But there is something I need—"

"Daddy!" Athena interrupted. "*Yiayiá* said she's going to smash a pomegranate on her door for good luck and I can help if you let me." Athena bounced up and down. "Can I, please?"

"It's very late, Angel." Max sighed. "I should be getting you home soon."

"Please?" She clasped her hands together as if in prayer.

"And why are we doing this?" Max queried.

"You never did this?" Kally asked. "It's a common Greek custom. It's done for good luck. First, the kindest and most innocent person, usually a child, steps foot into the house. This person determines the kind of year the family will have," Kally explained. "I'll bet *Yiayiá* wants you," she told Athena, tapping her on the tip of her nose, "because you're such a sweet girl."

Athena nodded her head vigorously. "That's what she said!"

"What does smashing a pomegranate have to do with this?" Max asked.

"On Christmas, *Yiayiá* hung one above the front door of the house. After Athena completes the *Kalo Podariko*, or first footing, she will take down the fruit and roll it on the door, smashing it until the seeds fall out."

Max raised a skeptical eyebrow.

"The more seeds that fall, the more good luck the family will have during the year," Kally said.

"Well … if that's the custom then we have to do it," Max agreed.

"Thank you!" Athena hugged her father quickly before calling out to Kally's grandmother.

"I suppose I've been lacking in passing on all of these traditions to her," Max admitted with a flicker of guilt.

"You're doing the best you can. She's a happy child; that's what matters the most."

✶ ✶ ✶

Max and Kally hung back on the walkway while *Yiayiá* and Athena made their way onto the front porch. After Athena stepped into the house, she hopped back over the threshold to join *Yiayiá* and the rest of the family. Together, they held the ruby red fruit in their hands, laughing as they pounded it against the weathered door. Plump, crimson seeds scattered around their feet.

"That was fun!" Athena giggled.

"It was," Max agreed. "But I better get you home and in bed if you want to come back tomorrow for dinner."

"Go, *kuklítsa mou*," *Yiayiá* said to the child, cupping her chin affectionately. "I have more surprises for you tomorrow."

✷ ✷ ✷

The next afternoon, Max and Kally returned to her family's home with one very excited little girl. All morning she kept asking her father if it was time to go and when the time finally came to bundle up and head over, Athena was practically bouncing off the walls.

After being guided by Melina to the Christmas tree in the Andarakis living room, Athena squealed with delight. Blue eyes as round as saucers looked up at Kally's mother. "Are those for me?" Athena asked in amazement.

"They are!" Melina said. "St. Basil left them for you. He must have known you'd be here today."

"Is he like Santa Claus? Cause he already came."

"In Greece, Saint Basil brings gifts to the children on his name day," Melina explained.

"Your family shouldn't spoil her this way," Max whispered to Kally. "I want her to come here without expecting something every time she's invited."

"In a blink of an eye, she'll be grown," Kally replied. "She should have the magic of childhood while she can."

Max, standing behind Kally, wrapped his arms around her. "After what she's been through, she deserves it."

"She was so little. I'm sure she has no recollection of those days." Kally hoped and prayed her words were true.

"She still has occasional nightmares." Max turned Kally around by the waist to face him. "I'll never forgive myself for not taking her out of that situation sooner."

Her heart bled for this man who she loved so much. The memory of those days and the part he had played in it haunted him still. She could see it as his expression darkened.

Kally cupped his cheek. "You're a good man, Max. A devoted father. You need to leave the past where it belongs."

Max sighed deeply and nodded. Watching his daughter open gifts with Mia and Krystina lifted some of the heaviness from his heart.

"You know ..." Kally smirked. "... tradition suggests that today, you should only speak of the good, not the bad, or you'll jinx yourself with a year of poor luck."

"Superstitious much?" Max laughed. "I remember my mother telling us when we were young that superstition was against church beliefs, that we should trust only in God. I suppose that's why I've never heard of these customs."

Kally shrugged. "She was technically correct, but I think over time myths and lore stuck, and now it's done more for tradition than belief."

Max rolled his eyes but it was clear he was amused. Athena sat in jubilant contentment amongst a plethora of L.O.L. dolls and accessories.

"As it is, I keep stepping on them every time I enter her bedroom," he complained. But Kally could see by the tenderness of his expression that he didn't really mind.

"A girl can never have too many of the latest dolls." Kally grinned. "But let's separate her from them long enough to eat dinner."

Dinner, as always, was plentiful. In the center of the large banquet table, platters of *pastitsio, moussaka*, and chicken *oreganato* with lemon potatoes dominated the space. Melina passed around a tray of *meze*: black cured olives, rice-filled *dolmathes* and grilled *kefalogra-viera* cheese.

The number of simultaneous conversations was almost as abundant as the food and wine being consumed. Melina and George discussed his ailing father in Athens, while Krystina did everything she could to avoid Loukas, who poked her with his fork each time she refused to acknowledge him. Mia explained to her cousins the day to day role she played at the magazine while Max and Kally tuned everyone out, speaking in quiet whispers to each other. *Yiayiá* and her cousin, Rhea, in an effort to school the child, counted out in Greek, urging Athena to repeat after them.

When it was time for dessert, *Yiayiá* scurried into the kitchen, returning moments later with a golden, sugar dusted cake that looked to be around the same circumference as a pizza pie. "It's time to cut the *Vasilopita!*" she exclaimed with delight. "*Athená, éla, moró mou.*" *Yiayiá* extended her hand to the child.

Athena bounced over to her and with an aged hand resting over the child's small fingers, together they scored a cross into the top of the cake as everyone looked on.

"The first piece goes to Christ," *Yiayiá* said, as she cut the first wedge, plating it and setting it aside. She did the same with the second slice, announcing it was for the *Theotokos* - The Virgin Mary. She whispered in Athena's ear and, when they cut the next slice, the child proudly stated it was for Saint Basil. "The one who left all the toys for me!" she added, and everyone laughed. After the piece for the entire household was cut, a slice was offered to each person present, from the oldest to the youngest.

"Nobody takes a bite until we all have a slice," *Yiayiá* reminded. She waved a wrinkled finger in warning. Inside the cake, a golden coin was hidden for one person to find. But who would be the lucky recipient?

Finally, the last piece of cake was dedicated to the poor. This was done in remembrance of the charitable life Saint Basil lived and as a reminder to follow in his example.

"Now?" Athena asked impatiently.

Yiayiá nodded, opening her arms, gesturing for everyone to take a bite.

"It's me! I got it!" Athena shouted. "I got the gold coin."

Applause broke out and Athena's smile widened. She examined her prize. Confusion took hold as she turned it between her fingers. "What do I do with it?" she asked. "It doesn't look like any coin I've ever seen."

"That's a drachma," Kally said. "It was the money they used in Greece before they switched to the euro."

"I held on to some of them for the *Vasilopita*," *Yiayiá* explained. "Save it for good luck," she told Athena.

"I think we will have the best luck ever!" Athena declared.

"I believe you're right, my sweet girl," Max agreed. "It's going to be a very good year."

Chapter 25

Max

An eerie silence loomed over the streets of the normally lively village. Absent was the revving of motorcycle engines or the honking of horns. No patrons spilled from restaurant doors. Not a soul was out and about. It was an absolutely bone-chilling February night and the only feet pounding the pavement belonged to officers Max and Leo.

They cut through clouds of condensation made by their own breath as they headed to Rocketship Park. It was doubtful the officers would stumble upon any mischief tonight. Black clouds blanketed the moon, impeding illumination. The sinister sky threatened snow and, as the wind picked up, the flakes began to fall.

Much to their surprise, they heard voices in the distance. Max flashed a light in the direction of the playground slides and saw three male figures. Two of the boys, upon seeing the officers, turned to run, the other stood frozen in place.

"Don't move," Leo warned, his tone commanding.

"What are you boys doing out on a night like this?" Max asked. As he approached, he sighed, disappointed when he recognized one of the boys.

"Loukas, I don't think your father would approve of you being out here at this time of night," Max reprimanded.

"He's too drunk to know any better."

"What are the three of you up to?" Leo asked.

"Just hanging," said a tall, blond boy with a cocky attitude.

"Is that so?" Leo stared him down. "Hands in the air. I'm going to frisk you."

"What for, man?" he objected. "I have my rights!"

Leo curled his lip and nodded. "You're correct. Would you like me to read you those rights and take you in?"

The boy huffed and lifted his arms while Leo patted him down, halting at his coat pockets. Reaching inside, he withdrew a clear bag containing a white powder. In the other pocket was a handful of capsules. The boy groaned.

"You're under arrest for the possession of illegal narcotics," Leo stated. "You have the right to remain silent."

Leo continued reading the Miranda rights while Max frisked the other two boys.

At the station, Max asked Leo to handle the two being arrested. He would deal with Loukas himself. Forcefully grabbing him by the collar, Max escorted the boy out of the building. "You and I are going to have a serious chat," Max said, pushing him into the squad car.

"Are you going to tell my father?"

"I should," Max replied.

"He'll just beat the shit out of me."

Max scraped his fingers through his hair. "Fuck." He shut the passenger door and swiftly went around to the driver's side. Turning to face the boy, he huffed out a breath, trying to gather his thoughts.

Max pulled a small, clear bag from his pocket and held it in front of Loukas' face. "This will solve nothing. Trust me I know," Max emphasized. "It almost destroyed me."

Loukas' eyebrows shot up, his mouth agape.

"Yeah, you got that right," Max confirmed. "But I came to my senses before I lost everything. Came damn near close enough though."

"Why didn't you just arrest me then?"

"Because you're a good kid. This isn't like you." Max poked him in the chest. "I stuck my neck out for you and I could lose my badge for this."

"I know." Loukas dropped his eyes to his lap.

"Your father might be a prick but the Andarakis family loves you like their own. How would they feel about this?"

"Are you going to tell them?" Loukas asked quietly, looking up to meet Max's punishing stare.

"Are you going to pull this shit again?"

"No."

"Then no. But I'm keeping an eye on you," Max warned. "You have a bright future ahead of you. Don't screw it up."

Loukas nodded.

"You need to talk, you come to me, okay?" Max turned the engine over. "I'll take you home."

Tension emanated from Loukas. Fear. Foreboding. Max sensed it.

"You want to bunk with me tonight until whatever happened with your dad blows over?"

Tentatively, Loukas nodded. "Yes," he whispered in relief.

Chapter 26

Kally

Kally floated about the café as if dancing a well-executed waltz. She scrubbed down the counters, covered baked goods with clear wrap, and set the tables for opening the next day. Business had been busier than expected that day, considering the frigid dampness that should have discouraged people from leaving their homes.

At five p.m., the unwelcome state of a shortened winter's day had fallen upon the island as the sun began to set and twilight darkened the sky. But nothing could dampen Kally's mood. These were the happiest days of her life and even while doing the most tedious of tasks she smiled, daydreaming of Max.

Kally jumped at the sound of the rap on the front door. Who could it be? She'd sent everyone home and locked the door behind them. But when she saw Max peeking in through the glass, her face lit up. She skipped, literally skipped to the door and opened it.

"Hi! I wasn't expecting you!"

Kicking the door shut behind him with the heel of his shoe, he wasted no time, pulling her in by the waist to draw her in for a kiss.

"I thought I would escort you to my home," Max said. "And I love you a latte too!" He grinned.

"What?" Kally looked confused for a moment but then remembered her apron. It was no secret that they often expressed her mood.

"I'd be a little worried if you were wearing the one that said, 'I don't give a frap,'" he joked.

"Oh, but I do. I give plenty of fraps!" Kally laughed. "I'll give you all the fraps you wish."

"Hmm." Max nuzzled her neck, his face getting lost in the soft waves of her hair. "I'd like a frap right now."

"You can have a frap when I wash away the crap from the day," she promised.

Max chuckled. "Okay. I'll take you home to shower and I'll pick up Athena at Lena and Paul's, and then I'll swing back by to pick you up."

"Sounds perfect." The Vardaxis men were out of town and, for the first time, Kally would be spending the night with Max and Athena in their home.

Kally shut off the lights and locked up.

Once home, Kally showered quickly, washing away the icing stuck to her hair and the coffee splotches on her skin. She hunted for her favorite Disney movie, along with another she had just bought to surprise Athena. Yes, Kally had quite a collection, even saving the outdated and now useless videotapes from her own childhood.

The Vardaxis family home stood at the top of the cliffs of Belle Terre overlooking the Long Island Sound. From the floor-to-ceiling windows, all of Port Jefferson Harbor was visible. It was as though Greek Gods lived perched in the clouds, looking down, watching the comings and goings of the townspeople. But tonight, there was no movement down below, save for the rocking of the few boats left moored in the water for the winter.

Max lit the fireplace while Kally made hot chocolate. Athena gathered her stuffed animals and the cozy throw blanket she used to snuggle under while they watched the movie.

"Can you guess which movie I brought?" Kally asked Athena.

She'd emerged from the kitchen holding a tray. "This snack is a hint."

Athena twisted her face in thought. After a moment, she shrugged. "I don't know, but churros are my favorite!"

"Yesterday, chocolate chip cookies were your favorite," Max teased, tapping her on the nose.

"Everything's my favorite!" She lifted her hands, palms up.

"Fair enough," Kally agreed. "Churros are a Mexican treat. I just happen to have a copy of *Coco* with me."

Athena jumped up and down with excitement. "I've wanted to see that my whole life!"

"Your whole life, eh?" Max chuckled. "That's pretty wild since it only hit the theaters a year ago."

Athena oohed and aahed at the vibrant colors flashing across the screen. By the end, the movie lost against her battle to sleep, the child's eyes growing so heavy that no matter how hard she fought, she couldn't manage to stay awake. Kally had her own problems. She'd gone through half a box of tissues, her eyes drowning in a puddle of tears.

Unexpectedly, Max's cell phone vibrated. Excusing himself, he retreated to an adjoining room. With a serious frown, he shortly returned.

"I just got called in. I hate to ask you but could you stay with Athena?"

"Of course." He didn't need to ask. Kally would help Max in any way she could, especially where his daughter was concerned. "Is everything okay?"

"Serious car accident. Possible fatalities. The department is short-handed. I could be gone hours."

"It's fine." Kally kicked off the blanket, stood and walked Max to the front door. Kissing him, she told him to take as long as he needed.

It was after eleven o'clock, past Athena's bedtime. Now she would have to find her bedroom in this palace of a home. Kally roamed the space. It didn't escape her that this lair, inhabited solely by men and one small child, still breathed of the feminine life who'd permanently imprinted herself not only on the beautiful structure but in the hearts of those who dwelled here.

A man didn't place the photos in the rhinestone encrusted picture frames resting on the fireplace mantle. Or run a fringe-edged runner down the length of the dining table topped with a silk arrangement of peonies. And a man didn't choose the chalkboard sign that hung over the kitchen entranceway—*The fondest memories are made when gathered around the table.*

Max's mother took pride in creating a loving home. Kally didn't need to meet her to know this. It was clear in every detail and crevice. She ran her hand up the solid wood banister as she climbed the winding staircase. Right or left? she wondered. Which way to Athena's room? Eeny, meeny, miny, moe! There had to be six bedrooms up here.

Feeling as though she was a privacy invader, Kally hesitantly opened the first door at the top of the steps. The oversized, dark wooden furniture and pewter-colored walls were clearly not a room inhabited by a small girl. Neither was the next room, which she surmised must belong to Milton. The style of décor was similar to her *yiayiá's* bedroom, right down to the crocheted doilies on the dresser and the replicated ancient Greek vase set on the window sill.

"Wow!" was all Kally could say when she stepped into Athena's room. Pale lavender walls, clean white furniture and a storm of fluffy pillows on a full-sized canopy bed greeted her at the third room she'd peeked into. It was every little girl's dream. Not to mention the corner of the room dedicated to her American Girl dolls and their accessories.

One by one, Kally removed the pillows and placed them on the upholstered chair by the window. She turned down the comforter and headed back down the steps to carry Athena to bed.

It was after two in the morning when Kally was awakened by the ringtone of her phone. Disoriented, she'd forgotten where she was, but as she rubbed the sleep from her eyes, it all came back to her.

"Hello," she croaked out.

"Sorry to wake you," Max apologized.

"It's fine," she said. "I nodded off on the couch."

"I know you have to open up in a few hours. I'm not sure when I'll be able to get home."

"It's okay," Kally said. "I called Egypt. She'll open and she's calling in extra help. I've got you covered. I'll take Athena into the café with me."

"Kal, I don't know what to say. Usually someone is here to help me if I need it. I hate to take you away from your work."

"It's what you do for the ones you love." Kally breathed in, contented, happy—at peace.

"You're the best thing that's ever happened to me, Kal. *Sagapo.*"

Kally threw her head back onto the couch pillow and chuckled. "Did you say that in Greek because you didn't want the guys to hear you say that you love me?"

"Pretty much. Sorry."

"You can say it in any language," she said. "It's still nice to hear."

"Oh, before you hang up," Max added, "there's an extra set of keys to my car in the blue parka in the hall closet."

"I completely forgot I don't have my car here," Kally said. "Okay, see you later."

Slivers of sunlight forced their way through the slats of the window blinds, one of the rays forming a golden stripe over Kally's face. She squinted from the brightness until her vision adjusted to the daylight. Padding to the bathroom, she took a good look at herself. What a sight! Her clothing was crumpled, her curls unruly from a restless sleep and yesterday's cosmetics were smeared around her eyes like a raccoon. She was happy that no one else was in the house to witness what a mess she was.

In a house inhabited by men, it was highly doubtful she'd find makeup remover. She settled for the liquid soap in the bathroom, freeing her face from looking as though she was auditioning for *The Walking Dead*. She was about to search for anything to moisturize her face when the doorbell rang.

"Just a minute," she called out, sprinting down the hallway. Kally opened the door, puzzled to see an attractive blonde woman dressed in a very fashionable, winter white wrap coat standing at the doorstep.

"Can I help you?" Kally asked, wondering who she was and what she could want at eight o'clock on a Saturday morning.

"And who are you?" the woman asked petulantly. "The maid? A nanny?"

The audacity and condescension in her attitude drew up Kally's defenses.

"Who I am is none of your concern." Kally glared at her. "Now what is it that I can do for you?"

"You can tell my husband his wife is here."

Kally gripped the doorknob. This woman either had the wrong house or she was insane. Either way, she was prepared to close the door on her at any given moment.

"I'm sorry, you must be mistaken," Kally told her.

"No," she insisted. "I'm quite certain. This is the Vardaxis home, isn't it?" The woman raised a challenging eyebrow. "So where is Max?"

Kally gasped. The pulsing muscle of her heart felt as though it had suddenly gone leaden, sinking to the floor. This was impossible. Impossible! "Who are you really?" Kally asked. Her voice came out in a frightened whisper. "Max's wife is dead."

"Dead!" She lifted her arms in the air, laughing humorlessly. "Ta da! Surprise! Is that what he told you? He lied." She wriggled her nose, her eyes sparkling with what looked to be sinister enjoyment.

"I don't believe you," Kally said. "You need to leave."

"Not before I see my baby girl."

A shot of adrenaline ran through Kally's entire being. Athena, she thought suddenly. She had to protect her from this woman. Her mother? Could it possibly be?

"You can come back when Max is here," Kally said, holding her ground. "Until then, you're not setting foot in this house. As far as I'm concerned, you're a stranger." She slammed the door shut and locked it.

The woman pounded the door, shouting her demands to open it.

"I'll call the police if you don't stop."

That seemed to quiet the woman but, before Kally turned away, she noticed a slip of paper pushing its way through the crack under the door. Kally picked it up. Turning it over, she discovered it was a photo confirming the woman's claims; it shattered everything Kally believed to be true. With shaking fingers, she released her grip on the snapshot. Tears ran down her face as she watched the picture slowly, almost tauntingly, float to the floor. Max and the woman—their wedding photo. Bridget was indeed very much alive.

Chapter 27

Max

Max entered Kally's café through the kitchen entrance, assuming that's where he would find his daughter. Even if Kally was overseeing the front, Athena was sure to be pestering Luis for a spoonful of batter or asking if she could help in some way.

What he walked into was not out of the ordinary. Krystina was showing his daughter how to neatly stack macarons in a glass dome, Luis was piping pink icing onto cupcakes and the door leading to the front swung back and forth as servers bustled in and out of the kitchen.

But something was off—way off. Kally was nowhere in sight. Krystina glanced up at him and frowned. Frosting shot out of Luis' pastry bag as though propelled from a cannon as he glared at Max.

The tension could be cut with a blade of grass until Egypt stepped in with a tray of dirty plates. She stopped dead in her tracks, the door smacking her in the ass. But her focus was trained on Max, green, laser sharp eyes burning fury straight into his. But why? He furrowed his brow, confused, and made his way over to her, relieving her from the cumbersome tray.

"Is Kally out front?" he asked, still wondering what had irritated her.

"No, she is not," Egypt answered in a clipped, snippy manner.

"Did I do something?" he asked. "I'm confused."

"Well, that makes two of you then, doesn't it?"

"What—"

"Daddy!" Athena called out. With Krystina's help, she carried the glass case of macarons. "I'll be right back," she told him proudly as the two of them walked the pastries out front.

"Hey, Krystina," Max greeted but he received no reply. No eye contact. No smile. Not even a wave.

"Am I living in an alternative universe?" he asked. "Would someone please tell me what in hell is going on?"

"Do alternative universes involve wives coming back from the dead?" Raising one accusing eyebrow, Egypt crossed her arms in front of her.

Max stared at her, completely flummoxed. She shook her head in disgust. Rolled her eyes. Huffed out a loud breath. What was she not saying? He repeated what Egypt had said in his mind and, when it finally struck him, his eyes grew wide with understanding.

"That's right, you lying, cheating piece of shit." Egypt spewed the words with great contempt but kept her voice too low for his daughter to hear.

"No, it's not what you think." Max ran his hands through his hair and leaned his head back in frustration. "How? Where?"

"She came to your home this morning asking for you." Egypt poked him in the chest. She flashed him a sardonic smile. "Said she was your wife. Not your ex-wife and obviously not your dead wife— your wife."

"Did Athena see her?" he asked. He clenched his fists. "Please, tell me she didn't."

"No," Egypt said slowly, her anger abating. Tilting her head as if to assess him, she continued, "Kally wouldn't let her near Athena."

"Thank God." Rubbing at the back of his neck, Max expelled a sigh of relief. "I have to speak to Kally."

"She doesn't want to see you, Max."

"She has to. I need to explain," he said. "She's home?"

Egypt nodded. "But you need to leave her alone. You can't explain away a lie."

"Give me your order pad," Max demanded. "Just give it to me," he insisted when Egypt only stared at him, puzzled. "And your pen." He scribbled on the top sheet of paper and handed the items back to her. "This is my sister-in-law, Lena's, number. Call her and ask her to pick up Athena. In the meantime, if you and Krystina wouldn't mind watching her a little longer, I'd really appreciate it."

Reluctantly, Egypt nodded.

Max had to set Kally straight. He had to make her understand. He just had to.

Chapter 28

Kally

Men. She hated them. Untrustworthy beings. The whole lot of them. She knew this to be true. At least in her experience, it was. This was exactly why she hadn't allowed herself to get involved with anyone since Jaxon. For despite the short-lived moments of happiness, there was always destruction in its wake. Shreds of sinewy matter peeled away, layer by layer, from what used to be her beating heart.

Kally felt dead inside. This time was worse than the last. She had not only fallen in love with Max, she also adored his daughter. Now what? His wife comes back to town to take her rightful place and Kally has to step aside. A wife who she was told had died. And now for the second time in her life, she had unknowingly been involved in a relationship with a married man. She was either the stupidest person on earth or the biggest fool.

Tears ran in streams down her face, landing on the pillow Kally clutched at her chest. Sitting upright on her bed, cross-legged, still as a statue, she stared at a crack in the wall in front of her. Yesterday, she had so much to look forward to. Today, the world was bleak, empty—tenebrous.

The doorbell rang but Kally ignored it. It rang again and again. Her cell phone vibrated, but she let it go to voicemail. She had no energy or desire to speak to anyone. Then the pounding began. Pound, pound, pound!

"Open the door, Kally!" Max shouted. "I know you're in there."

She ignored him. He would have to leave eventually.

"I'll stand out here all night if I have to," he called out. "I'm not going anywhere until you hear me out."

She believed him. He would stay until she relented. Even in the cold. But why? What would it change? Sliding off the bed, she made her way to the front door and yelled back at him. "Go away! Go home to your wife."

"We need to talk. I can explain everything."

Kally groaned. "Famous last words! Unfortunately, your explanation is a little too late."

"Come on, please, I can't keep shouting through the door," Max pleaded. "Give me five minutes. That's all I ask for and then you can throw me out if you don't like what I have to say."

Kally placed her hand on the doorknob. Her grip tightened as her mind waged war with her heart. But her heart had gotten her into this mess. Yet she knew she'd have to face him at some point. Better to get it over with now. She'd have to cut all ties with him and, as much as she would never want to hurt Athena, it would be in her best interest not to see her either.

Slowly, she turned the knob and opened the door. Neither she nor Max moved. She stood on one side of the door, her makeup smudged, her arms defensively wrapped around herself. He on the other side, waiting anxiously to be invited to step over the threshold.

Kally spoke no words but sidestepped to the left, unblocking his entrance into her home. She'd barely closed the door when he began to speak.

"We're not married," he said in a rush of words. "We're divorced."

The split-second relief of his confession didn't arrest her anger. "But she's not dead," Kally reiterated. "You told me she was dead. You lied to me."

"No." Max shook his head. "That's not quite true. I said she was no longer with us. I never once said she was dead."

"You have the audacity to play word games with me right now?" Kally pointed to the door. "Leave … just leave!"

"You granted me five minutes and I'm taking all of them," he insisted. "I'm not playing games with you. Everything I told you about Bridget was true."

"Except that she's still breathing!"

A load groan of exasperation came from deep within him. "Look, I know I should have told you. I meant to. I even tried to a couple of times," he said, scratching his forehead. "I knew you assumed she died from the overdose and I didn't correct you. But to me, she was dead. I have full custody of Athena and, as far as she knows, her mother no longer exists. Once she'd taken off with my boss, she never gave her daughter another thought. She wasn't even allowed visitation because of the trauma she'd put Athena through."

"I can understand why you wouldn't say anything at the beginning, but you had plenty of opportunities later on to tell me. This wasn't an insignificant detail," Kally emphasized. "You may no longer be married but the woman is alive and well, and I was far from equipped to deal with her. What if Athena had come to answer the door with me?"

"I don't even want to think about that."

"But you have to," Kally insisted.

"I'll deal with Bridget," he said. "Right now, I only want to talk about us."

Kally turned her back to him. "There is no us."

Max stepped swiftly to her side, taking her in his arms, but she broke free of him. "Kally, no. We'll work this out."

Kally looked at him as though he was a complete stranger. "I don't even know who you are, Max." She shook her head, more in disgust at her own foolishness. "I used your car to take Athena to the café. Keys weren't the only thing I found in your coat pocket. When did you start using again, or did you never stop at all?"

Max looked as though he was utterly confused until his expression changed to mortification. "I picked up a kid at the park for drugs. I didn't want to arrest him. You have to believe me," Max pleaded. "He's a good kid and I gave him a lecture and took the stuff from him."

"You always have a story," she deadpanned. "Who was this kid that you would stick your neck out for?"

"I can't tell you."

She laughed bitterly. "Of course, you can't."

"Kally, this can all be worked out. Give me a chance."

"You need to resolve your situation with your ex-wife and protect your daughter. That's why you came back to this town in the first place," she said. "What you don't need is a third person to complicate matters."

"Kally—"

"Max, I told you once that I wasn't meant for all of this. It's not in the cards for me." She shrugged. "This is the way it always turns out for me and I should have known better. I'm drained. I can't do it again. I want you to go. Please leave."

Without hesitation, Kally brushed past him and headed to her tiny foyer. Keeping her eyes trained on the floor, she opened the front door. Eye contact would have broken her resolve. There was little left to say and what few words she could think of were balled up inside the lump in her throat.

The tension released from her body as he stepped onto her porch, but as she was about to shut her door, Max's hand shot out, blocking it.

"Don't use this as an excuse to run away. You're letting fear drive you, the past control you. But I don't and won't give up so easily. This isn't the end of us." His voice held conviction.

But so did Kally's. "Goodbye, Max."

Chapter 29

Kally

A crocheted lilac blanket and *avgolemono* soup was *Yiayiá's* anti-dote to all of Kally's ailments, both physical and emotional. She had wrapped her granddaughter in a cocoon of purple wool while she whipped the eggs and lemon together to top the chicken broth.

It was her grandmother she often ran to for comfort and advice. Only she was to be able to soothe Kally. She listened without judgment and seemed to truly understand whatever it was that was bothering her.

Kally, while going through nearly an entire box of tissues, told her grandmother the whole story. As she wiped tears and blew her nose, *Yiayiá* repeatedly made her cross and sighed, "Oh, *Panayia mou,*" in reference to the mother of Christ. Her grandmother had grown attached to Athena and the very idea that she had been neglected or mistreated by her own mother pained her.

"Kallyope *mou,*" *Yiayiá* began, "I understand what you feel inside. Lied to. Betrayed. Disappointed that the relationship with Max was not intimate enough for him to reveal this important piece of information."

"Exactly," Kally confirmed with anger.

"Step outside of those emotions and thoughts for a moment," her grandmother suggested. "This was probably the most emotionally scarring time of his life. Not only because of the things his wife did to him and herself, but more because of how it affected his child. He walked away from everything he worked for."

"Yes, but he told me all of it except that one very important fact."

Yiayiá took Kally's face in her hands. "Sometimes the ones we love do things we cannot explain. Often, we may never know the reasons behind their decisions." A tear formed in the corner of her eye, the lone droplet spreading into the creases of her wrinkles. "You need to feel in here," she said, pressing a hand over her heart.

"Feel what?" Kally asked.

"The love. The trust. The faith that whatever happened was done to protect you in some way."

"Are we still talking about me or are you referring to yourself?" Kally asked.

"Both of us."

"After all these years and no answers, not one word from him, you still believe he loved you?" Kally had asked this question before, years ago when she first heard the story. After all this time, her *yiayiá* still had faith.

"I do."

"But if he's not dead, and you keep saying you know in your heart he's not, why doesn't he come for you?"

"I don't know," she answered. "I only know there must be a reason."

"What you leave behind is not what is engraved in stone monuments, but what is woven into the lives of others." Pericles

Chapter 30

Kalliope

Kalamata, Greece 1967

August in the southern part of Greece was typically hot, but at nine in the evening and with a gentle breeze drifting across from the marina, Kalliope took a few minutes to sit on her third-floor apartment balcony to gaze at the full moon.

Melina, her three-year-old daughter, named for the actress Melina Mercouri, was fast asleep after a full day spent at the beach. At any moment, she expected her husband, Panayiotis, to walk through the door, tired, soaked in perspiration, yet still gloriously handsome.

Kalliope missed the evenings they'd spend together, chatting over a meal, sipping wine on the terrace and later making love until they fell asleep in each other's arms. But since Panos took that third job, they spent little time together and, when he finally arrived home for the night, he could barely keep his eyes open.

Turning at the sound of footsteps, Kalliope smiled. He'd already shed himself from his soiled shirt. Even with only the moon to cast light on his form, she could see the definition of his muscles and the tanned glow of his skin.

Before she could stand to greet him, he was at her side, brushing his lips along the nape of her neck, tickling Kalliope with the golden tips of his wavy hair.

"You must be tired," she stated.

"Hungry, dirty, tired," he said, wearily.

"Well then," she teased, "I'll just have to feed you, wash you and take you to bed."

Picking her up, he carried her into the apartment. "But not necessarily in that order."

Wrapping her arms tightly around his broad shoulders, she laughed.

Kalliope did as she'd promised. Waiting for him was a grilled, red porgy and a tomato salad, which he consumed in record time. After taking a hot shower to soothe his muscles, Panos crawled into bed, pulling Kalliope in beside him.

He'd guided ferry boats into port in the early morning, spent all day catering to the needs of yacht owners moored at the docks, and in the evening, bartended a sunset tour on the water. Yet tonight, he'd made love to her with the same passion as he had the first time he'd claimed her as his own. Each time he thrust inside her, he called out, "*Zoi mou.*" My life. Now he looked down at her, a serious expression suddenly taking hold of his features. "*Alítheia. Eísai yia pánta e zoí mou.*" Truth. You are forever my life.

"What's wrong, Panos?" It wasn't what he said. He often spoke in sweet endearments. It's how he said it, as though it was the last time he might breathe those words to her. She knew her husband and something heavy was weighing on his mind.

"I'm concerned about our future here."

"In Kalamata?" she asked, a bewildered look on her face.

Panos rolled to his side, propping his head up with his hand. "In Kalamata ..." He sighed. "In all of Greece."

"You need to stop listening to those men you call your friends. They're looking for trouble," Kalliope chastised.

"Don't be naïve. Your king has betrayed us, allowing Papadopoulos and his Junta to take over."

"He's our king and it's clear he isn't happy about it," Kalliope argued. "One way or another they would have forced his hand."

"And you know this how?" His tone wasn't cross, even as he was in complete disagreement with her. Gently, Panos brushed loose strands of hair from her face. "He wanted Papandreou out and he made a deal with the devil. I fear the gates of Hell are about to open and I don't want you and Melina here when it does."

"What are you saying, Panos?"

"I've been putting away money, enough to send you and Melina to America." He sat up, sliding himself back to rest against the headboard.

Kalliope stared at him in astonishment as Panos nervously rubbed the palms of his hands back and forth along his thighs.

"That's why I've been working the extra job," he explained.

"And you didn't think it was important to tell me about this plan of yours?" she asked, hurt laced with anger coating her words.

"I was hoping it wouldn't come to this. I'm more on the inside than you know and if we don't fight for our rights, soon we won't have any."

"You're scaring me, Panos." Kalliope latched onto his forearms. "What have you involved yourself in?"

"Protecting my country and my family." He fisted his hands in her hair, drew her near and kissed her passionately. "*Zoi mou*. Never forget it. Everything I do is for you. Every step I take is to walk closer to you. Every decision I make is to keep you safe and for our future."

Tears rolled down her eyes, the tiny droplets spilling onto his hands as Panos tried to wipe them away. He was sending her and their child off to a strange land alone. Panos all but admitted that he'd be throwing himself into a precarious situation.

"I want to stay. Where you go, I go. If you fight, I stand by you," she stated adamantly.

His eyes swam with emotion—sadness, pride, determination— love—so much love. "It's all arranged. I have your plane tickets and you'll be going to stay with Rhea. She's expecting you."

"You did this behind my back." She broke free from his hold. Frowning, she rose from the bed, slipping her robe on. The light from the moon drew her attention as she walked to the window. Her street. Her town. Her Kalamata. The only corner of the world she had ever called home. The place of her birth and that of her daughter's. She was wed here. Melina was baptized here. Her parents lived and died here.

"When?" she asked, not turning to look at him.

"One week from now," Panos answered.

She swung around, fury in her dark eyes. "I am so mad at you!"

"I know. But you'll forgive me because I love you more than my life."

* * *

Panayiotis couldn't chance the ride to Athens with his wife and child. These days, suspicious eyes were on everyone. The Junta had military patrolling, searching for insurgents or anyone who didn't agree with their politics.

The three-hour bus ride would have given Kalliope a few more precious hours with her Panos, however it was not meant to be. She'd been granted a nine-month visa to visit family in America. After that, she was required to return. Panos instructed her to ignore the deadline and stay put until he either joined her in the States or sent money for her passage home.

The bus pulled up. Riders bumped around them, heading to board the bus.

"How will I know if you are … safe?" She wanted to say alive but couldn't bring herself to utter those words.

"You'll know it in here." He pressed his hand over her heart. "My heart beats for yours and yours for mine. We are of one soul." He kissed her deeply—lovingly. "The linger of my touch will always be with you as long as I am on this earth."

Kalliope brushed her fingers over the fullness of his lips. "And if I can't feel it?"

The bus driver announced the last call to board.

Panos kissed Melina on the cheek. He cupped Kalliope's chin and gave her one last meaningful kiss. "Then … you'll know."

Her eyes welled with tears; her expression begging him to let her stay.

"Go," he whispered. "I love you. *Zoi mou.*"

Chapter 31

Kally

Yiayiá's lip quivered. She pulled a fresh Kleenex from the box on her lap and blew her nose.

"That's so sad. And that was it? You never saw or heard from him again?"

"Once. Only once. I waited for over a year to receive that one letter," her grandmother said. "It came very unexpectedly because Panos had told me it would be too dangerous for him to attempt any communication with me. But he figured out a way. He didn't send the letter directly. He asked a young woman who wouldn't alarm suspicion to send it for him."

"I don't understand why it would be so suspicious—a man writing to his wife overseas?" Kally asked.

"The Junta was looking for reasons to arrest people. If they thought he sent his family away because he was conspiring with the resistance against the dictatorship, they could imprison him."

"I never realized things were that bad."

"It's bad when enemies invade your country," *Yiayiá* said. "But when Greeks fight Greeks, now that's a crime. *Mia dropí, sou léo.*" She stood, gathering a pile of used tissues and an empty teacup. "Enough about me. What are we going to do about you?"

"Me?" Kally asked weakly. "Nothing. I'll pull myself together and run my café. Eventually, my life will go back to how it was before. Before Max."

"*Koritsaki mou*, did you not learn anything from my story?"

"I don't understand the connection, no."

"The choices we make aren't always the ones we hope for. We live on Earth, not in Eden." Pointing her wrinkled finger, she shook it in Kally's direction. "Don't be so quick to judge or to let go of a good man."

"It's more complicated than that, *Yiayiá*, but I'll keep it in mind."

* * *

On the following Sunday, the last thing Kally wanted to do was to spend the day at her parents' home surrounded by her family—the whole family. Aunts, uncles, cousins. The whole shebang! But there she sat as though she was submitting to an out-of-body experience, observing the world around her but not engaging in it.

The thought and smell of food tied her stomach in knots. Thalia and her mother's incessant jabbering was grating on her nerves, her sisters had their heads together discussing some boy Krystina liked and Theo and Loukas were shouting at the TV over a soccer game.

But it was her father's conversation with Thalia's husband, Markos, that caught her attention.

"Right now, he's still in the hospital," her father said. "After, he'll be in a rehabilitation facility so that will buy me some time to figure things out."

"Dad, who are you talking about?" Kally asked.

"*Pappou*." He sighed. "Didn't your mother tell you? My mother called yesterday. He's been a little unsteady on his feet lately. He tripped last week and broke his hip."

"Oh no! Is he okay?"

"He had surgery. A hip replacement." George pulled at the back of his neck. "Now I need to figure out what to do. *Yiayiá* can't care for him and manage the store on her own."

"Are you thinking of going to Athens?" Kally asked.

"Somebody has to. But I have to see who can run the restaurant. Now if you were still working for me—"

"Dad!"

George threw up his hands in surrender. "Okay!"

"Kally." Melina walked over, cordless phone in hand. "It's Egypt."

"On the landline?" That was very odd, Kally thought.

"She tried your cell first," Melina explained.

"Hello? What? Are you joking?"

The alarm in her voice had everyone in the room turning to stare at her. Kally, not remembering where she had dropped her bag, frantically searched the room. "I'm leaving now," she told Egypt as she found it under the coffee table.

"What's going on?" her father asked.

"My café is on fire! Leo called Egypt and told her to call me."

"How did that happen?" Melina asked.

"They think it started next door." She was halfway out the door as she answered.

"We'll come with you," her father said.

"No, please. Stay put. The fire department is there. I'll call you when I have news."

Chapter 32

Kally

Kally slowly managed to negotiate around the fire trucks to see exactly how her café was affected by the fire that began in the neighboring store. More than once, she was asked to stay back, and after becoming frustrated by explaining over and over again that it was her place on fire, she eventually pushed through.

Her frustration was followed only by complete desolation as she watched everything she had dreamed of and finally built literally go up in flames.

"Ma'am," a firefighter called to her over the loud whir of the fire engines and the deafening sound of water shooting from the hose to fight the blaze. "You need to stand back. There's nothing you can do."

"That's my place," Kally cried. "I'm not leaving."

Startled by a tall figure jumping in front of her and pushing her back, she shrieked.

"Watch out!" he said when the remnants of her custom-made sign came crashing down.

It was Leo, she realized, turning to face him. "Leo." The devastation was written all over her face.

Resting his hand on her shoulder, he said softly, "I'm so sorry. It's Max's night off but I can call him for you."

"No."

"Kally, come on," Leo pleaded. "He'd want to be here for you."

"There's nothing he or anyone can do." She looked back at the smoldering building. The fire had finally been extinguished and, along with it, her hopes for the future.

A little past midnight, Kally was finally able to go home. The damage to the café was extensive and it looked as though little could be salvaged. It seemed about right, she thought, feeling defeated. Everything good in her life managed to fall apart one way or another. Now, the only thing she had left to fulfill her passions had burned to ashes.

She was done. So completely done. Worn to the bone. At that moment, Kally made a decision. It would be she who would go to Athens to care for her grandfather. Her father could handle the insurance on The Coffee Klatch while she was away and use the money to pay out the remaining months on the lease. When she returned, she would go to work for her father. That's what he'd wanted all along anyway, she relented.

The next evening, she called her parents.

"Are you sure?" her mother asked.

"Yes. There's nothing holding me here now. My going makes the most sense."

"That's a sensible solution," her father agreed from an extension on the cordless phone. "I'll make the arrangements. Thank you, Kally. This takes a big weight off me."

Before she closed the call, a deep sigh echoed from the other end. She knew it came from her mother and wondered what she was thinking.

* * *

Two days before Kally was to leave for Athens, Egypt forced her out of her home and hopefully her funk, dragging her out East for a ride.

The landscape as they drove along the rural roads looked to be as dismal as her mood. Spring had not yet arrived and the trees were bare, as were the dozens of vineyards they passed. Kally saw no sign of hope in the creepy, scraggly branches. Not even a single bud to show some sign of life. And that's how she felt. No hope. No future. Everything she ever dreamed of and thought she was building was gone, ripped from her world without a second thought.

Egypt pulled off the road when she came to the Angelidis Vineyard. Years ago, Kally had befriended Evvie, one of the winemakers working here, in the oddest of circumstances, both of them at a crucial point in their lives—Kally crying over Jaxon's grave and Evvie visiting her *yiayiá's* burial site for comfort. That day they had consoled and supported one another, forming an unexpected bond.

The tasting room was more crowded than they'd expected for a late March day. There was standing room only at the bar and almost all the tables were occupied. Kally spotted Michael Angelidis, the owner of the vineyard, and waved to him. Smiling, he strode toward them and kissed Kally on the cheek.

"I'll tell Evvie you're here," Michael said. He led them to an unoccupied table not too far from the French doors leading to the patio. "What can I get you, ladies?"

"I heard you have a Rosé this year," Egypt said.

"Evvie's idea. Yup. All of a sudden, it's all about the Rosé." Michael grinned. He lifted his hands, palms up. "You have to keep up with the trends. I'm a Pinot man myself." He raised two fingers. "Two Rosés?"

Not five minutes later, Evvie came to the table with three glasses of wine and a charcuterie platter. Kally popped from her seat and engulfed Evvie in a warm embrace.

"You remember my friend, Egypt?" Kally asked.

"Of course! It's so nice to see you again," Evvie greeted her with a warm smile. "What brings the two of you all the way out here this time of year? Not that I don't wish you visited me more often."

"Do you have a couple of hours," Egypt said sarcastically.

"I have time," Evvie, said, eyeing Kally suspiciously. "Do I have to worry about you?"

"No, I'm heading to Athens in two days to help out my grandparents. My grandfather broke his hip."

Egypt rolled her head and shot her an incredulous glare. "Nothing like starting a story at the end!"

Egypt went on to relay every bit of information from her romance with Max, to the break up, finally explaining the fire. Kally, with her elbows on the table, massaged her temples, not even bothering to interject. Thankfully, she refrained from the more personal details and only told Evvie that the man she'd been dating turned out to be married. That wasn't entirely accurate but Kally didn't have the energy or the wherewithal to correct her.

She looked up as Egypt continued to chat away. Then, suddenly, through the French door windows, she saw her. Kally felt the blood drain from her face. Outside, the patio was closed to guests but the tulips were in bloom and a small child held hands with Evvie's four-year-old twins as they dipped their noses into the flowers. Athena! What was Athena doing here? Her answer came when Evvie's husband, Zak, and Max came into view.

"I have to leave," Kally said frantically.

Both Egypt and Evvie looked to see what had panicked her so.

Following Kally's gaze, Egypt frowned. "What the fuck is he doing here?"

Evvie looked confused; Kally looked stricken.

"Kally?" Evvie inquired, grabbing onto her arm. "What's going on?"

Evvie looked back and forth between Kally and Max. Upon seeing Evvie through the window, Max waved but was then struck with a stunned expression similar to the one on Kally's face.

Kally watched as Max tugged on the door only to discover it was locked.

"Is Max the man you were speaking of?" Evvie asked.

"Yes," she answered breathlessly.

"But he's not married."

"I know. It's a long story." She picked up her bag and slipped her jacket on. "What's he doing here?"

"He's Zak's cousin."

"Of course, he is!" Kally wanted to curse the gods. Would they ever be on her side?

"Kally." She heard Max call to her. She turned around coming practically nose to nose with him.

"Excuse me." She walked around him. "I was just about to leave."

"Give me a minute," he pleaded. "I've been calling and texting and you haven't answered."

Evvie urged Egypt away to the bar.

"There's no point."

"The point is these last few months together. The point is what we had. No, have, and what I feel for you. The point is for us to work through this."

"There is no us," Kally stated definitively. "You broke my trust. It's over."

"Just like that?"

Her resolve wavered slightly. Inside, she wanted nothing more than to say, 'No, not just like that.' She was crumbling inside. Standing before him was tearing her apart. But allowing another man's dishonesty to ruin her would be worse.

"You may as well know I'm leaving for Athens. My grandparents need me and ... and there's nothing left for me here. So, yes. Just like that."

Kally turned and began to walk away but she halted at his words.

"I'll be here when you get back. I'll gain your trust back. There will always be an us."

She didn't think there was any of her heart left to shred, yet more of its layers peeled away, cell by cell. Kally headed for the exit without another word.

"Kally," Evvie pleaded. "Talk to me."

But she didn't have the strength to look back. Shaking her head, she choked out a small sob. "I can't." She collected Egypt, waved a weak goodbye to Evvie and Michael and left Max behind.

Chapter 33

Kally

With a heavy heart, Kally looked out the window as the airplane gained altitude and the life she once knew was left behind. Ordinarily, she would have been beaming with enthusiasm to visit Athens, however, the circumstances of this trip held no excitement for her.

Naturally, she loved her grandparents and wanted to help them during this challenging time. But playing nursemaid day in and day out when her heart was ailing and her future was bleak seemed completely dismal for her.

Once the flight crew instructed passengers that they were able to recline their seats, Kally did just that. All she wanted to do was sleep for the next nine hours. Hell! Wouldn't it be nice if she could sleep straight through until the heaviness in her chest lightened?

Kicking off her shoes, she wiggled her toes, pulled a neck pillow from her tote bag and relaxed into a comfortable position. Or as comfortable as one could get in the coach section. It didn't take long for Kally to drift off but the sleep was not a good one. She felt as though she was in a semi-conscious state and she was aware of the dreams that occupied her.

The images ran through her mind like a jumbled, unedited movie reel. At first, they were all pleasant and a content murmur escaped her lips. The wide-eyed expression of happy disbelief on Jaxon's face as she told him she was carrying his child—his hands pressed against her stomach—his whispers of love. Their whole affair flashed before her—that first motorcycle ride—dinner under the stars and the first time they made love.

A flight attendant roused her, asking her if she'd like a beverage. Confused, it took a moment to gain clarity as to where she was. *Not with Jax. Jax was dead.* Kally refused the offer for a drink and nodded off again. This time, thoughts of Max filled her mind. Cupcakes and children's parties. Holidays and family. Confessions of love when she never thought it possible again.

The commanding voice of the pilot came through the loudspeaker. "We'll be hitting some turbulence folks, so please remain in your seat."

A few minutes later, Kally was awakened by a jolt. "I'm so sorry," she apologized to her seatmate when her shoulder bumped his. The turbulence had indeed gotten rough. She felt as though they were driving along a road of deep potholes and the occasional drop was enough to make her heart race with nerves.

She drew in slow, deep breaths, trying to calm herself. Kally willed herself not to think about it and, hoping for slumber, she closed her eyes once more.

Max and Jaxon each were in a corner of a boxing ring, with Kally planted in the middle. The men were arguing for possession.

"She was mine first," Jaxon shouted.

"You don't deserve her," Max yelled back. "She loves me!"

"We're having a baby," Jaxon declared. "Back the fuck off."

"That baby died because you're a lying, cheating bastard."

"You are too. I'm not going to let you turn Kally into a drug addict like you did to your wife."

Kally covered her ears and sank to the floor of the boxing ring. "Stop! Both of you!" Images of both men polluted her brain—the stricken look on Jaxon's face when he left her that last night—the realization that Jaxon was not only lying in a casket, but that he had a wife mourning over it. She saw visions of herself, hunched over in pain, pressing at her belly and being wheeled into emergency surgery. The loss of the only part left of Jax she'd ever have.

Jax tried to reach for her but the entire platform of the ring lifted on one side. Kally slid closer to where Max was waiting. Reaching for her, she rejected him. "No! Stay away from me, Max," she demanded. "You're no better than he is."

The movement was making her dizzy but it didn't stop her from seeing Bridget in Max's doorway, claiming to be his wife. Photos of the two of them rained down on her—hundreds of them—each of the same wedding image.

As the two men encroached on her, she felt trapped and cried out over and over again, "Go away. Go away."

"Miss, Miss," the man next to her said, shaking her awake.

Kally looked at him, dazed.

"I think you were having a bad dream," he explained. "You were moaning incoherent words."

"Oh, thank you. Yes, I was having a bad dream," Kally admitted. "I hope I didn't disturb you."

"Not at all."

She smiled back at the elderly gentleman. Weird, weird, weird, she thought. Maybe it's best I get out of the country for a while after all.

Chapter 34

Max

A hazy mist fogged the windows. Max was seated on the sectional in the den, his feet resting on the coffee table. An ignored open-faced paperback copy of David Baldacci's *The Fallen* was spread across his lap. He'd read the same paragraph over and over until finally setting it down to stare out into the dreary nothingness of the day.

He missed Kally. There was a hopeful, albeit false, sense of security when she was in her café, so close yet so far away, in the town they both called home. But now, with thousands of miles between them and her resolve to break free of any form of contact with him, Max found it difficult to pull himself from his melancholy.

Lost deep in thought, he tapped his forefinger against his lips as an idea began to bloom. Pressing the home button on his iPhone, it came to life and Max tapped a call in to a number programed in his favorites. Five minutes into the conversation, the doorbell rang. Killing the call, he told his father he'd call him back to discuss the details of his plan further.

"Coming!" Max shouted, running for the door. But when he opened it, he aimed his furious glare at the person standing on the other side. "What are you doing here, Bridget?"

"You really didn't think I was just going to go away without a fight, did you?" she asked.

"There's nothing to fight over," Max said in a sarcastically sweet tone. "My life doesn't include you and I sure as hell want no part in yours."

He began to shut the door but Bridget blocked it with the toe of what Max was sure were ridiculously expensive boots. "I want to see my daughter. I have rights." She bobbed her head around looking for the child.

Max laughed. Half nervously—half incredulously. "You jeopardized those rights when you locked our daughter in a room while you fucked my boss," he spat. "You lost every privilege when you signed your rights away to your daughter for a quickie divorce and a cool five million."

Bridget bowed her head, her blonde tresses falling over her face. "I wasn't in my right mind. I'm a different person now."

Any sympathy he once had for her had died long ago. He wasn't buying this contrite display of conscience. "If you were honestly different and any kind of a real mother, you would know that Athena wasn't here. She's in school where she belongs at this hour."

"I just want to see her. Please, let me come in and wait for her."

Max's jaw tightened. She was truly pathetic and, on some level, he felt pity for this woman who had lost everything through her own poor choices. But Athena's wellbeing was his first priority.

"If you sincerely want to do what's right for our daughter, you'll turn around, get in your car and drive out of town," he said as calmly as he could muster. "Her nightmares are more infrequent now. She's happy and, as far as she knows, you don't exist."

"I never wanted any of this," Bridget cried.

"Neither did I, but you made your choice." He looked her over, eyes glistening, mascara streaking down her cheeks. "Why now?" he asked softly. "It's been two years."

"I want to try again. I made a mistake. We were a family."

"Where's Martin?"

"We're not together." She looked down at her feet. "He doesn't want me anymore."

"Ah! I see, and so you thought you'd take a shot at getting your old life back." Max raised an eyebrow. "Newsflash! We've moved on just fine without you. But no worries. You still have your settlement to keep you warm." He snapped his fingers. "Oh, wait! Do you have it? Or did that go up your nose too?"

"You're a cruel bastard," she barked.

"You get what you give, babe. Now get out of here before I file an order of protection against you." Max shut the door. He didn't bother to see whether or not she lingered on the steps. Shaking off the encounter, he tapped in a call to his father again. "Hey, Dad. Sorry, I got interrupted. Here's what I'd like to do …"

Chapter 35

Kally

The apartment in Athens was not the same one Kally remembered visiting as a child. That flat was on the fourth floor with a bird's eye view of the Acropolis, unlike this ground level one nestled between two buildings on a narrow street.

At eighty years of age, Kally supposed the walk up would have been too many stairs for her grandparents to climb.

There was no question that this was the home of an elderly couple. Inside, the place was simply decorated. Her *yiayiá* had long ago packed away the knick-knacks that would add to her daily cleaning. A dark, mahogany dining set dominated the living area, the remaining space occupied by a beige sectional. Finely stitched doilies sat on every surface. Each stick of furniture looked nearly ancient to Kally and, on the eastern corner of the room, hung an *iconastasis* with a collection of icons larger than she'd ever seen.

Sakis, Kally's *pappou*, still remained in the Athens Rehab Center when she'd arrived in Greece. That was a blessing, she thought. It would have been too much for her slight grandmother to lift her grandfather and put him to bed each night or help him with the many other responsibilities that came with caring for him while he recuperated.

Day after day, Kally and *Yiayiá* took the metro to the rehab center during visiting hours. In between visits, Kally took advantage of her free time by wandering the streets of Athens, a liberty she indulged herself in while she was still able to. Once her grandfather came home, she would be kept busy caring for him, and any chance at the tourist experience would most likely be gone.

With the sun shining down on her face and the April temperature a comfortable sixty degrees, Kally was not at all missing the New York spring weather, which still bordered on the colder side. She ate a *horiatiki* salad at one of the Plaka tavernas and took a *frappé* to go for her steep eighty-step climb to the Parthenon. Later, she shopped the boutiques of Monastiraki while enjoying a pistachio gelato.

Under other circumstances, Kally would have found pleasure in every moment. The spring in her step would have made her enthusiasm obvious. But her pace was slow and her sighs heavy. Distance hadn't erased her troubles. If she could only rid herself of this gnawing pain in her chest and the incessant battling voices in her mind, she'd be fine.

* * *

It was mid-April when Sakis finally came home. At eighty-years-old, his advanced age didn't hinder his ability at self-sufficiency. He still ran his jewelry store, even if he had cut back his hours and relied on a trusted manager. But the man had energy and now he used a good portion of it to act out his frustration by barking orders.

"He's not usually like this," *Yiayiá* told Kally apologetically as she ladled food into a deep dish. She had made a pot of *youvarlakia* for her husband but, upon taking his first bite, he'd pushed it aside with a scowl. 'The meatballs are cold,' he complained and 'the sauce wasn't as lemony as she normally made it.' Wordlessly, she snatched the plate from him, her face carefully composed as she returned it to the kitchen. Oh, this is going to be fun! Not! Kally thought. Then she had an idea.

"What's *Pappou's* favorite dessert?" Kally asked.

"*Galakteboureko* and *Koulourakia*," *Yiayiá* replied. "He likes to have the cookies with his *kafes*."

"Simple enough." Kally rubbed her palms together. She was ready to get her hands in some dough. It had been less than two weeks but she already missed the everyday routine of running The Coffee Klatch. The knot in her stomach twisted at the thought that there would be no café to return home to.

After a few days, Kally fell into a routine. After helping *Yiayiá* dress *Pappou* and cook his breakfast, she'd leave to check on the store. She was grateful there was only one to manage. The other had been sold over ten years ago. Whenever she arrived back at the apartment, she almost always insisted *Yiayiá* get away to visit a friend or two for a much-needed respite.

The small patio of the ground-floor apartment was just large enough to fit a round table and pair of chairs. It was a warm night, a gentle breeze blowing by as Kally gazed up at the stars.

Yiayiá, sitting in the chair across from her, patted her hand. "*Koritsaki mou*, you don't need to stay home night after night." She waved her hand. "Go! Find some young people and have fun."

Kally laughed. "And where would you like me to find these young people?"

"Well, I have an idea." There was a sparkle in the old woman's eyes. "My friend has three granddaughters. They are going to Glyfada this weekend, staying the night at a hotel and going to the beach. I think it would do you good to join them."

"I don't even know them."

"Yet you have been invited and the girls are more than happy to have you."

Galaktoboureko

Custard
8 cups milk

1 ½ cups sugar

1 ½ cups semolina

6 eggs, beaten

3 tablespoons unsalted butter

1 tablespoon vanilla

Pastry
1 pound phyllo

1 cup unsalted butter, melted

Syrup
1 ½ cups water

1 ½ cups sugar

2 tablespoons fresh orange juice

2 strips orange peel

2 cinnamon sticks

Preheat oven to 350°

In a pot, place milk, sugar, vanilla and semolina. Stir until mixed through. Add the beaten eggs and stir. Place over medium heat and simmer, constantly stirring. It will take a while for the custard to thicken. Keep stirring. When the custard thickens, remove from the heat and add the butter. Stir until the butter has melted and mixed through. Place the custard in a bowl and cover with Saran wrap. Allow the custard to cool. Butter a 9x13 inch pan. Using half of the package of phyllo, butter each sheet with a pastry brush and place it in the pan. Keep layering the sheets until you have finished the first half of the phyllo. With a large spoon or ladle, add all the custard over the phyllo. Layer and butter the remaining phyllo one sheet at a time, covering the custard. Brush the top layer with butter. Tuck in the edges of any overlapping phyllo. Score with a sharp knife into squares and bake at 350° F for 1 hour.

In the meantime, combine the water, sugar, orange juice, orange peel and cinnamon sticks and simmer for 20 minutes. Set aside to cool. Pour the cooled syrup over the warm pastry.

Chapter 36

Kally

"I'm back!" Kally called out. It was Sunday evening. The past couple of days were spent on the beach by day and the clubs at night. Kally never did this at home. Egypt would have to drag her kicking and screaming to set foot inside anything resembling a nightclub. But she had to admit, here in Greece, it was fun.

"Look who's making progress!" *Yiayiá* exclaimed. Down the hallway, *Pappou* came, briskly rolling along with his walker. No more tentative baby steps. He was not wincing in pain with every movement.

Kally clapped her hands. "*Bravo!*"

"Maybe when I see the doctor on Tuesday he'll let me get rid of this hunk of junk," *Pappou* growled.

"That hunk of junk kept you on your feet," Kally scolded. She set her overnight bag down, pushing it against the wall with the tip of her toe. "Why don't I get you settled on the patio and I'll pour us all a glass of wine."

Kally led him outside, *Yiayiá* at their heels. A few minutes later, she returned with a tray and an old letter she stuffed into her back pocket—her grandmother's letter. Kally had asked if she could hold onto it for a while and her *yiayiá* hadn't objected. Under the light of the moon, they made small talk, discussing the finer points of her weekend away. She left out the details of how drunk Antonia got or about the random hookup Petra had with a German tourist. The last thing she wanted was those bits of information to get back to her grandmother's friend, and, if the Greek hotline telecasted remotely as much as it did in the States, well ...

"I want to ask you both about something," Kally began. "What do you know, if anything at all, about my other *pappou?*"

Sakis stared at her blankly but her grandmother's forehead creased. Examining Kally closely for a motive to her question, she inquired, "What makes you ask? It's not something your mother likes to talk about."

"I know," Kally replied. "But my *yiayiá* told me all about him and how he promised to come for her." She pulled the letter from her back pocket. "It's all in here. A letter he wrote to her. I believe he meant to come for her. My mother thinks they were both abandoned by him but *Yiayiá* never believed it for one second. She had such faith in him and, after reading this, I do too."

Sighing deeply, her grandmother said, "Yet we have no information on him."

"*Típota!*" *Pappou* exclaimed. "Nothing. Your father tried to find some information on his whereabouts with no luck."

"When?" Kally asked. "When he was separated from Mom?"

"Yes," *Pappou* answered. "He thought if he could find her father it would be one step toward her forgiveness."

"He was trying to prove how much he loved her but, since his efforts came up empty, he never told her that he'd searched," *Yiayiá* added.

"How does someone disappear without a trace?" Kally asked.

"I suspect he wasn't the only one," *Pappou* said. "He was openly against the Junta. At the time, they suppressed free speech, banned the work of artists and musicians and jailed those who spoke out."

"It's so hard to believe that happened here and not so long ago."

Kally blew out the tension from her body.

"He could have been one of many who were tortured or killed," *Yiayiá* said sadly. "We have no way to know for sure."

"That's the odd thing," Kally pondered. "She is certain, adamant really, that he is still alive somewhere and can't get to her."

"What do you think makes her so sure?" *Yiayiá* asked.

"Denial," *Pappou* blurted.

"No," Kally disagreed. "It's more than that. It's the promise in the letter. A feeling in her heart. A connection she feels to his soul. She insists that connection has not been severed." She thought if opportunity and time presented itself, she would try to gather some information on what may have happened to her grandfather. It's the least she could do for her grandmother.

"Can I see the letter?" *Yiayiá* held out her hand and Kally willingly gave it to her.

The faded ink on the yellowed envelope did not hold the return address of Panayiotis Nikopoulos, but that of a woman: Stella Demopoulos of Kalamata. Kally saw the confusion reflected on her grandmother's face as she gingerly removed the weathered paper from its sleeve. Softly, she read it aloud.

March 10, 1968

Kalliope mou,

I pray this letter makes its way to you. I think of you every day. Know that I love you with my soul and all of my being. Give my Melina a kiss from her baba. It is not possible to say more except that I must take great care and few risks if I am to see you again. I am always with you in my heart and mind. Nothing but death can keep me from returning to you.

All my love,

Panos

"This is all very sweet but I don't see anything more than a love note," *Yiayiá* said. "I don't believe this man would have deserted his wife but there's nothing to indicate he might still be alive."

"1968 was a bad year," *Pappou* said. "If he was one of the many stirring up what the Junta considered trouble they probably arrested him … or worse."

"What if I went to Kalamata to find this Stella?" Kally asked. "Maybe she knows something."

"If she's still alive," *Pappou* said. "We don't know if she was a young woman or a much older one."

Kally chewed on the tip of her thumbnail. "Good point. I'll do a little research on the computer first."

* * *

The next morning, Kally slipped her laptop in the blue and white canvas tote bag she had purchased from a boutique in Glyfada and strode to the nearest internet café. Once she waved away the smoke billowing in her direction, she went to the counter and ordered a coffee and croissant. "Greeks and their damned coffee and cigarette breakfasts," she muttered under her breath.

Finding a seat, she opened her laptop, took a much-needed sip from the steaming cup and got right down to work. It didn't take long to find the name Stella Demopoulos. Sixty-eight years old. Resides in Kalamata. Proprietor of the *Paralía Fourno*. Cool! She owns a bakery. That common thread just might get her talking, Kally thought.

For the next two hours, she researched her options to get to Kalamata. Finally, after three coffees, the croissant and a slice of cinnamon toast, Kally decided she would rent a car and explore other towns throughout the Peloponnese along the way.

Later that evening, after she had checked in on the store and stopped at the market, Kally went home to share the news with her grandparents.

"I found her!" she declared at the dinner table. "Stella. I found her. She still lives in Kalamata and owns a bakery."

"Now what?" *Pappou* asked. "That was so long ago. What makes you think she knows what happened to him?"

"It's a start," Kally replied. "I have nothing else to go on. I would really like to find out for *Yiayiá's* sake. I think she should know if he's dead or alive."

Her grandmother patted her cheek. "You're a good girl, *koukla mou*."

"I'll wait, of course, until the doctor says you're able to get around on your own," she addressed her grandfather. "I was thinking I might go for a few days and stop in Corinth since I'll be heading in that direction."

"You shouldn't go alone," *Pappou* suggested.

"I was thinking of asking Vivi along." The other two sisters she'd spent the weekend with were a bit too wild for her. Vivi was more level-headed and the one closest to Kally's age.

"Oh, yes! You should ask Paraskevi." Her grandmother was eager for Kally to make friends in the neighborhood. It was no secret that she was hoping her granddaughter would lengthen her stay with them.

* * *

"Take me to my store," Sakis demanded. He walked from the doctor's office sporting only a cane. Gone was the walker that had been the bane of his existence these past weeks.

"You still can't overdo it," Kally reminded him, "or you'll end up setting yourself back. Is that what you want?"

He waved off her nonsensical talk. "Take me or I'll get on the metro alone."

"He's not going to listen to a word I say, is he?" she asked her grandmother in defeat.

"No, but it will get him out of my hair for a few hours," she laughed.

Peals of excitement erupted when they walked into Andarakis Jewelry. "Sakis! Maria!" the employees exclaimed. And that was that! The beginning of her *pappou's* true rehabilitation. To feel useful again. To regain some semblance of his routine. Within a week's time, he was working nearly full time and Kally wasn't as vital to their day-to-day needs. It was time for a road trip to Kalamata for a little investigation.

Chapter 37

Max

Max was seated on a stool behind the counter of the newly renovated Coffee Klatch waiting for Kally's father to arrive. Only a few final touches needed to be addressed and the café would be restored to its original charm. That and the final walk through inspection were the only roadblocks holding up a grand re-opening. Aside from, of course, Kally herself not knowing any of the work on her place had transpired. She had been away for almost two months and was expected home in less than a week.

When Max had approached George with his plan, he'd stubbornly refused. George had already set his mind on Kally working for him once she returned home. But Max wouldn't take no for an answer. The Coffee Klatch was part of Kally's identity and cornering her into the family business when she clearly wanted a place of her own, one she'd built from her own passions, would surely stifle her spirit.

So Max did the only thing he could think of. He appealed to Kally's mother and grandmother. He had to admit, he was a little nervous. He wasn't sure if he'd be received as kindly as he had in the past or feel as though he was walking up against a firing squad. But they had greeted him just as warmly as always.

"I completely agree with you, Max," Melina said. "George and

I have been arguing over this. He said when the insurance money comes through, he will pay off the lease as Kally instructed. I asked him to hold off. She wasn't in the right frame of mind to make decisions at the time."

"If the two of you can convince him to use the money to rebuild, I'll handle the rest," Max said.

Yiayiá's eyes sparkled with delight. Pinching Max on both cheeks like a schoolboy, she cooed adoringly, "Such a good boy."

"Before we get ahead of ourselves," Melina interrupted, "you're forgetting a few important points."

Max leaned into the plush cushions of Melina's sofa, running his hands through his hair. He was about to get shot down with both barrels but for very different reasons than George's.

"First." Melina latched onto her pointed finger. "Kally doesn't want to see or speak to you, so what makes you think she'll allow you to take charge of fixing her place?"

Max was about to answer when Melina shot her hand up. "Wait! Second, even if she agrees, the money from the insurance payout won't be enough to cover all the damages and get the café up and running again."

"*Skáse tóra!*" *Yiayiá* scolded. "Let the boy talk."

Max winked at the old woman. She was always on his side. "If the two of you can convince George not to end the lease and to use the money toward the renovation, I promise you I will get the place back to what it was before the fire."

"How?" Melina asked.

"I've already spoken to my father and brothers. They're willing to put some of their crew on the job. We can get the materials at builder's cost."

"We can't expect them to work for free," Melina said.

"The insurance should cover the labor and a good part of the materials. I've got the rest covered."

Melina shook her head. "Kally would never go for it."

"That's why we won't tell her." He scrubbed at the stubble on his jaw. "Listen, I'm not doing this for me or to win Kally back. If anything, she might see this as a manipulation on my part to convince her to forgive me. I don't want her to feel obligated toward me or feel that she owes me anything."

"But Maximos *mou*, lying to her is what got you into trouble with her in the first place," *Yiayiá* pointed out.

"I didn't lie," he grunted. "You need to understand that. I was waiting for the right time to explain." He tapped his fingers against his forehead. "This is for the best. Kally will get her café back and it will make me feel better knowing I had something to do with some part of her happiness."

"Okay," Melina agreed. "I'll handle George. You take on the rest."

* * *

Max waited for Kally's father to arrive at the restored and renovated café. Thinking back, he chuckled to himself. George hadn't stood a chance with those two ganging up on him. Looking up when he heard the sound of the creaking door, Max rose from his seat to meet George and shake his hand.

Kally's father jiggled the loose change in his pockets, nodding as he looked around. "I have to hand it to you. The place looks even better than before."

"I'm glad you approve." Max motioned for George to follow him into the kitchen. "I'm waiting for the oven but look at this refrigerator."

George whistled. "The one she had was second hand. The oven too." He sighed. "She's going to wonder where the money came from for all of this."

"You're in the restaurant business," Max reminded him. "Tell her you called in some favors."

"I know I was against this but ..." George cleared his throat. "I want her to be happy." His voice was thick with emotion. "This was

215

her dream." He trained his eyes on the floor as he brushed the toe of his shoe back and forth.

Max clapped him on the shoulder. "I know you want what's best for her."

"You shouldn't give me the credit for this. She should know it was you," George insisted.

"No, she needs to come to me on her own. When she's ready. If she ever becomes ready," he trailed off.

Philotimo - meaning a way of life for Greeks which includes ideas and virtues such as honor, justice, courage, dignity, pride, self-sacrifice, respect, freedom, gratitude and hospitality. Literally translated it means friend of honor.

Chapter 38

Kally

The music of pop singer Nikos Mertzanos blasted through the speakers as the wind whipped about Kally and Vivi's hair. Kally had rented a white Audi A3 convertible for their road trip to Kalamata. She figured driving two and a half hours south to the Peloponnese Peninsula deserved a splurge.

About an hour into their journey, they arrived in Corinth, a small detour Kally had planned after reading about the ruins, the seaside village and the breathtaking landscape. Instead of simply passing though, the girls decided to spend the entire day and book a hotel for the night.

"Do you want to try it?" Vivi asked.

They had stopped by a spot at the Corinth Canal to watch, to Kally's horror, fearless individuals bungee jump off the bridge.

"Not on your life!" Kally exclaimed.

"They don't do this in the States?"

"Oh, yes. *They* do, but I sure as hell don't!" Kally said. "It is amusing to watch though."

They drove on to visit the ruins, particularly the Temple of Apollo.

It gave Kally pause when she stopped to think this structure was built over twenty-five hundred years ago, the seven towering columns before her created by the sweat and labor of men who lived in the year 560BC somehow still standing through the test of time.

"There are ruins all over Athens," Vivi said, sounding bored. "Have you not seen them?" She tugged on Kally's arm. "I'm hungry. Let's get something to eat."

They drove to Loutraki and pulled into a seaside resort on the Gulf of Corinth. Once they'd checked into their rooms, they headed directly to an outdoor café. Seated at a table shaded by a blue market umbrella, they sipped the natural spring water the area was known for and ordered lunch.

"Are you ladies here to use the spa?" the waitress inquired.

"We are!" Kally confirmed. "I read it feels amazing on the skin."

"More than that," the woman said tucking her order pad in her apron pocket. "It's good for the body and the soul. The water has healing powers."

In less than a week, Kally would be back home. She had left her problems behind, but soon they would be unavoidable. "Can the waters heal a broken heart and a business gone to cinder?" she asked miserably.

The woman gave her a sympathetic look. "I'm afraid not."

"Oh, Kally," Vivi said. "Why don't you stay longer? What do you have to lose?"

"Nothing. It's all gone. But I have to face my life, such as it is, sometime."

* * *

"I feel like mush," Vivi said with a content sigh. "Relaxed mush. Are you sure we can't stay another day?" she pleaded, melting into the comfort of the healing waters of Loutraki.

"No. I need to get to Kalamata and hopefully speak to Stella." Kally closed her eyes, sinking neck deep into the pool. "It sure is tempting though. Every bit of tension seems to be draining from my body."

"It's the magnesium in the water," Vivi murmured almost sleepily.

"Ten more minutes and then we have to get moving," Kally said reluctantly.

But ten more minutes turned into another ten and then another, until their bodies pruned to the point they had no choice but to step out of the water and towel off.

The next morning, they were off in the rented Audi, heading toward Kalamata, sad to say goodbye to the pretty seaside town with its magical waters. In no time at all, Kally pulled up at the address she'd programmed into the navigation system—*Paralía Fourno*—the bakery owned by Stella Demopoulos.

Shaking out her nerves, Kally checked her bag for the letter tucked in the zipper compartment and, with Vivi by her side, entered the bakery. The smell of fresh bread and sweet pastry lingering in the air was comforting if not a little sad. It made her miss her café all the more.

"How are you going to approach her?" Vivi whispered.

"I don't know. I guess I'll just ask for her."

"Let's buy something first and then start a conversation," Vivi suggested.

"What are those squiggly things?" Kally pointed to a tray of fried dough in the glass display case.

"You've never had *lalágia*?" Vivi asked, appearing outraged. "And you call yourself a Greek baker," she admonished.

"I'm a pastry chef, and I'm not limited to making Greek confections," Kally defended. "Honestly, I can't be expected to know the desserts of every region in this country."

"*Boró na se voithíso*?" A young woman behind the counter around Kally's age asked.

"Yes, thank you," Kally replied. "I'll take a pound of those," she said, pointing to the *lalágia*."

"And one of those rosemary olive breads, *sas parakaló*."

After wrapping the items, the woman placed them on the counter, pricing them up for her. Digging into her bag, she handed her five euro and told her to keep the change. But as she handed over the money, Kally stayed rooted in one spot, staring at the woman. Suddenly, she was very nervous. How did she start such a conversation? Would the woman be forthcoming or even willing to speak to her at all? So many thoughts rolled around in Kally's mind as her mouth went as dry as beach sand on a scorching day.

"Is there something else?" the woman asked with a raised eyebrow.

Fixated on the woman as though she'd grown a unicorn's horn, Kally nervously bit the inside of her cheek.

Stepping forward, Vivi took command. "Is Stella Demopoulos here?"

"She's in the back. I'm her daughter, Lia." She eyed the two of them curiously. "Whom may I say is here for her?"

"She won't know me by name," Kally admitted. "I think she knew my grandfather and I'd like to ask her a couple of questions."

"I'll get her."

After a few minutes of anticipation, an older woman appeared. It was evident that in her youth she must have been a beauty, despite the streaks of gray in her dark hair and the lines spidering out from the corners of her hazel eyes. Her apron was covered in flour and splotches of cinnamon marked her cheeks, yet there was something regal and proud in the woman's manner.

"Hello?" she said quizzically. "I'm Stella. What can I do for you?"

Kally extended her hand to the woman. Wiping her hands clean on the dishtowel she held, Stella set it down and accepted the proffered hand.

"I … my name is Kally Andarakis. This is my friend, Paraskevi. I believe you once knew my grandfather, Panayiotis Nikopoulos?"

A ghost of a smile crossed Stella's face as she examined Kally from head to toe. "Yes, I can see it. You have his eyes." Softly, she cupped Kally's chin. "And the bone structure of your grandmother."

"So you did know them both?"

"Ah, yes," she said, her smile widening. "I watched their daughter, Melina, from time to time."

"My mother."

"I thought it would be. I assumed there were no other children."

"No." Kally drew the letter from her bag. "You mailed this letter for my grandfather. It has your name and return address." She handed Stella the envelope.

"That was fifty years ago," Stella murmured, recalling the memory.

"Can you tell me anything about that time? About him? Or what might have happened to him?"

In the corner, there was a four by four weathered wooden table and three mismatched chairs. Stella motioned for the girls to follow her. When they were all seated, she clasped her hands under her chin, a faraway look taking her from the present.

Kally waited patiently. Stella seemed to be collecting her thoughts.

"Those days were a time of great turmoil. I was only a teenager but the politics of the time controlled every conversation at home and in the streets. The Junta unseated our Prime Minister and the King pretty much let them take over."

"Pretty much?" Kally asked.

Stella laughed humorlessly. "They did take over. The king's hands were tied. Had he fought them, there would have been much bloodshed. Papandreou—the Prime Minister—," she clarified, "was arrested. He was greatly admired so this didn't go over well with the masses."

"My mother told me of the protests of her time," Vivi said.

"Yes, and the king attempted and failed at a counter-coup, which only made matters more volatile," Stella said.

"That's when he was exiled," Kally stated. "Where does my grandfather fit into all of this?"

"He was quite vocal regarding his opposition of the Junta. The more he spoke out, the more dangerous it became for him, so he did the only thing he could do—send your mother and grandmother away."

Kally didn't understand. Not when her grandmother explained it and not today as this woman shed a more serious light on the situation. It could have all been so different had he just kept quiet. What more could he have wanted than to happily live out his life with his family?

The letter rested in the middle of the empty table. Kally laid her hand on it. "He loved her. It's so apparent in these words that she and my mother meant everything to him. Why would he risk it all?"

"For a better life." Stella closed her eyes. A moment passed as she sat deep in thought. When she opened them she cupped her hands over Kally's. "For a better Greece."

"So he stayed behind in Kalamata and did what exactly?" Kally asked.

"He got involved with an underground newspaper." Stella gestured her disgust with the sweep of her hand. "You don't know what it was like. Our freedoms were taken from us. No more free press. Music by bands like The Beatles and our own Mikis Theodorakis were banned."

"The Beatles?" Kally couldn't believe it.

"That's not all," Stella exclaimed. "Works by Tolstoy, Chekhov, Mark Twain!" She lifted her arms, shaking her hands. "Socrates. Socrates! All prohibited."

Kally was stunned. "I had no idea."

"Citizens were arrested for speaking out and many were never seen or heard from again," Stella said.

An ominous silence came over the three women. Kally was afraid to ask the question hanging in the air for fear of the answer. "Is that what could have happened to my grandfather?"

Stella squeezed Kally's hand in comfort. "I don't know." She sighed. "About a week after he gave me the letter to mail, he left for Athens.

He said there was more he could do there to join in the fight against the dictatorship."

"Athens?" Kally couldn't believe it. "Please tell me he returned at some point."

"No." Stella frowned. "I never saw him again."

"So I'm right back where I started," Kally mused in frustration. "The last place we think he'd been was the very place I've stayed these last two months."

"It seems so," Stella said. "I wish I had more information for you."

Kally stood, Vivi following her lead. "You've been a great help." She hugged the woman and, in turn, Stella kissed her on each cheek.

After offering goodbyes, they exited the bakery.

"What now?" Vivi asked.

Kally shrugged, a deflated expression crossing her face. "We head back to Athens," she said with a sigh. "There's not much else I can do for now. I leave for home in two days."

Chapter 39

Kally

The ride down Route 112 toward Port Jefferson Harbor should have brought a sense of comfort to Kally. Once her father's car drove over the railroad tracks, she knew she was truly home. She was seconds away from the view of the Long Island Sound, the commuter ferry loading cars on and off the dock, and the seagulls squawking as they circled overhead. She had left at the tail end of winter and returned to the beauty of rebirth. Azaleas were in full colorful bloom, flowerbeds were freshly landscaped and the leaves on the oak trees lining the narrow side streets reached over to touch, forming a natural canopy.

But she was coming home to a life very different than the one she'd designed for herself over these past few years. George patted his daughter's knee to show his understanding as they turned the corner to East Main Street and passed what used to be The Coffee Klatch. It wasn't in the shambles she last saw it but Kraft paper covered the windows, making it impossible to see inside.

"I suppose it's already been rented?" Kally asked, the pain in her voice evident.

George nodded. "I noticed some renovations."

There was a ghost of a smile on his face but it wasn't one of sympathy. Surely her father wasn't gloating over the misfortune that led to his victory. At least she hoped not.

Her father pulled into her driveway. Slamming the door, she curtly told him not to bother getting out; that she could handle her luggage. Mumbling her thank you, she gave him a perfunctory peck on the cheek and disappeared into the cottage she'd missed for the past two months. Emma greeted her at the door, screeching out an excited bark and jumping all over Kally.

"Hi, girl! I missed you so much!" Picking the dog up, she was treated to a slobbering of kisses on her face. "And I thought I was going to have to get you from Mom's house. What a nice surprise!"

Once Kally unpacked her luggage, ran a load of wash and gave the house a dusting, she slipped into a t-shirt and sleep short set. Making herself comfortable on her sofa, she pulled her laptop from her tote bag and began her search.

When she had returned with Vivi from Kalamata, she pumped her grandparents for every bit of information they could remember about the time period that would coincide with her other grandfather coming to Athens during the overthrowing of the government. Now, it was up to her to research to see if he was one of the many who had fallen victim to the tyranny.

She opened an article regarding the funeral of the unseated Prime Minister Papandreou in November of 1968. As she read, her eyes grew heavy and before she could finish the article chronicling the show of reverence for the man and the protests in the streets against the current regime of the time, she fell fast asleep with her fingers lingering over the keyboard.

* * *

The next morning, Kally heard the simultaneous knocking of the door and the ringing of the doorbell.

"All right, all right!" Kally shouted, clambering from the sofa where she'd spent the night. "I'm coming!"

"What took you so long?" Egypt complained when the door swung open.

"Welcome home to me!" Kally retorted. "What's got your knickers in a twist?"

"You need to put some clothes on," Egypt said urgently. Circling her pointer finger around her face as though she were about to land a small plane, she commanded, "And put on some makeup. You look like you just rose from the dead."

"And again, welcome home to me!" Kally brushed her loose curls from her face. "I did just wake up."

"You have ten minutes and then I'm stealing you away to a surprise location."

"I think I've had enough surprises for one year," Kally said. "No, thank you."

"Trust me," Egypt urged innocently. "You do trust me, don't you?"

"Yes, most of the time," Kally huffed.

"Good, now get dressed and then I'm taking you out of the house in this blindfold." She pulled out a black sleep mask trimmed in pink ostrich feathers.

"You have got to be kidding?" Kally planted her fists on her hips in defiance. "I am not putting that on."

Egypt pushed her toward the bedroom. "You are and that's final. Now go!" she ordered.

Ten minutes later, Kally emerged wearing white skinny jeans, a navy scoop neck t-shirt and a pair of leather sandals she had purchased at a shoe store at the Plaka. The scant amount of makeup and the messy bun was enough to squeak by Egypt's approval before she tied the blindfold over her eyes.

"This is just silly," Kally complained. "What are you up to?"

"You'll see." Egypt guided her into the 2013 Barcelona Red Prius she drove.

"Where are you taking me?" Kally asked. "You're making a lot of turns."

"Just trying to throw you off track."

After ten minutes of driving around, Egypt parked the car along a curb. Hopping out of the car, she swung around to the passenger side to help Kally out. When she opened the door to lead her into their destination, thunderous clapping startled Kally along with at least a dozen voices shouting, "Surprise!"

Kally flipped the blindfold off and slapped her hands to her mouth. Tears sprung to her eyes and her throat went dry. She was standing in her café. But how was this possible? Stunned confusion was plastered on her face as the crowd descended upon her, hugging, kissing, asking her what she thought. She didn't know what to think.

She looked over to her parents, completely stunned. "How?" Before they could answer, she turned to Egypt, who was filming it all on her iPhone. "It's exactly as it was before," Kally stammered, not believing her eyes. It was all there. Every detail, including Luis as he stepped out from the crowd with a tray full of ornately decorated cupcakes.

"Mom? Dad?"

"This is your dream, sweetheart," her father said, coming up next to her to plant a tender kiss on her cheek. "It's where you belong. I didn't have the heart to take it from you."

"Especially after we all worked him over," *Yiayiá* added.

"Oh, *Yiayiá*!" Kally giggled.

"She doesn't lie!" Kally's mother exclaimed. "We had to do more than a little arm pulling."

"I love you for this." She hugged both of them. "I love all of you!" she cried addressing everyone who had come out to share in this moment with her. They were all here. Her entire staff, her sisters, aunt and cousins. Leo, Mr. and Mrs. Lawson. She crossed her hands over her heart when she saw them. And Spyro and Milton too. Milton, Max's *pappou*. But no Max and no Athena. And in that joyous, insanely unexpected turn of events, that stabbing inconsolable pain lodged a little deeper in her heart. My choice, she told herself. I sent him away and for good reason.

She shook it off, forcing a smile back on her face. Luis passed around pastries. Krystina and Egypt were at the coffee station making *cappuccinos* and *frappés*. This was really happening!

"Tomorrow is your grand re-opening," her father said. "Time to get to work." He handed her a new apron, white with black trim. On the top right-hand corner of the bib was a graphic design of a blending tool. Lavender lettering spelled out a quote. "Where there's a whisk there's a way," Kally read out loud. Tilting her head toward her parents, she smiled. "There sure is. I don't know how you did it, but I'll be forever grateful."

"Put it on," Mia said. "I want to snap a photo. Plus, I have one more surprise for you."

"I don't know if my heart could take another surprise!"

"Do you remember when I interned at News Channel 12?" Mia asked.

Kally shrugged. "Uh-huh."

"Well, I tapped into a few of my contacts there. I told them your story about the fire and how you lost everything. I asked them if The Coffee Klatch could be the focus of one of their Dishin' Long Island features for tomorrow's re-grand opening."

"And?"

"And … would I be telling you all of this if they didn't agree?"

Kally's eyes widened. "Are you joking? Seriously? I'm going to hyperventilate." She began to shake her hands and rock back and forth on her legs. Suddenly, she had so much pent up energy, she thought she'd take off like a missile about to launch into space. "There's so much to do" She threw her hands up. "I don't know where to begin." Kally was spinning in circles.

"Take it easy," her mother said. "It will be fine."

"Tomorrow you'll come in early like you have in the past," Mia said, rubbing her shoulders.

"I'll be here with Luis, Krystina and the full staff," Egypt said, taking command. "Everything will get done."

"You'll go home around eleven-thirty or so to freshen up and put on something nice," Mia interjected. "And the camera crew will be here at one o'clock ready to take some shots of the place and interview you."

"Can someone pinch me? This has to be a dream." This was her place, just as it looked before the fire. It hadn't quite sunk in as she looked around the room.

"If you think you're in La La land now," Luis said, "wait until you see the kitchen." He grabbed her hand, tugging her toward the swinging doors.

It all pretty much looked the same—shelves stacked with bakeware, tools and supplies, a large stainless steel work station inlayed with both wood and granite boards for rolling dough, a holding and proofing cabinet, a commercial size refrigerator and ... oh! Where did that come from? she wondered. Walking toward it as if by magnetic force, she laid her hand on the beautiful appliance before her to make sure it was really there.

"Nope, not a mirage," she confirmed. The oven was more than twice the size of the one she had before. And that one had been second hand. This was shiny and new and ... huge! But how?

"There is no way the insurance covered all the renovation and this oven too." She turned to Egypt, Luis and her parents, who had followed her into the kitchen. "Is someone going to tell me how this is possible?"

"Sweetheart, stop with the questions and just be happy," her father said. "I have many connections. It's all taken care of."

"Okay." She shrugged.

All the well-wishers soon departed, leaving Kally to delve into work. She hadn't a moment to waste. There were pastries to bake, cupcakes to decorate, counters to adorn with her confections. Everything had to present flawlessly for the news feature. She would make sure of it.

Chapter 40

Kally

"That went even better than I expected!" Egypt exclaimed. The News Channel 12 crew had just finished packing up and she joined Kally in her office as she sank into her chair, exhausted from nerves.

"It did go well but I'm so glad it's over." She breathed out a sigh of relief.

"It will be interesting to see how they edit the feature," Egypt said. "I hope they really work the angle of the fire and this rebirth of the store." She lifted her palms to the heavens. "Like a phoenix rising from the ashes."

Kally giggled. "That's a little over the top, don't you think?"

"It doesn't matter one way or another. The glowing review of your delicious pastries and the rave over the various coffees you offer will have the customers coming in droves!"

"That's the hope."

"Speaking of hope and love and destiny ..." Egypt trailed off.

"We weren't actually, but go on if what you have to say involves you and Leo."

"No ... I was wondering if you gave any thought to Max while you were away."

"Of course, I did," Kally admitted. "I just can't scrub him from my mind like soap scum on bathroom tile."

"Whoa! Seriously?" Egypt's head bobbed in sync with the finger she aimed at Kally. "You are not comparing Max to soap scum," she berated. "He doesn't deserve that. Max is a really good guy who cares about you." She stood from her chair. "If you only knew, Kally. I love you but you're too stubborn for your own good. I have to go before I say something I'll regret." As she walked out of the office Kally heard her mutter under her breath. "If she only knew."

Only knew what? Kally was completely befuddled over Egypt's strong reaction to what she'd said. She didn't even give her a chance to finish her thought. Her friend had always been on her side. Always went to bat for her, protected her. Why was she suddenly siding with Max?

"We need you out front!" Krystina called in a rush of panic. "It's crazy out there. The curiosity over the news trucks out front have brought the crowds in."

"I'm coming," Kally replied. "Well, that's one way of letting people know we're back in business."

As she burst through the doors leading to the front room, the wave of chatter and laughter almost blew her away "Holy crap!" Kally exclaimed. Thankfully, no one heard her. Not only was every table occupied, but a line had formed out the door for takeaway orders. She had underestimated the staff she'd need on a day that was not only her re-grand opening but also the warmest day of the spring so far this year.

Pulling her cell from her apron pocket, she made a few quick calls for some extra back up and then quickly got to work filling orders for café lattes and a new specialty chilled Mexican chocolate drink.

* * *

By the time Kally closed for the day and went home, she was so exhausted she collapsed on her bed with her clothes on. Hours later, she awoke, took a quick shower and crawled back into bed.

The next morning, the fatigue from the previous day was all but forgotten. With a spring in her step, she bounced her way to the café. Instead of one of her usual music or audiobook selections, she turned on a small flat screen TV she now kept in the corner of the kitchen. Sometime between nine and ten a.m., Dishin' Long Island would be airing their feature on The Coffee Klatch.

Turning when she heard the squeak of the back door, she stared as Egypt entered.

"I wanted to be here with you when the show aired," she said.

"So you're talking to me now?"

"I wasn't not talking to you. We were busy yesterday."

Kally cocked her head to one side. "Cut the bullshit. I can see right through you."

Egypt raised an eyebrow. "It's good you can see one thing for what it really is."

"There you go again." Kally threw up her hands in frustration. "Spit it out! Just say what's on your mind."

"Never mind," she said dismissively, turning back to the TV. "I'm out of line. Let's watch the program before we miss it."

∗ ∗ ∗

With the extra publicity, business was better than it had been before the fire. In particular, requests were coming in for those pretty garden cupcakes, the Greek pastries and the high tea towers. It was rare for there to be a lull in the day but one afternoon as Kally leaned over the counter closest to the doorway, she saw Max pass by as he patrolled the street in his uniform. He didn't so much as look in her window or glance her way. He walked by as if the place didn't exist at all.

With a heavy heart, Kally felt as though knots were being twisted in her stomach. The anguish was unbearable. He was undeniably done with her. Of course, he was, she berated herself. She made it clear she wanted nothing to do with him. Yet, he still occupied every bit of real estate in her brain. She couldn't do anything without thinking of how Max would love this or laugh at that. While out shopping or walking the mall, she would spot a cute outfit at a children's boutique and have the urge to buy it for Athena.

Speculation over what Max was up to drove Kally crazy. She could have asked a question or two, but was too afraid to ask. So instead, she let her imagination run wild. Milton came to her surprise opening but didn't so much as mention Max. What did his sweet but sad smile mean? Kally wondered. Was Max back with his wife? Had she convinced him to give their marriage another try? If so, she and Max never had a chance in the first place. Bridget was, after all, the mother of his child.

This was all her fault of course. She didn't learn her lesson the first time. Jaxon lied to her. Max lied to her. She was a magnet for deception. No more. No more. No more. She had her café back and that's all that mattered. All she would focus on. The only drama in her day from here on out would be a cake failing to rise in the oven.

Chapter 41

Egypt

Dr. Alvita Basu found herself with a rare morning off. Between her private practice and her rotations in the hospital's ER, she was afforded little free time. So it was a treat for her to sit and enjoy a caramel latte and a lemon poppy seed scone at her leisure surrounded by the peaceful atmosphere of The Coffee Klatch.

"Can you sit with me for a few minutes?" Alvita asked her daughter when Egypt placed a second scone down for her to sample.

Egypt scanned the room and sat in the seat across from her mother. "It's pretty slow right now, so sure, but only for a few minutes."

"I'm so pleased this all worked out for Kally," Alvita said. "Now what about you?"

"What about me?"

"Your loyalty is admirable, Egypt. But when you dropped out of college it was to pursue your own dreams."

"I am, Mother," she said, her voice tinged with annoyance. "Is that why you're here? To grill me?"

"No, no," her mother replied in her calm, controlled manner. "I'm just making conversation."

"Well, for your information and in the interest of *con-ver-sation*," Egypt snipped, "I just shipped off a large order of my jewelry to a store on the West Coast that has been carrying my line." From the corner of her eye, Egypt noticed a patron enter and she stood to greet her. "And I just got another decent sized order from another store." She wanted to add a, 'so there!' but that would have been childish. Instead, she turned her back on her mother and greeted the woman who was curiously examining the room as if expecting to find something she had lost.

"Can I help you?" Egypt asked.

"Yes. Is Kally Andarakis here?"

"She is." Egypt eyed her with suspicion. "Who may I say is asking?"

"She won't know me by name but it's important that I speak to her. My name is Susanna."

"Have a seat," Egypt said, directing her to the table adjacent to her mother. "I'll go get her."

She found Kally in the kitchen, elbows deep in frosting, her apron smudged with sea green icing. The quote of the day on the bib was not a good sign. Nope. Egypt had no idea what business this Susanna had with Kally but the poor woman was in for it because written across her chest in bold, black letters was 'I don't give a frap.'

"There's a woman out front who wants to see you."

"What does she want?" Kally asked.

"She didn't say but she said it was important."

Kally dropped the pastry bag and huffed out a puff of air. After washing her hands and removing her soiled apron, she smoothed her hair as best she could before stepping out front.

Egypt pointed the woman out and Kally walked over to her, extending her hand and introducing herself. "I'm Kally Andarakis."

"Hi," the woman said nervously. "I'm Susanna. It's nice to finally meet you."

Kally looked puzzled but, as she stared into Susanna's eyes, she thought there was something vaguely familiar about her. Egypt, who had taken a seat by her mother, was eavesdropping, curious as to who this person was and what she wanted.

"What's so interesting?" her mother asked.

"Shush! My antennas are up," Egypt whispered. "I don't know why but something about this woman worries me."

"We've never met before?" Kally asked. "I almost feel like we might have."

"No, not formally anyway." Susanna fidgeted with the strap of her bag, her concentration focused more on the pointless action than on Kally it seemed. "I came here to talk to you about Jaxon."

Egypt clamped a hand over her gaping mouth.

Kally could barely repeat his name. "Jax … on? What about him? Who are you?"

"If I tell you who I was to him you'll get the wrong idea. I need to explain everything to you so you'll fully understand. And I have some questions I hope you can answer about the night he died."

"Did she say Jaxon?" Alvita said softly.

"Yes." Egypt put her finger to her lips.

"That's not a very common name," she mused, almost to herself. "Neither is Kally, for that matter."

"What are you getting at?" Egypt just wanted her to be quiet so she could hear what was going on.

"Nothing."

But Egypt could see her mother was lost in deep thought.

"This Jaxon, did you know his last name?"

"Reed. Why?"

Alvita rose from her seat. "I have to go. I forgot I have something pressing I need to attend to." She kissed her daughter's cheek and dashed out the door.

Chapter 42

Kally

The color drained from Kally's face. Who was this woman and why was she here to speak about Jaxon? It had been eight years now since he passed. Anything to do with him was history long buried and, even then, no one knew about the two of them.

"What do you want from me?" Kally asked in a strangled sob.

"I want to set the record straight. Jaxon would want me to."

"I don't understand. Even if that's so, why now? Why after all these years?"

"I didn't know how to find you," Susanna admitted. "Jaxon only referred to you by your first name. The only other thing I knew of you was that you were a pastry chef. I had no last name, no address and no clue as to your place of employment."

"Jaxon talked to you ..." Kally pointed to her. "... About me?" she asked tapping her chest. "Why?"

Susanna scrubbed her hands over her face. "Because, technically, only technically, I was his wife."

And it all became crystal clear. That's why she looked familiar. It was only for a brief moment but her face was seared in her mind. The hair was now blonder and the pregnant belly gone, replaced by a lithe, enviable figure, but it was her—the woman the funeral director pointed out as the deceased's wife—Jaxon's wife.

Covering her face with her hands, Kally closed her eyes, her heart pounding in her chest. "I'm so sorry. I didn't know. He didn't tell me he was married."

"No, you're not listening. I said we were technically married." Susanna grunted. "Jaxon made a promise and he did the honorable thing. I didn't find out about you until it was too late."

"The honorable thing because he got you pregnant?" The thought of it sliced through Kally like a hot knife.

"No! I need to back up and start at the beginning." Tables at the café were filling up. Susanna blew out an agitated breath and looked around. Too many people were within proximity to hear them. "Is there somewhere more private we can go?"

Kally nodded dumbly. "Follow me." As they headed toward the back, Kally tapped one of her servers on the shoulder. "I'll be in my office if you need me."

Kally closed the door behind Susanna and offered her a seat in front of her desk.

"I know this is so after the fact," Susanna started, "but again, I had no idea how to find you. It wasn't until I saw the feature they did on this place the other day that I put two and two together. I recognized you immediately even though I only saw you for that brief second before you walked out of the funeral home."

A sick feeling came over Kally as the memory of that night played over in her mind. "And why did you feel the need to find me all these years later?" Kally asked weakly.

Susanna leaned forward, keeping her eyes trained on Kally. "Because Jaxon loved you. Really loved you. And if you thought otherwise it just wouldn't be right. He'd want you to know the truth."

"He never told me about you." Kally looked away. "A lie, an omission—it's all the same," she said, thinking aloud.

Rummaging through her bag, Susanna pulled out an envelope containing a few old photographs. "This is Jaxon and my boyfriend,

Dillon, when they were about ten years old. They were thick as thieves. Like brothers."

Kally took the photo from her, examining it. Jax had never spoken of Dillon to her but one night he had been talking in his sleep and called out the name several times. "Your boyfriend?" Confused, Kally glanced up at Susanna.

"Yes." She handed Kally another picture. "That's the three of us in high school. Dillon was my first love. We broke up for a couple of years and then once we got back together, we were inseparable."

"Yet you married Jax."

"Let me explain," Susanna urged. "Dillon and Jax started to hang with a bad crowd. I wanted no part of it. I warned them that they were looking for trouble and nothing good would come of it."

"What made them take up with them?"

"Who knows? Rebellion maybe. Both of them had rough upbringings." Susanna waved off the thought. "Anyway, one night the whole bunch of them got into a brawl with some guys who were way tougher than they were. Gang related, you know?"

Kally's eyes widened. "What happened?"

"Jax was stabbed multiple times."

Kally gasped. "The scars! I asked him about them but he wouldn't talk about it."

"He lost his spleen and both kidneys were punctured. He needed a blood transfusion due to the internal bleeding." Susanna clutched her chest at the memory. "The doctors weren't sure if he'd make it through the night. Both kidneys were damaged beyond repair."

"Oh my God!" There was so much about Jax she knew nothing about.

"Dozens of people from town and high school, work and the surrounding area answered the plea to be tested as a donor. As it turned out, Dillon was a match."

"Really?" Kally wished she had heard all of this from Jaxon's mouth.

"Crazy, huh!" Susanna exclaimed. "What were the chances? But they always felt like brothers, so in a way they were. Dillon didn't have to think twice. He saved Jax's life."

"So when did you and Dillon get back together?"

"During all of this insanity," Susanna admitted. "I couldn't stay away from either of them. I basically nursed them back to health. And they swore off hanging with anyone who spelled trouble. Partly because I threatened to walk out the door for good if they didn't."

Kally folded her arms across her chest. "Good for you." So engrossed in this tale, she almost forgot it was Jax she was speaking of.

"Fast forward," Susanna exhaled, closing her eyes. "I got pregnant. We were planning to get married but then I found out about the baby and then before we could make plans ..." Tears welled in her eyes.

"What? What is it?" Kally reached for her hand, patting it tenderly.

"One night, Dillon had a seizure. It was out of nowhere." She lifted her shoulders. "He had no history of them. It lasted less than a minute and Dillon wanted to ignore it. He refused to go to the hospital. Until it happened again and I insisted."

Kally watched as Susanna struggled to formulate her words.

"It didn't take long for the doctors to figure out that Dillon had an inoperable malignant brain tumor."

"No ..." Tears sprung to Kally's eyes for the pain that news must have brought Susanna.

"Dillon was an old-fashioned kind of guy about certain things." Susanna's smile was melancholy. "He was dead set on marrying me before the baby was born. I think it was because his mother had him out of wedlock and his stepfather always called him a little bastard."

"What a terrible thing to say to a kid," Kally said disgustedly.

"Things got bad really quickly," Susanna sobbed. "It was painful to watch. He asked Jax to make sure his kid would be okay. He begged Jax not to let him be born a bastard like he was. Jax promised to marry me if it came to it but he assured Dillion that he'd be walking down the aisle with me."

"Oh my gosh!" Kally exclaimed. "Jax did the honorable thing and all this time I thought he was lying to me. Leading a double life."

"If you hadn't run out so quickly I could have explained," Susanna said.

"If Jax had told me all of this in the first place I would have understood."

"Would you have?" Susanna asked. "Deep down, do you believe you would have accepted it?"

"No." Kally admitted, meeting her eyes.

"But the bottom line is that I knew about you because he talked about you all the time. He was crazy about you and you need to know that."

"Did you ever sleep together?" Kally asked. "You were married after all."

"God, no! In name only. We were married in name only." Susanna closed her eyes and inhaled deeply. Exhaling as though expelling the toxins from her body, she opened her eyes slowly. "That felt good to finally get off my chest. I do have one question for you though. I'm not sure you'll have the answer but it's worth a try."

"I don't know what I can tell you. Obviously, you knew him way better than I did."

"The night of the accident—the night Jax died, he called me in a panic. Said he had to speak to me right away." Serious blue eyes looked for the answers in Kally's brown, grief-stricken ones. "He never made it to my place. Do you have any idea what made him race to see me?"

Kally knew. It all fit into place now. She covered her face with her hands to hide the tears running down her cheeks.

"That night," Kally said through sobs, "I told him I was pregnant."

"What?"

Kally nodded, wiping the tears from her face. "At first, he seemed so happy, but then he said he had something important to do," she said between short, gaspy breaths. "That's when he took off." She looked up at Susanna in horror. "Is it my fault he's dead? It is, isn't it?"

Susanna jumped from her seat, making her way to the other side of the desk to comfort Kally. "No, not at all. How could it be? You gave him wonderful news." Reaching over, she took Kally's hands in her own. "He would be so happy to know he had a child in the world."

Kally shook her head as the tears continued to stream down her face. "I lost the baby the night of the funeral."

"Oh, Kally. I'm so very sorry."

"Thank you. It was a long time ago." And then it dawned on Kally. "What about your baby?"

"A little boy. He's eight and a half now. I named him Dillon Jaxon."

"I'm happy for you," Kally cried. "At least a part of Dillon still lives in your son. Thank you for finding me. It really means a lot to know the truth."

"I truly hope you can make peace with it and know in your heart that you were loved. Jax was a good man."

Chapter 43

Kally

Yiayiá covered her ears with her hands as the ferry announced its arrival at the pier. Kally had suggested lunch on the outside deck of Danfords adjacent to the dedicated area for the two large ferryboats, the *Grand Republic* and the *Barnum*, to load and unload the many commuter cars traveling back and forth from Connecticut.

Few people knew about Jax and her miscarriage—her mother, *Yiayiá*, and Egypt. So on that sunny day in June, under blue market umbrellas, overlooking a string of small boats docked near the restaurant, Kally retold the entire story Susanna had shared.

Her mother tsk, tsk, tsked between bites of her lobster roll, while *Yiayiá*, adding to her mother's chorus, exclaimed *po, po, po!* at several points in the tale. Egypt remained unusually quiet, biting into her portobello burger as though it was a mission to finish it in record time.

"That sheds a different light on the matter, doesn't it?" Melina asked.

"It does clear things up," Kally admitted. "It's all ancient history though."

"Is it?" her mother questioned. "You can't tell me the past hasn't affected how you react to what happens in your present."

"What are you driving at, Mom?"

"That you assume the worst from men when it isn't always the case," her grandmother accused.

"Are you all going to gang up on me about Max again? He has a wife and child."

"He doesn't have a wife!" they all cried in unison a little too loudly.

"Oh, now you decide to speak," Kally said snidely to Egypt.

Egypt released the burger from her fingers, letting it plop onto her plate. "Kally, I have something to tell you. Since you told everyone what happened when Susanna came to see you, I'm not going to wait to get you alone." She wiped her hands on the napkin resting on her lap. "My mother overheard part of what Susanna told you before you went to your office. She heard her say she wanted to talk to you about the night Jaxon died."

"Okay …"

"I never told my mother about Jax, so that night in the ER it didn't register with her."

"What didn't?"

"That this man, Jaxon, kept saying 'Kally, need Kally, call Kally' over and over.

Kally froze. All eyes were on her. The sounds of the seagulls overhead, the clanging from the cars driving onto the ferry, the chatter of the diners around them, it all disappeared from her ears. All she heard in her mind were the words Egypt had repeated.

Finally, clasping her fingers together, she looked down at her plate. "I don't know how to process that information. I've been overloaded." She looked up at Egypt. "I was the last words on his lips? The last thing on his mind and I wasn't there for him? Kally! How many Kallys are there around here? Your mother should have called me."

Egypt opened her mouth but Melina beat her to it. "Wait one minute! I know you're upset finding all of this out after so long but Egypt's mother had no way of knowing you were the Kally he was speaking of."

"She tried to get the phone number for whoever Kally was off his cell phone but it was passcoded," Egypt explained.

"I'm sorry." Kally sighed. "This is all freaking me out."

"I think Susanna's point in telling you was to let you know Jax wasn't a cheat," Egypt said. "This should help you finally move on without all the distrust and suspicion you harbor."

"I get it," Kally conceded. "But that was then and this is now. One thing has nothing to do with another."

Collectively, the three women groaned.

"I think it's time for an intervention," Egypt said. "She needs to know."

"No, we'd be breaking a trust," Melina said. "We promised."

"*Áde kalé! Varéthika!*" *Yiayiá* exclaimed. "Enough with this *malakéa*. She needs to know the truth."

"What now?" Kally asked. "I'm just about at my limit."

"It was all Max's idea!" Egypt blurted out. "The café restoration. The upgrades on the kitchen. He arranged all of it."

"What?" Kally was stunned. She turned her attention to her mother. "I thought Dad took care of it."

"It was that beautiful boy," *Yiayiá* cooed in her thick accent.

Kally waited for her mother's confirmation.

"It's true," Melina admitted. "Max went to your father, begging him not to pay out the lease. He laid out a plan using his family's construction company, securing the labor cheap and the materials at cost. Between Max and your father, they made sure every detail was recreated exactly as it was before."

"But Dad was dead set on having me work for him."

"Max convinced him it would be a terrible mistake," her mother explained. "That you would be unhappy."

"Even with the insurance money and the discount on materials, I don't see how all of it was covered. Especially that oven!" Kally exclaimed. Suddenly, her spidey senses were tingling. Hopefully, her suspicions were off base. "Mom, please tell me Dad covered any amount over what the insurance paid out."

"No, you dumb ass!" Egypt chastised. "Max did."

Kally groaned. Hanging her head, she rested her arms on the table and plopped her head down. Her mass of curls shook with her rejection of the idea. "No, no no! Wait!" She popped her head up. "If this is all true, then why wasn't he at the opening?"

"I taped it for him so he could watch your reaction," Egypt admitted.

Kally sighed. Thin strands of dark brown ringlets fell over her face. Running her hands through her hair, she brushed them away. "He did all of this for me but he didn't want to see me," Kally whimpered.

"No, you idiot!" Egypt admonished. "You didn't want to see him. He was respecting your boundaries."

"A man doesn't go through all this trouble for a woman unless he loves her," Melina added.

"I know," Kally stretched out. "But he led me to believe his wife was dead. How am I supposed to trust him?"

"You just spent the last half hour telling us that everything you believed to be true about Jaxon was wrong," Melina reminded her. "Could you possibly have some misconceptions about Max's situation?"

"*Koukla mou.*" Her grandmother cupped Kally's cheek. "Don't let your pride or a miscommunication destroy your chance at a great love."

Kally examined her grandmother's face, trying to picture her as a young woman. Still, after all this time and so many years separated, the love for her Panos was evident. Such faith—faith that he didn't abandon or forget her. Faith that he was out there somewhere and would be with her if he could. Faith—the recipe for true love. And Max had faith in her—in her passion for what she had built from her talent and her need to succeed on her own.

"*Písti, Yiayiá,*" Kally said. "That's what you have. I wish I had an ounce of that faith." She looked to all three of the women sitting at the table with her. "I don't know what to do next. Ask him for the explanation I never gave him the chance to give? Thank him for what he did for the café and insist on paying him back for what he laid out?"

"No!" Egypt shouted. The diners at the surrounding tables turned to stare at her. "Sorry," she apologized. "Are you trying to make up with him or insult him?"

"I don't know." She flopped her head down on the table again.

"I know," Egypt said. "And I'll tell you." She wagged a finger at her. "The ball's in your court. You baked the cake, now it's time to frost it. In other words, it's your move."

"I can't just call him up after all this time. What am I going to say? 'Changed my mind. Don't care that you didn't tell me about your not-so-dead-wife.'"

Egypt slapped the side of Kally's head.

"Ouch!"

Melina and *Yiayiá* chuckled.

"You're a smart girl," Melina said. "You'll figure out the right way to handle it."

Kally sighed in defeat. "Come on, Egypt, we better get back to the café. I left Krystina and Loukas covering the front. God knows what I'll find when I get there. They may have killed each other by now."

* * *

Kally spent the remainder of the afternoon pondering what to do. Her anxiety level was at an all-time high and she chose not to subject her patrons to the current mood she was in. Baking was not only a source of happiness for her, it was also a form of therapy. And so, she baked—chocolate chip cookies, biscotti, and mini lemon tarts. Madeleines, scones and cream puffs. Then she had an idea. Kally would speak to Max in a language she knew best. Out came the cake pans and cupcake tins. It was time to batter up!

Red Velvet Cupcakes

2½ cups flour
1½ cups sugar
2 large eggs
1½ cups vegetable oil
1 ounce red food coloring
1 teaspoon baking soda
1 tablespoon cocoa powder
1 teaspoon vinegar
2 teaspoons pure vanilla extract
1 cup Greek yogurt

Preheat oven to 350° F.

Sift flour, cocoa powder and baking soda together. In a large bowl, beat the sugar and eggs. In a separate bowl, mix the oil, food coloring, vinegar and vanilla and then add to the egg mixture until combined. Add the flour and Greek yogurt, alternating dry and wet ingredients, starting with the flour. Pour the batter into paper cupcake liners. Bake for 25 minutes or until a toothpick comes out clean. Cool on a baking rack.

Cream cheese frosting

1 cup unsalted butter
2 - 8 ounce packages of cream cheese
1 teaspoon vanilla
2 pounds confectioners' sugar

Cream softened butter and cream cheese. Add sugar and vanilla, mixing until all the ingredients are blended and smooth. Fill a pastry bag with frosting and decorate the cupcakes.

"Dessert is like a feel-good song and the best ones make you dance."
Chef Edward Lee

Chapter 44

Max

A warm breeze, salted from the seawater, drifted in the air. The moon hung low, casting a golden illumination over the lively village. Competing music from The Harbor Grill and Danfords Deck overshadowed the chatter from the pedestrians passing idly by. After a winter that never seemed to end, everyone from mothers pushing baby carriages to octogenarians supported by walkers filled the streets. A line ran down the length of Chandler Square, leading up to the Port Jefferson Ice Cream Café window; an absolute tip-off that the summer season was in full swing.

Max and Leo patrolled the area, keeping a close watch for traffic violators by the blinking yellow light on the intersection of Main Street and Broadway.

Egypt, carrying a logo Coffee Klatch bag in one hand, approached Leo, whispered in his ear, and handed him the bag before disappearing.

"What was that all about?" Max asked.

"Delivery for you," Leo said, handing him the package.

Max, surprised and maybe a little nervous, pointed to himself for confirmation.

Leo's laugh rumbled deep in his throat. "Yes, for you."

He sat on the brick steps leading up to Christina's Handbag Store and pulled out the first box. Carefully, he opened the lid. Inside was a chocolate ganache cake. Written on the smooth surface was a simple 'Thank you.' Max uncovered the second, larger box, which, he discovered, contained a dozen cupcakes, each one iced with a single word to deliver her message — 'I couldn't have baked these without you and the oven you gifted.'

Max wondered who had finally told her. The last thing he wanted was for her to feel indebted toward him.

"Well?" Leo asked.

"I don't know, man," Max said. "I'm more confused than ever."

Leo grabbed the boxes from his lap. "Let me look at those." After scanning them, he picked up a cupcake, biting into one. "Mmm. Caramel. Seems like a peace offering to me," he said with a mouthful of cake.

"That's just it," Max grumbled. "It's such a Kally move. The polite thing to do. She wouldn't let it pass once she found out I was behind the renovations on her café."

Leo looked as though he was about to lose it. "Grow a pair, man, and go after that woman!" He lifted a finger when his phone beeped out a signal for a text message. Tapping out his response, he looked over to Max who was still contemplating the confection message Kally had sent. Leo snatched the boxes off Max's lap and chucked them in the back of the squad car. "Let's go, Romeo," Leo ordered with exasperation.

"Where?"

"Egypt said she needs us by the café. Somethings going on."

"It's closed at this hour," Max argued.

"You know, keep it up and you might just make detective," Leo said sarcastically, shoving him in the right direction.

Following along the narrow sidewalk, they wove between the crowds spilling out from the various restaurants and pubs until they turned onto East Main Street. Less crowded than the main drag, The Coffee Klatch was lit like a beacon guiding boats to shore.

"What on earth?" Max was perplexed. "I wonder if Kally is holding a special event?"

As they approached the café, Max looked in the window and upon seeing no sign of movement, he tugged on the door to see if it was locked. "This is very strange," he said when the door opened easily.

"Maybe Kally is in the kitchen," Leo suggested.

"She wouldn't leave the front door open this late at night if she was in the back," Max replied. "She knows better than that. I better have a look."

"Good idea," Leo said, practically shoving him through the door.

Nothing seemed out of the ordinary in the dining area, unless he considered every light being on after hours when not a soul was in sight. Striding over to the doors that led to the kitchen, he pushed one open, turning to see if Leo was joining him.

"I'll wait out here," Leo said.

Stepping through the door, Max stopped dead in his tracks when he spotted Kally standing, waiting for him, her dark, unsure eyes meeting his. She was wearing one of her aprons, but not her usual, elaborate custom styles. Plain and white, it was blank, but for two words scrawled in what must have been permanent marker. *'I'm sorry.'*

He kept his eyes trained on hers, hoping she could read the emotion swimming through them. She said not a word and, when he took a step toward her, she lifted her hand, pulling the apron over her head and letting it drop to the floor. Another apron layered under the first revealed itself and another message. *'You're worth the whisk.'*

Max smiled. He knew Kally had to come to him in her own time and in her own unique way.

She pulled the apron off to uncover the next one. *'If you still give a frap about me ...'*

Max threw his head back and laughed. She was so adorable. Did she really have any doubt?

Kally untied the apron to show him what he prayed was the last because he wanted nothing more than to erase the few feet between them. *'Maybe you'll take a whisk on me?'*

Max was at her side in a nanosecond, his arms around her waist, his lips pressed to hers. Releasing her, he took her face in his hands. "No risk. A sure thing. And I give a thousand fraps about you."

"Only a thousand?" she teased.

"Nope. All the fraps in Greece and America and anywhere else they make them." Max kissed her, pulling her in even closer. "I love you, Kally. I'm in love with you. Not young, naïve love. Not infatuation. Not obsession. True love. Adult love." He leaned his forehead against hers. "Am I making myself clear?"

"Crystal," Kally said with a smile. "Many things have been cleared up for me these past weeks. But what counts the most is that I've been miserable without you. You've occupied my thoughts every minute of every day because I love you so much, Max."

"Not just for my incredibly large and amazing oven I hope?"

Kally laced her arms around his neck. "Maybe a little," she giggled.

"Is this where you shut off your equipment and I carry you out in my arms with you wearing my officer's cap?"

"As long as you carry me up the street to my home, I say absolutely."

Chapter 45

Kally

Moonlight filtered in through the spaces between the window blind slats. A rumpled mess of discarded clothing strewn in the direct line of light laid on the floor—a lilac sundress, a hand-painted apron, the trousers of an officer's uniform.

Max had always taken Kally slowly, savoring each second, every kiss and caress. She happily drifted along, undulating softly as she was swept further into the depth of the ocean until the final satisfying crash to shore.

But this was a different side of Max—one she had not seen before. With an urgent and raw sensuality, he not only made love to her, but irrevocably staked his claim on her. Born from longing and need, missed time and apologies, soul promises and lust crazed desperation, they drank each other in like they never had before.

Kally herself had been freed from her ghosts. The insecurities were gone. The lack of trust, forgotten. She was no longer afraid to give her heart away. A new day was about to dawn and Max would awaken beside her.

"I love you," Kally said to Max as they lay face to face, naked on her bed.

"I love you, too. But talk is cheap." He smiled. "I'd rather show you."

"I think you already have."

"I've only just begun." He pecked her on the lips then worked his way down her neck, trailing kisses southbound down her collarbone until he found her breasts. Taking one in his hand, the other in his mouth, he flicked and licked the nubs, bringing them to hard peaks.

"Max," Kally groaned out her pleasure.

He smiled against the hollow of her cleavage. "More?" he asked.

Her answer was a muffled moan as she latched onto a fistful of his hair.

Continuing his exploration, he kissed down her ribcage, bellybutton and … well, as far south as he could venture, until she lost all brain function completely. She may never leave this house or this bed for days or weeks. She'll order their meals in and never allow either of them to see the light of day for a long while.

"More," she panted. "More of you. I need you."

"I don't need to be asked twice." But this time, he flipped her over onto her knees, entering her from behind. Turning her head, she met his gaze, his eyes darkening, wild with desire for her. Max took both her breasts in his hands as he found a powerful rhythm, thrusting in and out of her with greedy desire. The erotic ecstasy was almost too much and Kally shuddered as she gripped the headboard for support.

"Oh, God, Oh God, Oh God," she moaned.

"The name is Max but God works too," he grunted as they reached their crest together.

Collapsing into a fit of laughter, Kally sank into the pillow. "I see your self-esteem is at a low point."

But that was the thing with them, Kally realized. They could laugh, have misunderstandings, be separated for months, love each other, make jokes and be silly or disagree, but it wouldn't matter. At the end of the day, he would always be by her side and support her in whatever she needed. And for her part, Kally would always love him and Athena. They were hers and always would be.

Epilogue

Kally wasn't even halfway through the morning and it was already measuring up to be a very strange day. First, Egypt had called the night before to insist she take a much-needed day off. Since the feature two months ago on News Channel 12, The Coffee Klatch was busier than it had been before the fire. But at the height of the summer season, how could her friend suggest she take time off? But Egypt wouldn't take no for an answer, so Kally agreed to go for a mani-pedi and head back to the café by one o'clock.

Egypt: Wear that cute little striped romper u bought last week. Just a suggestion.

Weird text, Kally thought. Wear it where? To the salon or the café? But why?

Kally: Too nice to wear for a mani or work.????

Egypt: Just this once. No ?s

The romper did look good on her. It accentuated her long, lean legs and the draping at the neckline showed just a hint of cleavage. Admiring herself in the mirror, she slipped on a pair of navy sandals and headed out to the nail salon.

At twelve forty-five, a string of texts came flooding in from Egypt, asking if she'd be on time. First, she forced her to take time off, now she's begging her to come in. The girl just couldn't make up her mind.

Kally: I'm coming!

Egypt: Don't stop home to change. No time. Swamped here!

And this is exactly why it was a mistake to take the morning off.

Kally walked in the back door of the café. The kitchen was unusually quiet. Luis had his ear pods in and was singing along in Spanish while whisking a bowlful of eggs. Egypt was leaning on the counter, drumming her fingers along the stainless surface. The minute she spotted Kally walking through the door, she popped her head up.

"Yay! You're here!" Egypt called out.

"Yes," Kally dragged out, looking at her like she had lost her mind. "You told me to come straight over."

"And here you are!" she squealed. "Right Luis?"

"Oh, yeah," he said, lifting a large aluminum pot and dropping it to the floor. The clang was ear deafening. "Sorry, it slipped."

"Where is everyone?" Kally asked.

"Out front," Egypt replied. "It's busy out there." She grabbed Kally by the hand and led her to the main room.

Kally had barely made it past the swinging doorway when she halted.

"What on Earth?"

The entire room was ensconced in flowers. The glass counters, the windowsills and every table was set with vases of lilacs and daisies. The café was bare, save for the people she knew and loved. Her parents and sisters. Her *yiayiá*, aunts and cousins. Milton and Spyro, and all of Max's family as well. A sign hung in the window, 'Closed for a private event.' Kally was so confused.

From behind Max's family, he emerged, sporting a customized and somewhat masculine, if there is such a thing, black apron. Next to him was his daughter, nearly bouncing with excitement.

Kally warmed at the expression on his face as he looked at her. Raising his eyebrows, he pointed to the writing on his covering. '*I love you a latte.*'

Kally laid her hands over her heart and mouthed, 'I love you too,' and then she out and laughed when he pulled off the apron to reveal another apron.

"Copycat," she joked.

He puffed out his chest. '*I'm batter with you.*' Not giving her a chance to respond, he whipped off that apron to say, '*I donut want to go a day without you.*'

Aside from the ahs and occasional whispers, the café was silent. Kally's eyes welled with tears. He had gone to such lengths to show his love.

Max took three quick strides toward her, taking her hands in his. "I don't have a cute quip for this, so I'll say it straight." He took off the apron, dropping it to the floor. Kally took him in, handsome in tan trousers and a white linen shirt, the sleeves rolled up, exposing the tanned glow of his muscular forearms.

"Or rather I'll ask you." He bent down on one knee and Kally gasped. "Will you please marry me?"

Kally nodded, the tears running down her cheeks. She didn't even think to look at the ring he slipped on her finger when he kissed her. She only saw the love in his eyes and hoped he saw the infinite love she felt for him in hers.

"Do you like it?" he whispered.

"Oh yes," she answered enthusiastically, her eyes never leaving his. "I adore what I see."

"I meant the ring." He smiled.

Kally held her hand up and exhaled. "Max, it's so beautiful."

The two carat, oval diamond sat surrounded by a halo of smaller diamonds. Family and friends could hold back no longer. Cheers erupted. The crowd moved in for hugs and glances at the ring.

"*Na zisete, engoní mou,*" *Yiayiá* said, wishing her granddaughter a long and happy life. "You good boy," she told Max, cupping his cheek.

"Are you marrying me too?" Athena asked, sidling up alongside Kally.

This child craved what she never really had. She was as precious to Kally as Max was. "You better believe it! It's you, me and your daddy for life."

The end

An excerpt from Efthymia's Story

"Design creates culture. Culture shapes values. Values determine the future."
Robert L. Peters

Chapter 1

Mia

November 2018

Mia was convinced she was born in the wrong era. While her friends listened to pop music and followed DJ Khaled waiting for local concert dates, she preferred the classic sounds of Benny Goodman and Tony Bennett. Classic rock was as contemporary as she got, and the same could be said about how her tastes ran with just about everything.

Mia considered herself a 'Charlotte', the prim and proper character from the *Sex and the City* series. And although the sitcom represented women living in Manhattan from two decades ago, she shuddered at the thought of comparing herself to any of her contemporaries in the series *Girls*. If they were the representation of her generation with their highly dysfunctional lives and bizarre choices of male companionship, then she had to say a firm, 'No, thank you'. Charlotte was refined, cultured, and at least somewhat discerning with her men. And the clothing! Mia envied her sophisticated designer dresses, tailored to accentuate her slim figure.

In truth, Mia preferred to daydream of a more genteel time. She yearned to live like Audrey Hepburn in *Sabrina* or *Roman Holiday,* back when women dressed fashionably and men knew what it meant to be a gentleman. Give her the classic style of Jacqueline Kennedy in the days of Camelot, or the stylish dresses Lucy wore in her sitcom as she played bridge with the ladies. The iconic little, black sheath dress and string of pearls worn in *Breakfast at Tiffany's* was her go-to look for any occasion.

Mia was seated, perched upright at her computer, a support pillow resting at the back of her chair. Some days she could spend as many as eight hours focused on the monitor editing short videos or creating print layouts. Other days were spent running from department to department, directing photo shoots, attending pitch meetings, or hiring set designers for future campaigns.

Leaning back, Mia clasped her hands together and stretched them over her head, loosening out the kinks from sitting in one position for so long. She kicked off her black, spiked-heel pumps, removed her dark-rimmed glasses, worn only to magnify the images on the screen, and rubbed her tired eyes.

Homelife was one of Aris Publications' smaller staffed magazines. It was most likely Mia's diverse skills that had first won her the position she now held. It was rare for a graphic designer to have the capability to also take professional-grade photographs and edit the raw footage of a video shoot. But Mia could do all of it, and she hoped these skills would make her not only more marketable but also invaluable to her employers.

"Do you want to grab something to eat before we go to the CCP meeting?" Jenny, one of Mia's co-workers, asked, rolling her chair back so she could peer around the cubicle partition separating their desks.

Mia pressed the home button on her iPhone. The display read six-fifteen.

"Sure," she said. "We'll have to make it quick, though. I don't want to be late for our first meeting." She slipped back into her shoes, opened her desk drawer, and retrieved her bag.

Mia waved goodnight to her other co-workers as she and Jenny walked past long, white tables, partitioned with adjustable slats hosting several computers for employee stations. The walls were painted a soft rose, giving the room a fresh, light atmosphere, and despite a nearing deadline, there was nothing about this space that seemed chaotic. As they made their way to the glass door, etched with the magazine logo, leading to the elevator, Jenny turned to Mia.

"Le District?" Jenny asked.

"I never say no to French food!" Mia agreed eagerly.

Aris Publications was located in Brookfield Place, a shopping center and office building adjacent to the World Trade Center. Anything Mia needed was at her fingertips, from the high-end designer boutiques where she could only afford to window shop, to the more sensibly priced stores, to a couple of high-end food courts offering a variety of unique foods from which she could never tire.

Mia found two vacant high-top seats by a counter situated around the open cook station in Le District. They each ordered a glass of rosé and shared a charcuterie board while their paninis were being prepared.

"The guy was a total drip!" Jenny said, filling her in on her date from the night before.

Mia laughed into her wine glass as Jenny regaled her with her latest online dating disaster. Normally, she would have heard all about it when she'd come home, but Mia had fallen asleep early and didn't hear her roommate come in.

"I mean, I filled out this long, extensive profile with a ton of detailed questions, and they sent me that guy?" Jenny went on. "He droned on for forty-five minutes about the benefits of the statin his company developed over the competing pharmaceutical companies."

"So, no second date?" Mia joked.

"I didn't finish the first one. I went to the ladies' room and asked my sister to call me in ten minutes," Jenny said. "Then, I got the hell out of Dodge on some lame excuse."

"Have you sworn off dating apps now?" Mia asked, spreading

some brie on a paper-thin cracker.

"That one, definitely! But I'm on Zoosk now, and they have the best success rate."

With her auburn hair and green eyes, Jenny's face was striking. Her figure was a bit too curvaceous for her own liking but Mia pointed out to her more than once that women like Marilyn Monroe and Jane Russell flaunted their bodies proudly and that she needed to as well.

"Why don't you give it a try, Mia? What do you have to lose?"

"Precious time," Mia answered. "That's not for me. How did couples meet before all this online stuff? What happened to the old-fashioned way of meeting by chance, or at work, or through a friend?"

Jenny raised an eyebrow. "And how many men have you met that way?"

"Point taken." Sweeping her lustrous, sable hair from her face, Mia sighed.

"You know, for a person living in the most progressive city in America, you sure have some small-town ideals."

"Not small-town," Mia corrected. "I just like things to happen a certain way. I like romance and instant chemistry, not profiles and clinical checklists."

The grill man served up their plates, interrupting their conversation, and Mia thanked him. "We have about fifteen minutes before we have to make a dash for it."

After they finished dinner, Mia and Jenny headed to the bank of elevators. They rode up to the twenty-first floor and looked for the suite where the CCP meeting was to be held.

The Community of Creatives in Publishing held a yearly awards event. In addition, they introduced high school students to the many positions the publishing industry had to offer and helped to place college students with internships.

A portable stage had been erected at the front of the room; behind it a large viewing screen was set up. A podium was placed off-center, and seating had been arranged in rows beyond the stage. Seats were filling up quickly. Mia and Jenny found chairs in the fifth row, seated themselves quietly, and waited for the meeting to begin.

Mia was doodling on her notepad when the chairman of the organization stepped up to the podium. She didn't even notice until he began to speak, looking up when she heard a voice as smooth as velvet, laced with a slight indistinguishable accent, seduce her ears.

And then she saw him. Tall, dark, and handsome was too vague a description for this man. His double-breasted suit looked as though it had been tailored specifically for him, and she was sure it had been. He wore a cuffed shirt with gold and onyx cufflinks, and she'd bet any amount of money his ensemble cost more than she made in three months.

Mia wasn't one for dramatic overtures but she latched onto Jenny's arm. Her nails dug into her friend's skin in an involuntary reaction to the man standing on the stage before her. He was gorgeous.

As if his face wasn't perfect enough with his square jaw and the deep dimple in one cheek, he pulled out a pair of black-framed glasses and slipped them on before beginning his speech.

"Oh-my-God," Mia whispered, trying to contain herself. "Now that's a Clark Kent who doesn't need the Superman costume."

"He is hotter than hell," Jenny agreed. She glanced at Mia with a raised eyebrow. "I've never seen you react this way to anyone—ever."

"That's because I don't recall Adonis coming down from Mount Olympus before."

"You'll just have to find a reason to speak to him when the meeting is over," Jenny suggested.

"Shh, he's about to begin." Mia put a finger to her lips to silence her friend before adding, "Besides, I can't do that. I'd die of embarrassment."

She fell silent as he began his speech.

"Good evening and welcome. For those of you who don't know me, my name is Nicholas Aristedis of Aris Publications ..."

Other books by Effie Kammenou

The Gift Saga Trilogy:
Evanthia's Gift
Waiting For Aegina
Chasing Petalouthes

Love is What You Bake of It
The *Meraki* Series

If you enjoyed *Love is What You Bake of It* please consider leaving a review on Amazon and Goodreads.

Feel free to connect with Effie Kammenou on social media

Website - www.effiekammenou.com
Twitter - @EffieKammenou
Facebook - www.facebook.com/EffieKammenou/
Instagram - www.instagram.com/effiekammenou_author/
Goodreads - www.goodreads.com/author/show/14204724.Effie_Kammenou
Bookbub - www.bookbub.com/authors/effie-kammenou

Sign up for Effie's newsletter to learn about promotions and events - https://www.subscribepage.com/effiekammenoubooks

For additional recipes follow Effie's food blog
https://cheffieskitchen.wordpress.com

Made in the USA
Middletown, DE
12 April 2021